THE CLEARING RAIN

Suzanne Cass

S C
STORM CLOUD PRESS

The Clearing Rain

Storm Cloud Press, Perth Australia

Copyright © 2023 by Suzanne Cass

Edits by Evermore Editing

Cover by Vikncharlie

All rights reserved.

To the Tarkine, may it forever remain untamable and untouched.

CHAPTER ONE

Everything was perfect. Exactly how Lacey had envisaged it. The sun was setting in a brilliant show of pink and purple over the green-swathed mountains, and the evening air was warm and silken against the bare skin of her arms. The gentle buzz of an insect and the plop of a fish rising on the river below the only sounds to break the silence.

An ideal evening for what she had in mind. She'd been planning this day for over six weeks, since before Christmas, even before Nico had started recovering from his bullet wound. And now that Nico was almost healed, Lacey could start to focus on the bright future they might have together.

Nico was back on full duty now, pretending there was absolutely nothing wrong with him. But she knew different. He was still in pain sometimes; she occasionally caught him wincing when he lifted something heavy or moved too quickly.

Three days alone, just the two of them taking it slow, filling their days with sunshine and lots of simple food and gentle exercise was exactly what the doctor ordered. This was a dog-friendly area, so Smudge had accompanied them, and he now lay asleep at their feet, content and worn out from their day spent trekking.

It'd been her police partner, Linc, who'd planted the seed of this idea. She'd taken that thought and let it grow in her head until she'd come up with the perfect plan. A weekend away was an excuse to take the completely remodeled Dotti 2.0. Kombi van out for a run and christen her with an overnight stay. As well as the added bonus of getting away from their demanding jobs and chill for three days with no thoughts of murder or mayhem. She and Nico had finally arranged their schedules so they could both have a rare weekend off together. She gave a secret smile; Nico had no idea she had an ulterior motive for their holiday, but very soon, all would be revealed.

They'd driven Dotti down on Friday night and set her up in this secluded camp by the Pieman River in a tiny place called Corinna. It was no more than a scattering of huts offering rustic accommodation to tourists and an information center that was also a tavern, restaurant, and shop all rolled into one. The only way to cross the river was on a barge that carried one car at a time. Completely perfect for their romantic getaway.

Corinna was nestled in the heartland of the Tarkine, an indeterminate area of northwest Tasmania that was world-renowned for its ancient beech and myrtle rainforest. A person could get lost in this wilderness and never be seen again. But they'd die happy, Lacey decided. Lacey had never been much into photography, but even she had been in raptures as she snapped image after image of the lush Gondwana rainforest crowding in around them as they'd hiked the trails yesterday. It was so quiet here. Quiet and still. The place had a mysterious quality to it that she couldn't quite pin down. Perhaps it was the age of the ancient trees that'd seen so much over their hundreds of years standing guard over the river. Or perhaps it was the mysterious mists that drifted over the dark-olive treetops in wisps. There had been talk of protecting the Tarkine by turning it into a national park, but greedy mining companies were hampering the efforts of the conservationists. Such a shame. Lacey crossed her fingers and hoped the environmentalists would win this time.

This morning, when Lacey had peeped out of the van, the world had been shrouded in more mist, rising like gray, ghostly tendrils off the glassy water of the river. But the fog had soon cleared to a sparkling day, the sun bounding off the hillsides, making it sultry and so hot beneath the trees that Lacey had dived into the river more than once to cool off.

And now they were celebrating another day's hiking in the rainforest with wine and some local cheeses before dinner. Perfect. Raising her glass of pinot noir toward Nico who sat in the camp chair next to her, she said, "To the most beautiful place in the world." They clinked their glasses together as she met his indigo gaze and they toasted to this gorgeous little campsite tucked in next to the deep, slow-moving river.

"To the most beautiful woman in the world," Nico countered, and she smiled at him, his words hitting her in the solar plexus, then flowing all the way down to her toes.

God, how she loved this man. And he loved her. They were meant to be together. Forever. It was now or never. The timing was right. The ring nestled in its box snuggly in her shorts pocket. Her heart was beating so crazy fast she was scared Nico might hear it and ask her what was wrong. Should she get down on one knee in front of him? Or perhaps just hand it over all casual and easy as if it were the most natural thing in the world? Then watch his face, waiting with bated breath for his answer as the significance of the ring dawned on him. There was no doubt in her mind that Nico would refuse her. They were already as committed to each other as two people could be. Getting married was the next step along the trail of their love story. And rather than wait for him to do the asking, Lacey had decided to be the progressive, proactive, modern woman and ask him instead. Nico had been scarred by his ex-wife, Marietta. He'd married her for love, but it seemed she'd only married him to get her permanent residency. Lacey knew it might take him a while to feel himself worthy of that sort of commitment again. But she would show him that he *was* worthy. That together they were stronger; together they made the best team in the world.

Her pulse was an erratic pounding in her neck, her stomach awash with butterflies all of a sudden. How was it she could take aim and shoot at a fleeing criminal without so much as raising a sweat, but this…? This was doing her head in. Taking a few seconds to compose herself, to bring her breathing back to normal, she raised her wine to her lips and drew in a deep whiff of the dark-cherry liquid. Soft, fruity and familiar. But instead of her salivary glands watering, her stomach flipped over at the smell. Funny, she loved a good Tasmanian pinot. Why would the smell suddenly turn her stomach? Ignoring the warning bells, she took a sip, letting the wine sit at the back of her palate so she could savor the taste… And immediately spat it out onto the loamy earth. This time, her stomach did more than roil. It heaved.

Oh, God. She was going to be sick!

Putting the glass down with a clatter, she lurched out of her chair and half staggered, half ran to the nearest tree, promptly vomiting the remains of her lunch onto the bright-green moss below. Giving a low moan, she hardly noticed Nico's appearance at her side, his conciliatory hand on her shoulder not enough to stop her retching again and again until she had nothing left to throw up. Daggers stabbed into her abdomen and the terrible smell made her gag all over again. The rough bark of the tree beneath her palm was the only thing keeping her from toppling forward into her own mess.

"What's the matter, Lace? Was it something you ate? Maybe that chicken sandwich you had for lunch was dodgy," he said, rubbing small circles on her back, while trying to hold a concerned Smudge at bay. Lacey knew he was only trying to comfort her, but she didn't want him touching her suddenly. She wanted to be left alone like a wounded animal to crawl away under a log and wallow in her misery alone. She felt awful. Her whole body pulsed hot, then cold at the same time as sweat ran freely down her face, and she retched some more. Tears poured from her eyes. Oh, God, this was surely how dying felt.

When she didn't answer, Nico said, "I'll get you some water."

"Yes," she croaked. Water would be good. She was as parched as the desert. While Nico rushed off, taking the dog with him, Lacey gingerly straightened, one hand held tight against her stomach. The terrible retching seemed to have stopped now, the agonizing spasms abating, and she wiped at her mouth with the corner of her T-shirt.

Focussing on a shaft of fading sunlight piercing the jungle growth, she tried to figure out what was wrong. This was the third time she'd thrown up in the past four days. The first time she'd put it down to sour milk in her tea when she'd resorted to using the milk from the break room at the station on Friday morning. The second time, yesterday morning, she'd just made it to the small amenities block to take a shower when the nausea had overwhelmed her, but she'd put that down to needing a good hearty breakfast to fill the empty void in her stomach—and she had indeed felt better after Nico had fed her toast and tea. But today... What was today about?

The mere smell of wine had never made her sick before. A small kernel of worry gnawed at the inside of her chest. What if...? No, she couldn't be. It was impossible, and she pushed the idea from her head.

Nico rushed back with the water and a washcloth and Lacey cleaned her face, then took a few tentative sips.

"Thank you," she finally puffed. "I'm okay. I'm feeling better now." And it was the truth. Now that her lunch lay on the damp, jungle earth, her stomach was calm, no sign of the terrible hot flushes that'd tormented her body.

"Good. Because you scared me." Nico led her back to their little campsite, lowering her gently into her chair, his brow still creased with worry. Smudge was equally worried, resting his nose on her knee and lifting his brown, sympathetic gaze to hers.

Lacey looked at her glass of wine, then quickly looked away again. Nope, she wasn't going to try that again tonight. But the dry crackers seemed to be calling to her.

Oh, God. Dry crackers. You only craved dry crackers when you were… Again, she dragged her mind away from that thought.

"Why don't you sit here and enjoy the view, and I'll cook dinner tonight," Nico said. Irritation at his offer claimed her, unbidden, and she was about to snap at him that she was perfectly capable of walking to the van and turning on the cooker, when she stopped herself. Why was she suddenly so angry? Over nothing. Nico was being nice. She had no reason to jump down his throat. He hadn't meant it to sound like she was weak, unable to do even the simplest of things, like cook a meal.

Come to think of it, this wasn't the first time she'd become irritated at Nico for no good reason.

Oh, shit. She put her head in her hands. Mood swings were another sign, weren't they?

He was instantly by her side, crouching down, his forehead resting against hers. "Hey, babe, do you want to go lie down?" He'd misunderstood her dismay, possibly thinking she was going to be sick again.

Gathering her wits, she managed to raise a smile as she lifted her head. "No. I really am fine." She struggled to find something to explain her mood to him. "I'm just bummed that I ruined our night, that's all."

"You haven't ruined our night," he said, stroking her hair. "This has been the best weekend I've had in forever. We should do this more often. Just you and me and Dotti."

"Yes," she agreed. But she said it with an anxious heart. "And I'd love it if you cooked dinner. Thank you," she added. Dinner was going to be a simple affair tonight, anyway. Sausages done in a frying pan on the small gas stove housed in a hidden compartment in the van—along with a countertop, it became a handy outdoor kitchen. Nico could throw together a quick salad from the few vegetables left in the tiny refrigerator and they could finish it off with some crusty bread she'd bought from the tourist center this morning.

As she watched Nico duck his head, bending his tall frame to get to the fridge inside the van she pushed a hand in to her shorts pocket where the little box sat like a stone. But the romantic atmosphere had been ruined. And now that niggling worry was weighing down on her mind like a bloody ten-tonne anchor, she couldn't think straight anymore. She couldn't ask Nico to marry her now. Not until it was confirmed one way or the other. And she couldn't tell him of her suspicions. Not until she was completely sure herself.

CHAPTER TWO

Nico sat back in his office chair, emitting a deep sigh. It was only ten in the morning and he already wished he was anywhere but at work. The pile of paperwork stared at him from the corner of his desk. So many files to read and review, but he just couldn't find the energy. His boss, Chief Inspector Shadbolt had volunteered him to help the Hobart unit out by going over their case files on a tricky murder that remained unsolved four months down the track. But the words kept blurring together and he couldn't concentrate. Perhaps a cup of coffee might help.

But he knew the real problem; the reality of returning to work after his short holiday was dragging him down. The few days' reprieve he and Lacey had enjoyed on the weekend already seemed eons ago and it was only Tuesday. *Such a great getaway,* he thought as he put his hands behind his head and tipped the chair back. The peace and the beauty of the Tarkine was still lodged in his soul, and he couldn't figure out why he hadn't been there before. Lacey had picked the perfect place to take Dotti 2.0 out for her first run.

Walking the trails in the luminous rays of the summer sunlight with Smudge beside them had brought them closer together as the tranquility of the forest seeped into their bones, driving away the stress of everyday life.

It'd been six weeks now since he'd been wounded on top of Barn Bluff while in pursuit of the double murderer Sandra Brown. He'd been lucky that the bullet had been a through and through just above his hip, and hadn't pierced any vital organs. But his recovery had been slower than he would've liked, and he'd only returned to active duty two weeks ago. Light duties—which really meant deskbound—had been driving him slowly insane. Shadbolt seemed to be intentionally keeping him tied to his desk with this newest case, reading over files for days on end. But the easy strolling through the rainforest had lightened his heart somehow, chasing away the ache in his side until he barely remembered it.

And after their hikes, they'd gone back to Lacey's van at night and made unhurried love in her rooftop bed while watching the stars wheel in their lazy dance overhead, and he easily forgot that he'd even been injured. Despite their busy lives and hectic work schedule, they still had a great sex life. But even he had to admit that sometimes it was rushed or squeezed in between a late-night work call and the need for sleep. It was nice to slow down for once and take stock. Good for them both. And good for his still healing body to take it slow—not that he'd admit that to another living human being, including Lacey. Their connection was getting deeper and more substantial all the time, but this weekend away had cemented his commitment to her into the very core of his being.

Lacey seemed to have been slightly distracted, however, as if she had something on her mind. And then on Sunday night she'd become sick suddenly, which had worried him and put a dampener on their mood. But she'd seemed to recover quickly enough and was smiling at him throughout the rest of the night, even managing to eat half a sausage and some bread, but she'd turned her nose up at the salad for some reason.

That night, he'd held her in his arms and kissed the top of her head and they'd talked instead of making love. Lacey had finally fallen asleep with her head on his shoulder, her arm thrown over his chest, emitting soft snores, dueling with the sound of Smudge's snores from his spot on his doggy bed on the van floor below. And he was fine with that. He hadn't been able to sleep, feeling strangely energized and wide awake. So he lay there contemplating life and love and everything in between.

The idea of asking Lacey to marry him had been rolling around in his head over the past few weeks and it was getting stronger every day. Silently, he berated himself for not being better organized; he could've popped the question while they'd been in Corinna if only he'd decided which ring to buy. The owner of the local jewelry shop had been sworn to secrecy over Nico's increasingly frequent visits. But no matter how long he pored over the various diamond cuts and even the differing precious stones—like the large, square emerald or the marquise-cut sapphire—Nico couldn't find the exact right one for Lacey. It was driving him crazy. Maybe he should bite the bullet, ask her to marry him and let her pick out her own ring. Yeah, that might be the easier way to go.

Coward, a little voice in his head whispered. And he knew it was true. Something else was holding him back, and he could probably put it down to the way Marietta had shredded his heart into a million pieces so that he no longer trusted himself when it came to making a commitment.

He loved Lacey with all his heart. He wanted to get married. Even have kids one day. He could do this. And he was going to do it right. Making up his mind, he decided he was going back to the jewelry shop this afternoon to choose a ring.

Lacey was out on patrol with Linc and wasn't due back at the station until four. That should give him plenty of time to go down and make the purchase and then find a suitable hiding place in his office afterward. He needed to be quick and discreet, making sure none of the other officers saw him. Tyrell especially would know something was up; he was too good at reading people's faces. If Nico returned to the station with a little blue box in his pocket, Tyrell would notice something was awry and call him out. Nico liked and respected the African-American man originally from Detroit; they'd become great friends over the past two years. But he couldn't have Tyrell knowing what he was up to; he'd never live it down.

Linc and Lacey had been sent to check out a report from a farmer who said he'd heard screams and other strange noises during the night. The farmer ran an alpaca stud around twenty minutes outside of Burnie, but hadn't bothered to call in his concerns until this morning. Nico was dubious about the story, wondering if the old farmer had been hitting the booze just a little too hard last night. But Shadbolt decided with all the unusual criminal activity Burnie had encountered recently—including not one, but two murderers caught in the space of six months—that every lead should be followed up and put to rest. He wasn't taking any chances.

Nico respected his boss' wisdom, even if he disagreed with his rationale. Although, the uncertain specter of the mysterious serial killer hunting in the northwestern corner of Tasmania still hung over their heads like a stinking pile of dog shit. Nothing had been heard on that front for over six months now. There'd been no more murders and no fresh leads in that time. Perhaps the killer had moved on, away from the heat of an active investigation. Gone to find easier prey in an area where the cops weren't on high alert for his presence. Maybe he was no longer even on the island. Nico could only hope.

At the thought of Lacey following up a midnight distress call, he felt a spike of anxiousness. He always worried about her whenever she wasn't with him. Ever since that phone call from his father right before Christmas. The threat might've been a veiled one, but Nico had heard the intended malice behind his words and it scared him. Nico trusted Linc implicitly and knew that Lacey couldn't have been partnered with a better bloke. However, not even Linc understood the danger she could be in. He certainly didn't understand the panic that gnawed around the edges of Nico's thoughts day and night, wondering how he was going to protect her from his father.

Nico had informed Shadbolt about his father rising from the dead; he was duty bound just in case it impacted on any current or past investigations. And of course Lacey had filled Linc in; as her trusted partner, he had every right to know, since it may also put him in danger. But no one else at the station knew of his private pain. Lacey had downplayed the danger to Linc, saying that she was only telling him because Nico had insisted, and that she didn't believe she was in any danger. But she didn't know Serge like he did. Serge was canny, not book-smart, but street-smart, a sharp intelligence born on the battlefield. You needed to be smart to fake your own death and get away with it for seventeen years. They still hadn't identified the body they'd exhumed from Serge's supposed grave. Which was frustrating; if they had an ID for whoever that poor man in the burnt-out car had been, it might unearth a connection to Serge, lead to fresh clues as to his whereabouts.

Nico conjured up an image of his father, Serge. Or he should say Reginald Smith, as that was the alias he'd been using until a few years ago. Serge's aliases seemed to have changed over the years with rapid speed and it was hard to keep up. In his memory, Nico saw a long, hawk-like nose, forever slightly crooked because it'd been broken during his father's early years of playing rugby. A strong, determined jawline, not much different to Nico's, except for the shallow cleft in his chin. His brother, Brice, had inherited that dimple, but Nico was thankful his chin remained cleft-free. High, dark eyebrows that Serge had a habit of winging up sardonically whenever he was skeptical about something— which was often. And equally dark eyes, almost black, able to chill a person to the bone. Serge had always been clean-shaven, a hangover from his military days, but Nico suspected he might be sporting a lot more facial hair these days in an attempt to hide his identity. The man was tall, had an imposing way of towering over a person. Nico remembered with a shiver of trepidation how his father had loomed over him as a child as he meted out his strict rules and even stricter punishment.

Serge had spent fifteen years serving in the French Foreign Legion and a year fighting in the Gulf War in the early nineties before returning home to his family a changed man. Nico had only been two years old, and didn't remember much of that time. One of the few things he did remember was that Serge had been a hard man; a hard taskmaster to both his wife and his children. The French Foreign Legion, or FFL, wasn't easy to get into; only one in ten even made it through basic training, so Nico understood a man needed a certain edge to survive in that kind of environment. But Serge's edge was more than hard. He was completely inflexible, with a definite mean streak. The FFL motto was "Honor and Fidelity," but Nico doubted Serge had ever possessed either quality. When Serge had been pronounced dead after the fiery car crash when Nico was fifteen, he'd been secretly relieved to be rid of his father's tyranny. But it seemed the man had faked his death only to come back and begin tormenting Nico with his elusive presence all over again.

Unable to help himself, Nico pulled out his phone and checked his personal email, but there were no new messages. Damnit to hell. He'd been hoping for an update from Patrick McTernan, but there was nothing.

McTernan was a private investigator whom Nico had first hired back when he'd heard rumors that his father was still alive. McTernan had been thorough and was good at his job, eventually confirming that the rumors were indeed true. At the time, Nico hadn't wanted to hear the truth—that his father had betrayed his family and thought nothing of leaving them to cope alone and bereft, so he'd shut the investigation down. But just because Nico didn't want to believe it was true didn't make it so, and he and his mother, brother, and younger sister had to face facts that their father and husband was the lowest kind of rat fink who'd ever walked this earth. Not only had he verbally and emotionally abused them when he'd been around, but he hadn't even had the decency to leave them like a man; instead, he'd taken the coward's way out.

Nico's guts seethed at the thought he'd even wasted one minute grieving for that deadbeat. Serge was no father to him. Or Brice, or Gaëlle. Never had been, never would be.

He remembered with great clarity his father's words on the night he'd called him six weeks ago, right before Christmas. Serge had said, *"We have some unfinished business, you and I. I'll look forward to meeting you soon. I can't wait to look into my son's face and see what kind of man he's grown into."* Then Serge had laughed, a cold, calculating sound that had all the hairs on the back of Nico's neck rising to attention. He heard the implied threat in his father's words. And when Serge had mentioned how beautiful Lacey was, and how Nico needed to take care of her, there was no mistaking that he included her in his threat. Which was why Nico hated to let Lacey out of his sight.

Why was Serge disturbing Nico's hard-earned peace? It was a question he had no answer for. Yet. But he was getting closer. McTernan had been on Serge's trail since early January. It was costing Nico an arm and a leg, but money wasn't the issue here.

Six months ago, McTernan had been the one to uncover Serge's defection to Tasmania from a small town in Victoria two and a half years earlier. Back then, Nico had put McTernan off once he heard that news, unwilling to look too deeply into the consequences of that information. But a month ago, not long after that threatening phone call, he'd re-employed the man to continue the trail.

Using CCTV to trace the old Volvo Serge had driven onto the ferry in Melbourne two years ago, the investigator had uncovered clues to suggest that as soon as he landed in Launceston, his father had sold the Volvo and used cash to continue his travels, so it was near impossible to track him. Also disposing of the name Reginald Smith, Serge then went through a variety of new names over the next few years.

It'd taken McTernan nearly a week to pick up the trail again in Launceston and find the person Serge had sold the Volvo to, but that was the break he'd needed. Serge had not only swapped the Volvo for an even older, beat-up Ford the man was selling, but had paid him way more money than it was worth just to sweeten the deal.

Serge was a wily bastard, and he was clearly trying to hide his trail. He'd gone through two more vehicles after that on his way down to Hobart, as well as many iterations of his name. But McTernan had finally uncovered the details of a possible current vehicle Serge was driving—a rusty, vintage Subaru.

Two weeks ago that vehicle had been spotted driving

down the main street of Strahan on the west coast. Too close for comfort in Nico's mind, and the news had made his blood run cold. But that would make sense, because Nico was sure the intruder in their house six weeks ago had in fact been his father. If he were hiding out somewhere near Strahan, it put him well within driving distance of Boat Harbour Beach. McTernan had asked some careful questions around the small country town and a man who possibly matched Serge had been spotted at the gas station one night, as well as buying food from the local supermarket on another occasion.

But there'd been no word from McTernan for over a week now, and Nico was getting worried. He stood up and stretched his arms above his head. No point in dwelling on it. McTernan would get in touch when he had more information to share. And Nico would just have to grin and bear it until then. Now, it was time to get his head back into this paperwork.

Just as Nico prepared to retake his seat at his desk, Sally-Ann appeared in the doorway to his office, a frown wrinkling the spot between her eyes. "Linc and Lacey just called in a dead body," she said without preamble. "A young woman lying in a ditch on the side of Cutter's Road, right near that farmer's place."

"Shit." The word was out of his mouth before he could stop it. "Tell them I'm on my way." He surged out from behind his desk, the quick movement causing a tug deep in his side, reminding him that he still wasn't completely healed. Motioning Sally-Ann to follow him down the hallway, he asked, "Do we have any details yet?" His mind kicked into top gear, both surprised and alarmed that the farmer's tip-off had actually amounted to something.

Sally-Ann shook her head as she tried to keep up with his long-legged gait. "Not really. Linc just called it in. Said the farmer directed them to a gravel road that runs through the back of his place. That's where he heard the screams coming from. The body was clearly visible to anyone who was driving down that road. Not hidden at all. No particulars as to cause of death or injuries at the moment." Sally-Ann rattled off the few facts she knew. "But she was found naked," she added.

An eerie tingle ran down his spine. Naked didn't mean murder. But it certainly pointed to it. Along with the screams the farmer heard. Shit. Sally-Ann was smart enough not to say anything further. Not to extrapolate or put her thoughts into words. But he knew she was thinking along the same lines as him.

But more than that, this was becoming eerily familiar. Linc and Lacey had been first on the scene when the body of the girl had been found in the river before Christmas. And Lacey had been first on scene six months before when Rania's life had been taken by his best friend, Gabe. He hoped with all his might this wasn't an omen, and another killing spree wasn't about to start.

His immediate thought went to Lacey; he wanted to take her off the case. To keep her safe by spiriting her away. He knew it was a knee-jerk reaction and she wouldn't go for it in a million years. And rightly so. Her job as a police officer was to preserve the peace and protect the innocent, which sometimes put her squarely in the line of fire, and he knew better than to override her wishes. While he'd been up on top of Barn Bluff, he'd finally come to terms with the fact that no matter how much he wanted to, he couldn't protect her from everything; he couldn't be her shield all the time. But goddamnit to hell, he was having a hard time keeping the fear at bay right now.

CHAPTER THREE

"I heard some god-awful screams last night. Scared me so much, me hair turned gray." The farmer smiled, showing a couple of missing teeth. Lacey kept her features blank; screams in the middle of the night we're not to be taken lightly. The farmer had told them to call him Pacca—short for Alpaca. His son had thought it was hilarious when he'd first started to breed the animals and decided to call him that as a joke, but now he was the one laughing all the way to the bank. Pacca stared at them from the safety of his front doorway as his grin fell away.

Lacey shot Linc a sideways glance. He stood straight-backed in his dark-blue uniform, staring unblinking at the farmer, clearly unimpressed with the old man's form of humor too. Then she let her gaze slide around the dilapidated veranda as she waited for the farmer to elaborate. The house was weatherboard and had clearly seen better times. If this guy was making as much money from breeding his animals as he said, then he wasn't putting it back into keeping the place shipshape. Driving up to the house in the police cruiser, she'd noted how the roof sagged in one corner and the outside was in desperate need of a new coat of paint. The grassy paddocks had at least looked in better shape, with a healthy coverage of pasture and the wooden rail fences in good condition. A herd of alpacas eyed them warily as they'd crested the hill and come to a halt out the front of the small homestead, long necks erect as they stared down their noses like a haughty bunch of queens.

Lacey finally let her gaze come back to the old farmer. There seemed to be no Mrs. Pacca, or indeed no family at all, just the old man on his own, judging by the state of the place. Which was a little sad and Lacey reevaluated her perception of the farmer. Loneliness was a hard burden to bear.

When neither Lacey nor Linc responded, Pacca went on with a scowl, "Away over there it was. On the road out the back, sometimes called Cutter's Road, but I'm not sure that's official, like. I might've seen flashing lights too. Reminded me of the war. I thought I was back in Vietnam for a second." He waved a skinny, arthritic hand toward his rear fence as if trying to shoo the apparitions away. "That road ain't used by many people no more. Not even me. It don't go much of anywhere, the council blocked it off years ago." A coughing fit suddenly overtook the old farmer, and he needed a few moments to regain his breath while she and Linc waited patiently. "It's on my property. No one uses it without my knowledge. That's why I called you coppers to come and take a look see."

"Why didn't you call it in last night?" Linc asked as evenly as possible.

"I thought about it." Pacca shrugged. "But then I musta fallen asleep or something. It wasn't till I was feeding the paccas this mornin' that I remembered." A rueful look entered the man's red-rimmed eyes. One of regret, tinged with self-recrimination. "At first I thought I was dreamin' about the war again, but then I knew it was more than that."

Lacey thought that look might have something to do with the old bloke being too intoxicated to even dial a phone before passing out. She held in a sigh.

"But I know what I heard." Pacca stood a little straighter, his creased clothes hanging off his thin frame. "So I thought I'd better do the neighborly thing and report it, you know."

"Thank you, sir," Linc said stiffly, taking a small step backward. "We'll let you know if we find anything."

"Much appreciated, son." Pacca watched them with circumspect eyes as they turned as one and retreated down the rickety front steps to their cruiser.

Neither of them said anything until they were inside the vehicle and bumping down the dirt track leading around the side of the house toward the back paddocks, where a thin line of trees looked like it marked the road Pacca had mentioned.

"Screams and flashing lights," Lacey said thoughtfully, raising a skeptical eyebrow in Linc's direction.

"Hmm. It's probably nothing," Linc agreed. "The old bloke was probably hearing things. And seeing things. Did you catch a whiff of his breath?" Linc screwed up his face.

Lacey nodded. She'd been able to smell the stale whiskey and cigarette smoke coming off the old bloke in waves, even from her spot a few feet back from the door. Pacca clearly loved more than a little tipple every night. Together with his creased, dirty work clothes which looked like the old man had most probably slept in them, he didn't make the most credible witness. And his reference to fighting in the Vietnam War might also make him unreliable. Flashbacks and broken memories were the scourge of many returned war veterans.

But they were here now and needed to check it out so they could report back to Shadbolt. Lacey's money was on the false report. Then her mind drifted back unbidden to the day a little over six weeks ago when she and Linc had responded to a call out to the river near the outskirts of Burnie to discover the first body in a double homicide that'd changed all their lives.

A tingle of premonition fizzed through her veins. Surely, not another murder? Not so soon. This was a small town in the sleepy north of Tasmania. One killer in a year was unlikely, let alone two murderers and three bodies in six months. They'd had their fair share of murders. So this was bound to be another case of a false report by an old man who was too deep into his whisky glass to know any better. Yep, definitely an unreliable witness. Maybe it was the wind blowing in the trees, or a fox howling mournfully for its mate, or an owl hooting its haunting call as it sat in a tree watching in the dark. So many reasonable explanations.

"Sorry," Linc apologized as he drove through an unavoidable large pothole and Lacey grabbed for the bar above her head.

"No probs," she replied, gritting her teeth to try and hold herself steady, while keeping her eyes peeled for anything out of the ordinary. Just in case. This road hadn't been graded in years. In winter, this track may have been impassable for anything other than a four-wheel drive; it'd be muddy and treacherous. Lacey was thankful for the dry heat of summer as a plume of dust rose around the cruiser's wheels. And even more thankful they were in the air-conditioned comfort of the cabin rather than having to walk through the growing heat of the day. Summer in Burnie was usually mild, but on days like today when the air was still and the sun beat mercilessly down out of an azure blue sky it could get hot enough to fry an egg on the tarmac. They were about halfway to the line of trees marking the road at the end of Pacca's property and there was still a lot of pounding through potholes to go.

Lacey's mind wanted to leap back to the problem uppermost in her thoughts, but she kept firmly focussed on the job ahead of them. She'd already spent way too much time cogitating on the subject on the way out here in the cruiser. She'd been so quiet in fact, that Linc had commented on her silence, asking her if something was wrong. Something was wrong, but she plastered on a smile and told him she was merely wishing she were back in the Tarkine on an extended holiday rather than chasing down rumors and innuendos. But it was almost impossible to keep her concentration on the task at hand.

Because her pregnancy test had come back positive this morning.

Positive.

Her brain had gone completely numb when she'd seen those two little blue lines.

She didn't know what to feel. Or what to think.

Apart from the fact that her birth control had failed. Big time. But there was nothing she could do about that. A fact was a fact. And the fact was, she was pregnant. And it was no good berating herself for her practice of skipping the placebo birth control pills in the pack and taking the hormone pills continuously most months so that she didn't have to deal with a messy period. It was easier that way, especially with the long shifts she pulled as an officer on the beat and the very physical nature of her job. That was the reason she hadn't picked up she was pregnant earlier, because she wasn't looking for the warning sign of a missed period.

At the same time as fear and trepidation had flared in her heart, there'd also been a kernel of joy. A small but exquisitely bright flare of hope. But it was too soon to be buoyant. She needed to tell Nico. And they needed to decide what to do. So instead, she'd been draped in a pall of anxiety all morning. This wasn't the right time to be pregnant. She and Nico had never even discussed the idea. And if they had, they'd surely be waiting for a time much farther down the track. Not now. They hadn't even been together a year yet.

She should've waited until she was in the privacy of her

own home later tonight to do the test. But she couldn't bear not knowing, so she'd slipped into the bathroom at the station right before starting her shift and peed on the stick.

Her morning sickness—because she now knew with certainty that's what it was—was going to get harder and harder to hide. Especially from Nico. This morning she'd had to rush to the bathroom as soon as she woke, leaving Nico all sleepy and warm in bed. Then she'd tiptoed to the kitchen and swallowed a few dry crackers and some water and she'd started to feel human again. But she couldn't keep living off dry crackers.

Nico had emerged a few moments later, giving her a quizzical look—he was usually the first out of bed, bringing her an early morning cup of tea before he hopped in the shower—but not questioning her. Yet. The questions would come soon, however. And she needed to have the answers straight in her own head. She owed it to Nico to tell him soon. Tonight. Or tomorrow at the latest. This wasn't something she could keep from him. Didn't want to keep from him.

Pregnant. The word rolled around in her head. Even after seeing the absolute proof, she could still hardly believe it. But there were definite signs. And now she knew what to look for, she was beginning to see the signs everywhere. Tender breasts for one. She was surprised Nico hadn't yet commented on how much fuller they were looking. Then there was the newest development which meant she could hardly look at a vegetable without feeling ill. Normally, she loved her vegetables. A fresh salad on a warm night was one of her go-to meals. Now it seemed that all her stomach wanted was a little protein and lots of carbs, carbs, and more carbs. Salty or sweet, her stomach didn't mind. Hell, she'd even succumbed and had a bucket of hot fries for morning tea today from the local takeaway. Linc frowned at her unusual choice of meal, and said, "You okay, Shorty?"

She'd merely nodded and offered him one of her hot fries which he'd brushed away in favor of his berry smoothie.

Oh, God, how was she going to tell Linc that he'd be losing his police partner in a few short months? Was he going to hate her? Most female cops went onto light duties in the later stages of pregnancy. Of course, there were rules around discrimination in the force and she could never be forced to do anything she didn't want to. But it was a matter of logic and practicality. You couldn't hope to chase down a fleeing felon when you were encumbered by a huge, bouncing belly. And then there were the risks to the unborn child to consider. There was *so much* to consider, Lacey's head was spinning.

But first she had to tell Nico. Her gut churned at the idea.

"There's a gate between us and the road." Linc's gruff observation brought her tumbling guiltily out of her musing. She hadn't been paying attention, even after all her best intentions.

"I'll get it," she replied, already unbuckling her seat-belt, ready to jump out and unlatch the gate. But when she waded through the long, dry grass at the edge of the paddock, she found the latch so rusted from disuse, she could barely open it. At least this backed up Pacca's claims that he scarcely used this road anymore she thought. She grunted as she struggled with the latch. A small breeze tickled the leaves of the trees above, the tall, straight trunks marching away like a line of soldiers in either direction. Tugging with all her might, she finally got the gate to swing back toward the paddock, gaping open just enough that Linc could drive the vehicle through.

Lacey stood in the middle of the Cutter's Road—well, more of a dirt track—hands on hips, feet akimbo, studying the lay of the land, while Linc drove the cruiser a little way down the road and parked it off to the side. It was quiet out here now the car engine was off. Only the mournful sound of a crow cawing somewhere in the distance.

Linc exited the car and shaded his eyes as he squinted into the bright sunshine. "You want to go that way?" he asked, pointing down the road behind her. "And I'll go this way."

She agreed with a nod of her head. They could just drive along the road; it'd be much quicker. But they also might miss something. If there was anything out here to see. Turning around with a sigh, she kicked at the dirt with her black boots, raising puffs of dust as she trudged down the middle of the road. It seemed to have been unused for quite a while. There were no fresh tire tracks. Looking for anything out of place, she shaded her eyes much like Linc had done and kept her mind open for all possibilities.

Less than a minute later, she heard a shout. "Hey, Shorty, get over here."

She looked back to see Linc squatting, staring intently at something in the shallow roadside ditch only a few hundred feet back up the road. The dark skin of Linc's face had taken on a sallow hue and he was leaning back, as if unconsciously trying to get away from whatever was holding his gaze.

A flood of adrenaline flushed through her at the urgency in his voice. Surely not. Surely he couldn't have just found…

She began to run.

Skidding to a stop behind Linc, she swallowed a gasp of fear.

The body of a young woman lay in the ditch. Face up, eyes blank and staring, she was completely naked, hands crossed neatly over her chest. Fresh ligature marks formed dark bruises around her neck. There was no doubt that she was dead. Lacey's stomach churned, this time not from morning sickness, but out of fear and loathing.

There was another killer among them.

CHAPTER FOUR

Nico stared down at the body below him in the ditch. The poor young woman. She couldn't have been more than twenty-one or twenty-two. With so much living ahead of her to look forward to. All that now taken away from her. They were still waiting for Harry McCormick and his forensic team to arrive from Devonport, and so the body remained uncovered. Nico noted her forget-me-not-blue eyes staring unseeing into the sky and he was suddenly sickened. The depravity of people. How could someone do this to another human being? He should know better by now, but he was still shocked at the depth of hatred he felt toward whoever had done this.

He turned his back on the wretched scene to see Lacey standing beside the police cruiser watching him pensively. Her long, blonde hair was pulled back into her customary ponytail, contrasting starkly with the dark blue of her uniform. Linc was finishing off taping the area around the body and two other officers had formed a roadblock at each end of Cutter's Road. Not that it was needed; this place seemed deserted and Lacey had already told him the old farmer had said no one ever used this road, as it led to nowhere.

So why had the killer chosen this spot as his crime scene? Did it have something to do with the alpaca farmer? Was someone trying to send old Pacca a message? The farmer would be the first witness on his list to interview as soon as the forensic pathologist and local GP, Dr. Lagos, arrived and confirmed what they already suspected: death by strangulation.

Nico walked over to where Lacey stood, the sun beating down on the top of his head. It was hot. Nico shrugged out of his suit jacket and slung it over his arm as he leaned a hip against the cruiser next to Lacey. Her beautiful face was paler than normal, and Nico wanted to slip an arm around her shoulder, but he refrained because they were at work and she was a cop on duty.

"You okay?" he asked quietly.

"Not really," she answered in a voice low enough to be only heard by him. "I know we're police officers and we expect to see this sort of stuff all the time, but still…" She shrugged, and he saw the glint of unshed tears in her eyes. "I'm beginning to feel like I'm a jinx," she said, only half joking. "I am the common denominator in all the murders in Burnie ever since I set foot in this place," she continued, a sour tilt to her mouth.

"You know that's mere coincidence, nothing more, right?" He gave her shoulder a light squeeze.

"My cop brain knows that," she replied, but there was no reassuring smile to accompany her words. "But tell that to my small, but very vocal, superstitious side." This didn't sound like the Lacey he knew. She rarely doubted herself and would never think to let coincidences or random facts rattle her.

Linc called over, "All secure, Detective." His gaze flickered between Lacey and Nico as he rolled up the rest of the police tape.

"Thanks. Can you guard the body until forensics get here,

please?" Police procedure; a body was never left alone until it was taken away by the forensic pathologist. That could mean a matter of a few hours or sometimes even days, depending on the state of the body or how much ground there was to cover and evidence to collect.

"Sure." Linc packed the tape into the trunk of the police car and grabbed his police hat from the back seat before he took his place at the edge of the road. The sun was searing, even through the odd patches of shade cast by the trees along the roadside. But Linc bore it with stoicism, standing with hands behind his back, legs akimbo, tall, broad-shouldered and indefatigable.

"Walk with me," he suggested to Lacey, as much to keep her close as to take her mind off all those dark places it seemed to want to go. "I know you've already done a preliminary sweep of the area, but I'd like to take a closer look, see if we can find any clues as to how the girl died, where she died, and how the killer got in and out of the area."

"Right," Lacey agreed. But to Nico's way of thinking, she agreed too readily, not once questioning Nico's motives. Something was going on with her.

They walked in the middle of the road following Lacey's earlier footprints, careful not to disturb anything, shoulder to shoulder, neither of them talking. It was just nice to feel her presence, know that she was safe beside him for the next little while. But they found nothing. Not a single footprint that didn't belong to a police officer. Not a single tire track. It was as if the body had been spirited here and the killer had left without a trace. If it hadn't been for the screams the old farmer had heard, the girl might've gone unnoticed for a long time.

"Where does this road lead to?" he asked, not taking his gaze from his surroundings. "Nowhere," she replied. "Pacca said the council shut it off years ago. At least at the city end. Not sure about the other end." They both swiveled in unison and stared back in the direction they'd come. All the police vehicles had accessed the site through Pacca's property, and no one had yet traveled the length of the track. "I walked a little way along in that direction." She pointed toward where the road disappeared into a shimmering heat haze. "No tire tracks I could see."

"So how do we explain the screams the farmer heard? And the flashing lights?" he asked, posing the question as much for himself as to her. "If he killed her here, then there should be some sign, some clue. No one can scrub an outdoor crime scene of every single clue." That might be true for an inside crime scene, but not out here. A person was bound to leave tracks in the dirt, broken grass, snapped twigs, all signs of a struggle. But there was nothing that he could see.

"Shadbolt's probably going to call in extra help on this one," Nico said as they turned to make their way back to where Linc stood like a statue in the distance, on guard. During the double murder case before Christmas, Shadbolt had called in two extra detectives from Launceston, Pederson and Saito, to lend a hand with the high-profile case. If his hunch was correct, this was going to be an even bigger shit-show than the one previous.

"Why?" Lacey shot him a sharp look, and he grimaced. But she needed to know.

Nico drew in a deep breath. "Similarities with the suspected serial killer MO." He didn't have to elaborate, he could see the exact second comprehension hit Lacey as her fists clenched by her side and she closed her eyes for a brief second.

"I was afraid of that," she replied at last.

"So was I." It was the last thing he wanted, but everything about the dead woman screamed that this was the same killer who'd come to their attention less than a year ago. A spate of murders, all young women who worked in the sex industry, which started around nine months ago. Three women so far, cause of death had been strangulation. Two of the murders had taken place in Hobart, then there'd been a lull in activity until a third death had been reported over in Zeehan on the northwest coast, unsettlingly close to Burnie, six months ago. This was around the same time as Rania's death, and for a while they'd suspected she might've been one of his victims. But the MO didn't fit, and they'd disregarded a connection fairly quickly.

A profiler had come up with an outline of the suspected killer. Male, most likely a drifter. These were possibly not his first murders, as he seemed experienced with killing, and the crime scenes were always left spotless—the killer was careful not to leave anything behind that might give him away, one sure connection to this crime scene. The profiler also thought perhaps the suspect had a military or religious background, because when the bodies were found, they were laid out neatly on their backs, hands folded onto their chests above their hearts. Exactly the same as this poor girl Lacey and Linc had found today.

* * *

Nico smothered a yawn and sat upright. It'd been after one am when he'd crawled into bed last night, but he hardly felt like he'd got any sleep. He'd spent hours interviewing people yesterday afternoon, then more long hours back at the station collating the information and reading reports until his eyes were red rimmed, and then taking his findings to Shadbolt. The chief inspector had agreed with his preliminary theory that this could well be the work of the elusive serial killer and had immediately requested more manpower as Nico suspected he would. Nico would be lead on the case, the same as last time, but they'd need many more feet on the ground and minds on the case if they hoped to solve this one quickly.

Lacey had been fast asleep when he'd arrived home, and he hadn't had the heart to wake her. But when he'd opened his eyes this morning, she was already gone from their bed, which was unusual, especially given that her shift started at midday today and she often liked to lie in if she could. Smudge too, was gone from his cozy bed on the floor.

Dragging himself up wearily, his feet landed on the cool wooden floorboards as he sat on the edge of the bed, orienting himself into the new day. With yet another murder to solve, sometimes he wondered what he saw in this detective job; all the long hours and misery he often endured over another wasted life. The dead girl remained unidentified; there'd been nothing on her body or in the vicinity of the crime scene to help determine her name or where she was from. It was frustrating to say the least.

Nico dragged a T-shirt over his head and padded into the kitchen, wondering where Lacey had got to. There was a fresh pot of coffee made, and with a sigh of relief, he poured himself a mug. As he lifted it to his lips, he caught sight of Lacey outside on the back lawn over near the garage. She was practicing her judo moves. He caught a flash of movement behind her and saw Smudge nosing through the long grass in the orchard at the rear of the property.

His gaze returned to Lacey, as if drawn by a gravitational pull. Graceful and long-limbed, flowing from one stance to the next, she was beautiful. Dressed in skintight yoga pants and a small crop top, her outfit showed off her athletic body to the max, and he felt his cock stir at the sight of her because he knew exactly what it felt like to run a hand down those muscular thighs. Knew exactly how to touch her so that she sighed and urged him for more.

But watching her early morning workout made him

wonder. Her mood had been…odd yesterday at the crime scene. He'd been distracted by the newest murder, and so had she, but there was something else going on in her head that he just couldn't fathom. He'd become pretty good at reading Lacey's thoughts and state of mind. But yesterday, she'd been a closed book. It was a little peculiar, considering the amazing weekend they'd just spent together which'd left him feeling more connected to her than ever. Now it was almost as if an invisible wall had gone up in her mind. But why? He didn't think he'd done anything wrong. Everything had been fine between them over the last two days.

Mug of coffee in hand, he opened the door and trod quietly down the back stairs, not wanting to disturb her. The morning air was cool against his bare legs, but the dew on the grass was already burning off and he knew it'd be another warm day—by Tasmanian standards.

She had her back to him as he stepped barefoot across the grass and he watched her unabashedly, drinking in every graceful movement. He must've made some sound, however, because she turned suddenly, already in a fighting stance, eyes cold as ice. Deadly and ready to defend herself. It shocked him how sharp and dangerous she looked. But just as quickly, the woman with the dangerous edge disappeared behind a self-deprecating smile.

"You scared me," she said, lowering her hands and opening her palms.

"You didn't look scared," he countered. "You looked… powerful." And he was reminded of that night when he'd first encountered Lacey; she'd knocked him to the ground in one swift move when he'd been unwise enough to approach her unannounced. So, of course he knew how dangerous she could be. But this little lesson was good; it helped him remember not to overstep, and to stop worrying about the vague threat Serge presented; she was indeed capable of taking care of herself.

"Really?" she asked, lowering her gaze modestly.

"Yes, really," he replied, kissing her on the cheek, then stepping back so she could continue her practice. Smudge came bounding across to say good morning, his cheerful antics making them both smile.

Instead of going back to her judo, however, Lacey came and stood next to Nico, bare feet buried in the damp grass, her gaze thrown out over the vista of the early morning sun glinting off the ocean in the distance. He could feel her mood change, a strange sort of tension descending over them.

"You're up early," he commented, not looking directly at her; instead, following her lead and letting his gaze drift over the view below. His cottage sat almost at the top of the hill, where they could look down at the rest of the small township of Boat Harbour Beach, as well as enjoy the stunning view of the little curved bay and the endless ocean stretching out beyond.

"I couldn't sleep," she replied, still not looking at him. "I've got a lot on my mind," she added cryptically. "But I didn't want to wake you, so I came out here to enjoy the morning."

"Okay." He took a sip of hot coffee. "Anything I can help with?" he asked lightly, knowing she'd either tell him what was worrying her, or not. It was her choice and he wouldn't push.

"Yes. No. I mean..." she dithered, a hundred different emotions flickering across her face all at once. The first stirrings of alarm fluttered in his belly. What was going on?

"Nico..." She stopped again and turned to face him. "I don't know how to say this, so I'm just going to say it." It almost looked like she was gritting her teeth, as if about to deliver some terrible news and his heart rate skyrocketed. God, she was sick. She was about to tell him that she had some incurable disease, he just knew it, and his knees wanted to buckle beneath him.

"What? Tell me," he demanded, also turning to face her, even though his heart was hammering in his chest and his mind was screaming that he didn't want to know. All he really wanted was for everything to stay the same. Stay in this perfect moment, unaltered, as they watched the sun rise over the ocean together.

"I'm pregnant." Her gaze locked with his, her green eyes wary and watching him.

It took him a few seconds to process her statement. *What?* She wasn't sick? Not dying of some terrible disease? Then the magnitude of those two words began to sink in. It was the last thing he'd been expecting.

"Pregnant?" As in, she was going to have a baby? *They* were going to have a baby?

"Yes." Her gaze never left his. "I did a test yesterday morning, and it was positive. Then I did another one last night, just to be sure. It was also positive," she added.

That would certainly explain her distraction yesterday.

Her mouth took on a strange tilt at one corner, an expression he'd never seen before entering her eyes as he continued to open and close his mouth like a fish gasping for air. It felt as if he were enveloped in a fog of bewilderment, as if his brain barely understood what she'd said, and he couldn't find the words she so clearly wanted him to say. He didn't know what to do in the face of this enormity.

"But you're on the pill," he spoke the first thing that came to mind, the cloud of confusion refusing to clear.

"Yes," she answered, clearly holding on to her patience with increasing difficulty. "And I'm just as shocked as you are. No birth control is one hundred percent effective, however, and we now have to deal with the consequences."

Yes, he knew all that. Logically, he knew all that. But their birth control had failed? And now she was pregnant?

"You're going to be a mother?" Even as he said the words, the enormity of the idea settled on his shoulders. "I'm going to be a father?"

"If that's what you want," she replied. And that's when he finally understood the look on her face. It was a mixture of dismay, disquiet, and also of fragile hope. She was as conflicted about this news as he was. But she'd had more time than him to digest it. And she clearly had a preferred outcome.

But did he want it? Did he want to have a baby with Lacey?

They'd never really talked about having kids. She'd had an unhappy, complicated childhood because of her narcissistic mother, and he wasn't even sure if she wanted kids of her own. Of course, Nico had already considered having children with Lacey in the privacy of his own head—would be happy to have them—but this had all come on much sooner than expected. They'd been together for less than a year. She'd just restarted her fledgling police career. And he was still establishing himself as a superior detective, and hopefully in time climbing the ladder all the way to the top. They had a brand-new unsolved murder on their hands, which'd take all their time and energy. What would throwing a baby in the mix do to all of that?

Then, there was the specter of his own father and his terrible years spent under Serge's threatening presence. The scars Serge had left ran deep. And they also made him question his own ability to be a good father. Was Serge's cruel treatment of his children somehow hereditary? That idea scared Nico the most.

But it was that kernel of fragile hope reflected in Lacey's eyes that finally undid him. She would never put it into words, but she was hoping with all her heart that he was on the same page as her. She wanted to have this baby; he could feel it deep in his soul. And if that's what she wanted…

"I'm going to be a father!" It was a proclamation this time, not merely a question. He placed one hand on her flat stomach and looked her square in the face. "We're going to have a baby." The fog suddenly cleared and he could see clearly, his heart swelling with pride and love. Love for this gorgeous woman. And love for something as yet undefined, but something they had created between them.

A brilliant smile lit up her face. "Seems like it, yes," she finally replied. Her eyes glistened with unshed tears. "If you're truly okay with this." She tilted her head to the side in inquiry.

"Of course I am." He pulled her into a tight embrace, and they stood holding each other with the rising sun lighting up the world behind them.

"It's not going to be easy," she warned. "There are a lot of things we're going to have to sort out before it comes." She pulled away slightly so she could look up into his face, a troubled frown replacing her ecstatic smile. "Like where is the baby going to sleep? How long can I keep working? Should we get married before? Do you want to take paternity leave?" The questions tumbled out of her mouth one after the other, like a torrent being released from a dam wall. Clearly, she'd been worrying over all the things, big and small, unsure of how he was going to receive this news.

"It's okay, Lace," he soothed. "We'll work it out. It'll all be good. One step at a time." He pulled her back into his chest, kissing the top of her head, enjoying the feel of her lithe body against his. A family. They were starting their own little family.

There was only one fly in the ointment that could possibly spoil Nico's joy right at this moment; the thought of his father, lurking out there somewhere. He was a threat to Nico and Lacey and now their unborn child. And Nico needed to do something about it. Sooner rather than later.

CHAPTER FIVE

Lacey sat in the back of the operations room watching Nico debrief the team with all the new information that'd come in overnight. Which wasn't much. They knew squat about the poor murdered girl. No new leads, no new evidence, no closer to IDing the victim. It was now Thursday, two days since she and Linc had found her in the ditch and they had nothing. It felt like the girl had been murdered by a ghost.

Some officers were nursing hot mugs of coffee, her included, while others wrote in their notebooks. But they all focussed entirely on Nico and the photos on the murder board at the front of the room. Jay Pederson and Tasman Saito were also seated in the room. The two other detectives from the Launceston unit sat down the front, staring fixedly at Nico. Lacey nodded at Linc who sat a few chairs away, but couldn't quite meet his eye.

Yesterday had been hard. Keeping a secret from her partner was hard, especially when they were cooped up in the police cruiser for most of the day. In some ways, Linc knew her almost better than Nico did. More than once during their shift he'd asked her if everything was okay. She'd told him she was just a little shocked at this new murder in their sleepy little town and he'd taken her answer at face value, then changed the subject to how they were going to catch this guy. But she knew it was only a matter of time before Linc's suspicions grew, and she wouldn't be able to lie to him forever. The morning sickness alone was going to be a dead giveaway. It was getting worse. She'd had to rush to the ladies' bathroom right before this meeting. She'd learned to carry those disgusting dry crackers on her at all times, as for some reason, they seemed to calm the swells of nausea.

Dragging her thoughts away from how she was going to break her pregnancy to her partner, Lacey instead let her gaze settle on the large image of the murdered girl, front and center on the whiteboard. If it weren't for the ligature marks around her neck, she could almost be peacefully asleep, using the long, dry grass as a pillow and the blue sky as her roof. Lacey's mind drifted, and she wondered what the girl's story was. What had she been doing before her life had been so cruelly cut short? Judging her age to be around twenty-one, Lacey knew she was on the cusp of adulthood. Fresh-faced and eager to face the world. Where was home for this girl? Did she have a boyfriend? Or girlfriend? Or family that were missing her? Such a shame this girl wouldn't be able to fulfill her potential and go on to live the life she was meant to.

The backs of Lacey's eyelids began to prickle, and she gave her head a quick shake. This bloody pregnancy stuff was a pain in the ass. Now she was getting teary at the drop of a hat. She was supposed to be a hardened cop, not be affected by death and carnage...Well, at least not show how affected she was. How was it going to look to her colleagues if she burst into tears every time she studied a crime scene photo of a dead or mutilated victim?

But then again, every death still reminded her of Cindi. She'd never get over watching that little girl take her last breath. The nightmares still haunted her sleep, but they were getting less and less. She'd suffered PTSD after the event where Cindi had been stabbed to death by her mother, but she was getting on top of her inner demons slowly, bit by bit every day. And being a cop was part of the process of winning back her old sense of purpose. It was just a shame that being a cop also brought these kinds of murders into stark contrast, reminding her that not every story had a happy ending in this world and she wasn't infallible.

Refocussing on Nico's words, she pushed images of Cindi out of her head, while also banishing questions about this new dead girl's previous life. The only way they could truly help the victim now was to find her killer and mete out justice for her death.

"The more we scratch the surface of this crime the more questions it poses," Nico said. "The only thing we know for sure is that she died by strangulation, and that time of death was around midnight on Monday. Autopsy confirmed that this morning," he added. "Other than that, we don't know where she was murdered. It could've been on scene, or somewhere else, and then her body dumped by the side of the road."

Nico stopped speaking giving his team space to ask questions. But when none came, he continued, "At first glance, this murder looks like it follows all the typical MO of the sex worker serial killer we identified mid last year." Lacey grimaced at the label. Someone in the team had bandied the term around after the third victim was found and the nickname had stuck. But Lacey found it crass and disrespectful to the women he'd killed so far, and she decided she'd have words with Nico afterward to see if they could come up with a better moniker.

"The precision with which the naked body was laid out postmortem, hands crossed over heart, the ligature marks, the age of the victim, the way the site has been left spotless, almost as if the killer was never there, no signs of physical assault, other than strangulation, all point to him."

At least that was one small mercy in the litany of other despicable acts. None of the other three murder victims had been raped or tortured.

"But there is one major difference. We can't confirm this yet, but it doesn't look like this girl worked in the sex industry. She was too…clean." Nico hesitated over the word, but Lacey got his meaning. Girls in that field often had drug habits or were involved in other substance abuse, the signs of which were unmistakable. There was often bruising or marks on a woman's body left by over enthusiastic customers. Poor nutrition, eating disorders, and lack of self-care leading to poor dental hygiene were also often an indication of mistreatment. And not to be indelicate, but inflammation or other injuries of the vaginal area were also common. The forensic pathologist would have been able to document any of these as evidence if they'd been there, but it seemed like she was just a normal young adult, living a healthy life.

"Like I said, this isn't definitive. But if it's true, this puts the victim outside the serial killer's normal scope of his preferred victim pool. Which is worrying. It might mean he's branching out. Taking on a wider sweep of prey," Nico said.

The room was silent for a few seconds as everyone digested this news.

"Or it could mean this isn't the work of our serial killer," Pederson said. And while it was what everyone else might've been thinking, Nico still threw him a blank look that fooled no one. Nico and Pederson didn't see eye to eye. Not since he and stablemate, Saito, had joined them in the Sandra Brown case before Christmas. Pederson was curt and had little to no bedside manner. He said things as he saw them. Saito was more circumspect, had a quiet manner, but a steely gaze that belied her small stature. Both were good detectives in their own way, and both might prove handy in the days and weeks to come.

"It could," Nico agreed. "Again, we're not discounting anything at this early stage." He turned on his heel to pace forward to the whiteboard, pointing at the photo of the old man on the alpaca farm and changing the direction of the conversation. "I've interviewed the farmer, Vincent McMillan —he prefers to be called Pacca—who made the report of screams during the night. His farm vehicles and building have been thoroughly checked, with no signs of evidence or any foul play. He has no alibi for the night in question, but I'm inclined to believe his story for now."

No alibi apart from the bottle of whisky Pacca had consumed that night, Lacey thought darkly. And then chastised herself for being so unkind. The old man was clearly battling his own demons, so who was she to judge.

"We need to dig deeper into his past, however, make sure he hasn't got any priors, or criminal connections," Nico continued, tapping his finger thoughtfully against his chin as he stared at the image of the old farmer he'd pinned to the board.

Lacey understood that Nico had to follow all avenues to make sure he didn't miss any vital clues, but she highly doubted Pacca was their killer. He wasn't the most sprightly of old men. She concluded he must be close to eighty, even though it was hard to tell, sun ravaged and wrinkled as he was. But the way he'd shuffled around on his front veranda spoke of arthritic joints and years of prolonged pain. Not like her lively neighbor Herb, who, with his wife, Margie, were cycling enthusiasts, keeping fit and trim even though they were now both well into their seventies. Pacca would've struggled to hold down a twenty-one-year-old girl, even if he did manage to drug her beforehand, let alone to strangle her, which was a very intimate crime and possibly spoke of a lover or someone else who felt passionately about the victim.

And that didn't even begin to answer the question of how he got the girl out into the ditch in the first place. He couldn't have carried her that far. He might have transported her in one of his dusty vehicles, but Nico said they'd all been checked and cleared of evidence. Which left the possibility that the old man had an accomplice. Or was an accomplice himself.

"Why did the killer choose that remote, unused road?" The question interrupted her musing, and Lacey glanced over to see it was Constable Karl Hickey who'd spoken up. Thick-necked and stocky, Hickey reminded her of a bulldog. But he was a good cop, with great instincts and she respected him, even if he was a little gruff for her liking. "Not a lot of people even know that Cutter's Road exists, it tends to be local knowledge only," Hickey continued. "Which means this guy is either a local, or he's spent some time and energy scoping out the place."

It was true. Pacca had told them—and it'd been confirmed by the council—that the end of the road, where it joined up with the highway had been permanently blocked off with a concrete barricade ten years ago at the request of the farmer himself to stop *"those stupid tourists getting lost on his property"*, as he'd so eloquently put it. The other end of the track terminated at a junction with another dirt road used by locals to access their properties from the main highway between Burnie and Strahan, around forty farms in all. Pacca's rear access road was blocked with a gate and cattle grid on that end. Not locked, merely latched closed, much like the gate she and Linc had driven through the other day. So anyone could access the road if they really wanted to. But it was clearly marked with a Private Property, Keep Off sign to keep trespassers away, and it seemed no one had the need nor the desire to travel down it anyway.

"Agreed," Nico responded. "I've got Sally-Ann and

Constable Lawson door knocking the area to see if any of the residents heard the same thing Pacca did. She's also going to ask for any security footage they have. Who knows, we might be able to identify a vehicle or a person visiting that road over the past few weeks." It was a long shot, Lacey thought, but they might get lucky.

"Do you think he might've had a specific reason to choose that particular crime scene?" Hickey continued, obviously on a roll, trying to make any connections he could between victim and killer.

"Possibly." Nico raised one shoulder in a bemused shrug. "And if he did, does it have something to do with Mr. McMillan? Is the killer sending him a message? Or sending us a message? Perhaps trying to frame him for the murder?"

"Yeah, right," Hickey mused, then lapsed back into a thoughtful silence.

The debrief continued for another twenty minutes with all the team members contributing something to the conversation. But it became more and more apparent the longer they talked how little they actually knew about the crime. No witnesses—apart from a drunk, old, unreliable man—no clues, nothing.

Nico released them all to their daily duties. While he and the other two detectives stayed on the case, she and Linc were back out on patrol. Sally-Ann and Dawn were out door knocking, and Nico had a couple of the junior constables searching through the databases to see if they could come up with an ID for the girl. The crime scene had been thoroughly and forensically searched and cleared, but with no real leads to follow up, the rest of them were on normal duties unless something else came up.

"Come on, Shorty," Linc called over as he stood and stretched his arms above his head. "Let's head out." He nodded toward the door, and then stage-whispered, "And grab a coffee from our favorite barista on the way." He gave a wicked smile; with so many brilliant white teeth flashing it almost blinded her. She was so glad to have Linc back as her partner. When he'd been struck over the head during the previous case and ended up in hospital, she'd been so scared that he might die. The incident made her all the more grateful that he'd made a full recovery and was back on the beat with her. She couldn't imagine working with any other partner.

She grinned back. "I'm sure Conner is expecting us," she quipped, also standing and resettling her duty belt around her hips. How long would this belt fit her until she had to let it out a notch? The wayward thought made her grimace. "I'm right behind you," she stated, waving him through the doorway before he saw her face.

Just before she slipped through the door behind him, she turned and caught Nico's eye, and they shared a secret smile. She had to look away quickly, scared someone would see their clandestine glance. No one could know that she was pregnant yet. It was too early; she was only seven weeks if her calculations were correct. And she still needed to have it doubly confirmed by the doctor; she had an appointment booked for tomorrow before her midday shift. But she was so happy, it was hard to keep it off her face. Lacey was almost bursting at having to keep the secret behind her closed lips. She wanted to shout it from the rooftops that she and Nico were going to have a baby together. Her thoughts of asking Nico to marry her had taken a back seat for now. But she hadn't shelved the idea completely. Now, more than ever, would be a great time to get married. For the baby's sake as much as their own. But she needed to pick her time, get it just right. It may come up sooner rather than later in discussions about how they were going to manage things. But for now, she and Nico were just digesting the news, letting it settle into their psyche and enjoy the notion.

Yesterday morning, after Lacey had blurted out the news—not how she'd intended to tell Nico, but she hadn't been able to hold in the words—they'd gone back inside to the living room and talked and talked. He'd held her hand as she recounted how she'd figured out she was pregnant while on their weekend away when she'd thrown up after drinking the wine, but she hadn't wanted to say anything until she was certain. Then they talked some more, about their hopes and dreams for the future. Nico should've been at work, but they both knew these few precious moments were a sacred time between them that shouldn't be lost. Nico had pulled her onto his lap and she'd rested her head on his shoulder, while he lay one protective palm over her belly—which was ridiculous because the baby was probably only the size of a raisin right now. Lacey had decided that she'd fallen pregnant during the make-up sex they'd had after their argument over Nico's ex-wife.

Things had progressed from there, and Lacey had found herself tugging Nico by the hand down the hallway toward their bedroom. Flooded with relief after sharing her growing joy with Nico, she wanted to feel his body cover hers, feel him moving inside her as the ultimate manifestation of their love.

They sank into the sheets. His mouth was on hers and she let herself ease into him. Softly, he ran a hand down her back, and she sighed at the simple pleasure of it. The comfort and passion he offered was like no other. Rolling her onto her back on the bed, he got rid of her yoga pants and tank top in one seamless motion. She stared up at him, enthralled by his handsome, familiar face. Then he speared his hands into her hair, spread like silk over the pillow, as his eyes speared into her soul and the emotion in the indigo-blue depths undid her. Every muscle ached at his touch and she knew he'd ruined her for any other man. She loved Nico like no other before.

He was her end and her beginning.

And now they had a new thread to add to their story.

She'd been lost in a world of sensation as Nico worked his magical hands over her body. But soon, his soft touches became demanding and needy as he divested himself of his clothes, and then they were both naked. Pinning her to the bed with his muscular thighs, his tongue ravaged her mouth then he moved down so that his teeth nipped at the sensitive skin of her neck. She moaned as waves of desire hit her. This moment had gone from soft and slow to hard and fast in three short seconds. She needed him inside her. Now. And she let him know, bucking her hips against his, urging his cock between her legs. Nico didn't need any more encouragement as he slipped into her and she clenched around him. She came fast and hard, and still felt the echoes of her own orgasm as Nico thrust three more times, then he shuddered like he was falling apart and cried out her name as he came, groaning and collapsing onto her as the waves of ecstasy washed through him.

It was hot and dirty and fast. This was something new they could add to their list of things they'd never done before. Sex while she was pregnant. Lacey remembered reading something about pregnancy hormones making a woman horny. If that was the case, they were going to enjoy the next seven months.

Shaking her head, she cleared away thoughts of sex with Nico and got her mind back on the job. It wouldn't do for Linc to see this dreamy look in her eyes.

Half an hour later, they were cruising along the back roads of Burnie, the crumbs of their oh-so-gloriously-rich-and-fresh croissants still littering their laps and the smell of the best coffee in the world permeating the cabin. Lacey was happy, her stomach full—for now—and she and Linc had settled back into their normal easy chatter. Their task today was to check out an old, abandoned warehouse on the outskirts of town where worried residents had reported a group of homeless people were using it as a drug den to shoot up. Then, if that was all clear, they were to set up a radar trap along the highway farther out. Lacey wasn't happy about issuing fines to speeding drivers—a lot of citizens saw it as nothing but a revenue raiser—but it was part of the job and she wasn't one to argue politics. She'd much rather be tracking down more clues on the supposed serial killer, but with no new avenues to follow up, that trail seemed to have gone cold. And Nico had the help of the two detectives from Launceston now.

"Did you see my uncle's expression yesterday, when Sally-Ann tried to set him up with that friend of hers?" Linc let out a loud laugh. Tyrell Jackson, Linc's uncle and the reason Linc was here in Tasmania on secondment from Detroit, had become the subject of Sally-Ann's laser focus lately. Sally-Ann was the mother hen of the police station, constantly taking the junior constables under her wing, and making everyone feel welcome and loved. But her one foible—some saw it as a serious flaw—was that she liked to see everyone happy. And in her mind happy equated to settled down with a good husband or wife. Sally-Ann conveniently ignored the fact that she herself was happily single and likely to stay that way.

"Tyrell didn't know which way to look." Linc roared with laughter. "He was brought up not to disagree with a woman. But when Sally-Ann said she'd already booked him a table at The Foreshore for him and his lady friend, he went white as a sheet."

"I thought Tyrell was due to head home to Detroit in the next few months," Lacey said.

"Yeah, he is. But that doesn't seem to put Sally-Ann off. Maybe she thinks if she can find him the right woman, he might decide to settle here and stay forever."

"Hmm," Lacey contemplated Tyrell's plight. "Maybe—"

Dispatch came through on the radio, interrupting their banter. "Unit one-two-nine, I've got a rather agitated man on the line who wants to talk to Constable Carmichael."

"Right," Linc said into the dash microphone. "She's here with me in the car. Any details on who he is and what he wants?"

"He says his name is Pacca, and he talked to you the other day. Carmichael must've made an impression on him, because he said he'd only speak to her." Lacey sat up straighter at the mention of the farmer's name and she sent Linc a look that said, *I wonder what he wants now?*

"Patch him through, Delilah, thank you," Lacey replied.

Pacca's scratchy voice sounded through the radio. "Is that you? Is that the girl in the uniform I talked to the other day?"

"Hello, Mr. McMillan. Yes, it's me, Constable Carmichael. My partner and I were the first officers to respond to your call the other morning regarding the murdered girl."

"Oh, thank Christ," he blurted. Delilah at dispatch was right; Pacca sounded agitated and slightly out of breath. "That tall detective fella gave me his card, but I threw it in the bin. I need you to come out to my farm immediately. Something else is going on."

Lacey shot Linc a look of alarm. "Calm down, Mr. McMillan, and tell us what's happening." Even as she spoke, Linc did a graceful U-turn and began heading in the direction of the alpaca farm.

"I think there's another girl. Out on my back road. Only this time she's alive."

CHAPTER SIX

Nico bent his knees and squatted down at the edge of the road, watching Lacey and the girl intently. It was hot, even in the dappled shade, and sweat trickled down between his shoulder blades as he pursed his lips and tried to figure out what was going on here. Absently, he picked a piece of dried grass and tapped it against his chin. This was all kinds of fucked up, and he was completely unsure of his next move. All he knew was that the old farmer had reported a naked girl walking up and down the same track at the back of his property where they'd found the murdered girl two days ago. She wouldn't let the old man near her, screaming and hissing at him like a frenzied cat if he approached, and that's when Pacca had called Lacey.

Linc told him upon arrival that the same thing had happened to him when he'd first tried to approach the girl. But when Lacey had waved Linc back to the cruiser and walked slowly toward her, the girl had calmed slightly, finally letting Lacey drape her police jacket around her shoulders to cover her nakedness. Then she'd managed to get her to sit and drink some water; the girl was so parched she'd gulped most of the bottle before Lacey could stop her. When Nico had arrived fifteen minutes later, Linc was looking on with a slightly bemused frown from where he was leaning against the bumper of the cruiser, completely unused to taking a back seat in something this important.

Lacey had shaken her head at Nico when he tried to come near, waving him off with the ferocity of a mother bear protecting her cub. It seemed Lacey had formed an attachment to the girl, and he was letting her run with it. For now.

Linc knew no more than Nico. He hadn't been able to leave his spot by the car; every time he made a move toward the women, the girl would get to her feet, darting him terrified glances and looking like she was about to bolt. So Linc had left Lacey to it. Now, Lacey sat in the long grass at the side of the road in the shade of a tall gum tree talking quietly to the girl. More police officers had arrived forming a cordon around the crime scene, but everyone had been ordered to stand back. The girl became agitated at the sight of another police officer, especially if they were male, and just as Linc had declared, it seemed like she might do a runner if they so much as looked at her sideways. Nico had made sure he was the exception, edging ever so slowly closer, which still wasn't close enough to hear what they were saying, annoying him to no end. Sensing a woman's touch was needed, he'd called in a female doctor, Mary Erikkson, instead of Imran, the male psychologist they normally used, to try and help talk some sense into this poor girl, and she should be here any minute.

Was this girl connected to the dead girl? And if so, why was she out wandering naked in the middle of the day? Had she escaped from the same man who'd killed the first girl? Or even more sinister, had he just let her go?

Nico had made no headway toward getting closer to Lacey and the girl by the time the psych arrived. The heat of the day had become oppressive and his patience at having to stay at this distance from a prospective lead in his murder case had just about run out. But when Mary arrived, walking briskly toward them along the dusty track, Lacey stood up and beckoned her over. It was the first time Nico got a good look at the girl's face, as she'd been hunkered down behind Lacey, almost using her as a shield, and what he saw made him forget everything else. Her face was ravaged by many tiny cuts and bruises, but it wasn't the physical injuries that floored him, it was the terrible torment in her eyes. Like she'd seen right down to the depths of hell and it'd ripped her soul apart.

Mary was by Lacey's side in a heartbeat, helping her get the girl to her feet. Then the three of them put their heads together for many moments in quiet conversation. Finally, the trio turned and with Lacey on one arm and Mary on the other, they began to walk slowly toward the ring of waiting police cars. The girl was still barefoot, and she wobbled and nearly stumbled. If it hadn't been for the two women by her side, she would've fallen into the dirt. Her thin legs were pale and also covered in cuts and bruises beneath Lacey's police jacket.

"She's agreed to go to hospital with me," Mary said in a tone that brooked no argument as they passed by him. "You can follow behind in your car if you like, but it might be a while before she's in any fit state to talk to you."

"Can one of my officers go with you?" he asked. It was imperative they keep her under guard until they had a chance to interview her. For her own safety as much as his need to find answers. Normally, Mary would understand this; it was standard protocol. But for some reason, this girl seemed to be engendering all sorts of maternal overprotectiveness in both her and Lacey.

"I'll go," Lacey offered immediately, and Nico grimaced. He needed to talk to her, find out what she knew. But he nodded curtly as she looked up for confirmation. Lacey's face was almost as pale as the poor girl, and that worried him. She was inclined to get too close to some victims, and sometimes took on their pain as her own. It was one reason why the little girl's death back in Melbourne had affected her so deeply. Why it'd resulted in her PTSD. The fact that she couldn't save Cindi. Every time she got close to a victim of crime, he secretly hoped she wasn't headed down the same path all over again.

He followed at a respectable distance behind the women. The girl seemed to shrink into herself as they approached the mass of police vehicles and officers clustered at the far end of the crime scene, but Lacey talked in soothing tones until they came up beside Mary's blue Honda SUV, and she helped to ease the girl into the rear of the car. Mary went around to the driver's side, but Nico snagged Lacey by the elbow right before she followed the girl into the car.

"Can you tell me anything?" he asked in a hushed whisper. This whole thing was completely unorthodox, but Nico was nothing if not adaptable. If this was what it took to make the victim comfortable enough to finally tell him everything she knew, then that was how it was going to be. But even a small morsel of information would help to ease his bafflement right now and give him something to work with in the interim.

Lacey glanced quickly into the car and then turned to him. The pain in her eyes was clear. "Her name is Taylor Longbrook, and she has no idea how she got here, or what happened to her. She keeps asking where her best friend Danika is. The last she remembers clearly is that they were backpacking through Strahan together. After that, she has no clear memories. Just flashes of a man. And pain. Lots of pain. That's all." Lacey closed her eyes briefly, as if the information was too much for her to process, too much to bear, then she got into the car without another word.

"Fuck," Nico said quietly as he watched Mary's car drive

away through the phalanx of cop vehicles.

For a second, he was torn. To follow Mary to the hospital in the hope he could speak to Taylor soon, or send someone he trusted to keep a watch over her and let him know the second she was ready to talk.

"Tyrell," he shouted to his colleague and good friend.

The man looked up from where he was studying a set of footprints in the dirt, his coal-dark skin glistening with sweat from the heat of the day. "Yes, boss."

"Follow Lacey, Mary, and the girl into town. Don't let them out of your sight and make sure you, and only you, stand guard at the victim's door until I get there. Don't let anyone in or out without calling me first. Including Lacey or the doc."

"Yes, boss." Tyrell was already opening the door to his cruiser. Nico knew the victim and Lacey would be in the best of hands with Tyrell. And Nico was sending him as much to look after Lacey as to guard the victim. She was pregnant. With his baby. He wasn't going to let anything happen to her.

At least he had a name now. Something concrete he could move forward with. Taylor Longbrook. Did that mean her best friend, Danika, was the one they'd found in the ditch? Nico dialed a number on his cell and relayed the information through to Sally-Ann. She was the best by far at digging up information, especially on short notice. Once he had her promise that she'd call him the second she found something concrete, he put his phone in his back pocket and concentrated on the crime scene. Hopefully, it might reveal more clues that'd help them piece together what'd happened here. Something to link the two girls, the dead one and the one left alive. Maybe, just maybe, this time the perp had slipped up and left some small detail for him to find.

Next on his list of priorities was to interview the old man farmer. To see if the girl had said anything to him, find out exactly what he'd seen and heard in the hours and minutes before he found Taylor. He'd already interrogated the old farmer once, and knew the man had an annoying tendency to waffle, going off on tangents when Nico needed him to stay on track. He talked about the war a lot, and how the whole country had hated his guts when he'd returned from Vietnam. Nico had Sally-Ann requesting his military records to see if anything suspect had happened during his service. Pacca also mentioned a son who was a greedy son of a bitch, and who'd tried to cheat him out of his farm. But when Nico pushed him for information, he waved it away as not relevant, saying he'd lost touch with his son when they had a falling out about the farm and he'd moved to the mainland. He hadn't spoken to his son in over ten years the old man had growled and wouldn't talk about it anymore. Apart from that, Pacca seemed to have no other family and very few friends.

But Nico couldn't shake the feeling there was something fishy going on here. This had to be more than coincidence. Twice in three days the old man had a girl dropped on his doorstep. What was the killer trying to tell them?

* * *

Two hours later, Nico stood outside the hospital room talking quietly to Tyrell. "I want a guard on this door twenty-four seven," he directed. He peered through the little window, trying to see what was going on in the room, but the curtains were tightly drawn around the bed and he could see nothing. "Is Lacey still in there?"

"Yes," Tyrell replied. "They've been in there the whole time. A female doctor is in there with them too."

"Right." Nico frowned at the door. "So you don't know anything more about the victim?"

Tyrell shook his head, keeping his gaze directed down the hallway. But Nico knew they were both wondering the same thing. What was going on in there? He needed to know. So he squared his shoulders, raised his hand to knock, but was surprised when he found himself hesitating, not wanting to intrude suddenly. Which wasn't like him. Not when he was on a case. Not when he needed answers. Something about the girl's obvious torment had gotten to him, and he wasn't sure why. Freud might say it had something to do with him seeing Taylor's distress and how that pain was affecting Lacey. Subconsciously, he wanted to take that pain away, so that Lacey was no longer suffering. But deeper than that, he knew how he'd feel if it were Lacey who'd been found wandering naked on that road. And that thought scared him shitless. Because it made him angry. So angry. Violence surged in his guts. He knew he wouldn't be reacting like this if Lacey wasn't involved in this case. And somehow, finding out about her pregnancy made it worse. Because it wasn't just her who needed protection now. There was another life at stake.

Drawing in a deep breath, he cleared his mind of all those wayward thoughts and knocked firmly on the door, then without waiting for an answer, he let himself in. "It's Detective Favreau," he declared to the drawn curtain. There was no way he was pulling back that screen without an invitation. "Is it possible to talk to the—to Taylor?"

"I'll be right with you, Detective," a voice that he assumed belonged to the doctor announced, leaving Nico standing on the outside of that screen listening to the low murmur of voices, his impatience building.

Finally, the curtains twitched aside, and both the doctor and Mary appeared. Nico caught a glimpse of Lacey, sitting in a chair at the girl's bedside, holding her hand, before his view was blocked by the two women as they stood before him. Mary merely nodded her acknowledgement, not speaking.

The doctor looked him directly in the eye. "I've conducted

my physical examination." He noticed a wayward strand of gray hair had come loose from her otherwise perfectly tight bun caught at the nape of her neck. She was to the point and professional, in a calm but maternal way. Nearly as tall as him, her white coat draped loosely over her thin frame. She swiped a hand across her forehead, and Nico suddenly discerned a deep fatigue in that one simple move. "I'll talk to you out in the hallway, if you don't mind?" She touched his elbow, and he found himself being led out of the room before he could object, Mary right on his heels. If he didn't know better, he might've thought he was being herded like some kind of animal. There wasn't even time to shoot Lacey one more look before he was past Tyrell and back in the hallway.

Once they were standing to the side of the nurses' station, the doctor said in a discreet tone, "I'm Dr. Monroe. I believe you've already met Dr. Erikkson." She nodded toward Mary. Nico held back his quip that he was the one who'd called her in, and merely nodded. "Good." Dr. Monroe consulted her notes before continuing. "Firstly, I can tell you that Taylor was not raped, or sexually assaulted in any way." She lifted her head to stare at him. "I'm telling you this now because I know it's usually the first thing you cops like to focus on."

Nico was a little taken aback. It almost felt like she was painting him as the enemy. "Thank you," he replied. That should be good news, but he had a feeling it wasn't. "The presence or not of a sexual assault can tell us a lot about the perpetrator, which is why it might seem like we focus on it." He stopped, not wanting to sound like he needed to explain himself, instead waiting for her to elaborate.

"Hmm." The doctor fixed her fierce, gray gaze on him for a second, as if weighing him up. He must've passed whatever test she was mentally putting him through, because she continued. "But there are worse things than sexual assault, if you can believe it."

"Okay." His skin began to crawl. What'd happened to this poor girl to make the doctor so cautionary?

Dr. Monroe pursed her lips. "Taylor has been subjected to physical torment, which has left her bleeding and scarred." The doctor glanced quickly at Mary. "But also mental torment, that has traumatized her immensely." The tall woman looked down at her notes. "There are hundreds of tiny cuts all over Taylor's body. I think they were inflicted as a form of torture." Nico remembered the brief look he'd had at the girl's face earlier and remembered the tracks of blood on her cheeks and forehead. His stomach clenched, but he gave nothing away on his face. "But I'm not sure what the aim of that torture was. Was he trying to get information out of her? Or was it merely for personal pleasure? I'm not the one to answer those questions." Dr. Monroe's face contorted with disgust. "But that's not the worst of it," she stated, then clamped her mouth shut as if unable to tell him the rest.

Mary took over the conversation. "Because of her trauma at the hands of this…individual…" Mary paused, and he was surprised to see how much she'd been affected by what she'd seen. "She has what we call dissociative amnesia."

Nico stood a little straighter. This wasn't what he'd hoped to hear.

"It's where a person blocks out certain events associated with trauma," Mary continued. "Sometimes their memory will return, often within a few days. But sometimes not for months, or ever. Taylor doesn't remember anything surrounding the other girl's death, and only a little about the few days before they were abducted."

Nico hid his grimace. He got what Mary was saying. This poor girl had been so badly marked by her harrowing experience that her mind had blocked it all out. Which meant she might not be able to tell him much about the killer. They were still desperately trying to ID the dead girl. It seemed highly likely it was Taylor's best friend, Danika, but they were yet to get concrete confirmation.

He tuned back in to what Mary was saying. "Taylor can't remember much of anything about the past few days. But her memories could be triggered by something in her surroundings, or even therapy," she added with a warning tone to her voice, but Nico felt a small rush of hope. So she *might* get her memories back. He needed to cling to that hope.

"However, it's most important, that Taylor feels safe. Both in her surroundings and in the people she talks to," Mary said.

Ah ha, that was what Mary was warning him about. She didn't want him upsetting her with his probing questions. How else was he supposed to catch this guy?

"Victims may suffer severe depression or anxiety afterwards, which I believe Taylor is experiencing right now, and I've prescribed some anti-anxiety medication." Both Mary and the doctor fixed him with baleful glares. He understood now that they saw him as the enemy because, by asking her questions, he was also asking her to revisit that terrible experience. But what choice did he have? Would they rather the perpetrator go free?

He chose his next words carefully. "Can I ask, in your personal experience, what do you think Taylor saw, or didn't see that might've caused the amnesia?"

Mary and the doctor exchanged a look. It was Mary who finally spoke. "I could be wrong, but I think the killer might've forced her to watch as he murdered her friend. There are signs that her eyelids were taped open, as well as other signs that she was physically restrained, her head held in a particular position."

Nico shook his head, shocked at the psych's answer. He wasn't sure what he'd been expecting, but that wasn't it. No wonder Lacey was being protective of this victim, as were the two doctors.

"Why on earth would someone do this to another person?" Dr. Monroe blurted. "I've seen some horrific things in my time, but this one takes the cake."

He knew there were sick people out there who did despicable things, and he'd seen some of that firsthand. But you never became completely indifferent to it.

"Can I talk to her? I need to know what she does remember." He held up his hands in supplication as both women glared at him. "I'll be as gentle as possible," he promised.

"As long as you keep it short. And as long as I can sit in on the interview, to be there if she needs me," Mary finally conceded.

"That would be good," Monroe added. "I still have ward rounds to complete." He could see her focus already moving on, homing in on the next patient on her list. Her disgust at Taylor's treatment had been real and raw, but the reality of being a busy doctor in a busy hospital was that she had other patients to care for.

"I'll go in and talk to Taylor, prepare her for the interview," Mary said.

"Could you send Constable Carmichael out, please?" Nico asked as Mary turned to leave. "She doesn't need to be in there for this." He wanted to debrief her before he went in; she may have some small but pertinent information that might help him direct his questioning. Besides, she'd already spent enough time with the victim. She needed to get back to the station and write up her notes, while the details were still fresh in her mind. Nico wouldn't admit to himself that a small part of him also wanted her out of that room for her own protection.

Lacey's gift was compassion. She often connected with a victim, or even a perp in some cases, in a deeper way than

Nico ever could. It allowed her to form a trust with them, draw out details from a victim that he might never achieve. This was a gift, but it was also a weakness. Because she felt things so intensely, she was often left with a residue of pain on the victim's behalf, especially if she was unable to help someone. And Nico could tell this case was special to Lacey. She was already a confidante to this girl, had already been drawn into her story in a profound way. And this worried Nico. Lacey was too close to this girl. She would hate to hear it, but he was scared this might trigger her PTSD again. Even though she kept telling him that with Imran helping her with therapy, and with Nico's love, she was slowly conquering the beast.

Perhaps his gift was almost the opposite. That he could detach himself from a scene—most of the time. To make a good detective, you couldn't allow yourself to get too drawn into the emotional side of things, or you might drown in those feelings, or become inadvertently biased.

Waiting beside the nurses' desk, he caught Tyrell's eye, conveying to the man that it was now doubly important he remain vigilant with this victim. If she had somehow escaped from this perp, rather than him just letting her go, then she might become a target again. The killer might want to come and finish what he'd started, especially if it got out that she couldn't remember anything. He needed to keep this whole thing under wraps and Taylor well protected until they understood what and who they were dealing with. Tyrell merely nodded at their unspoken communication and stood a little straighter.

Then he was nearly bowled over as Lacey came marching through the door.

"Why won't you let me stay for the interview?" she demanded, stopping her headlong rush mere inches from his nose.

"Because Mary will be there, so she'll be in good hands," he replied quietly, hoping that Lacey remembered it wasn't her job to sit by the victim's bedside. It was her job to help him catch the offender. "And because you need to go back to the station and write down everything she told you, the big and the small details, so you don't forget anything."

A little of the heat went out of Lacey's flashing, green eyes. "Fine," she spat, pursing her lips together, dropping her gaze to the ground. She was angry and unnerved and showing her distress by turning it into irritation toward him. He could deal with being her punching bag, if that's what she needed, but he hated to see her so tormented.

He took her by the shoulders and pulled her into his body. Wrapping his arms around her waist, he looked down into her face, not caring that Tyrell or the nurses could see them. He didn't need to say anything; his look conveyed it all. That he knew she was feeling helpless and angry all at the same time. But that he was there for her, both as a physical presence and to help her through the minefield of emotions this case seemed to have engendered.

"We have to catch this guy, Nico," she said, her voice muffled by his jacket. "You should see her poor damaged body. He cut her everywhere. And I mean *everywhere*." Lacey was close to tears, he could hear it in her tone, and he pulled her in closer, hoping to absorb all her pain to help her move past this terrible episode. He didn't make any false promises; he knew how notoriously hard these serial killers were to catch. But with every murder the bastard committed, they got a step closer to finding him.

Lacey melted against him for a few precious seconds before he felt her tense and then push him away, regaining her tough cop outer veneer. He led her to a row of plastic chairs on the other side of the nurses' station and they sat down together.

"You need to know what she's said so far?" Lacey said, requiring no prompting from him, so he just waited. "Right." She took a deep breath as if centering herself, preparing to recall the facts. "Mary told you about the dissociative amnesia?" At Nico's nod, she continued. "So, the first real memory she has is of waking up on the side of the road this morning. She has no idea how she got there, or how long she'd been there. He could've dumped her under the cover of darkness, probably drugged so that it took her a few hours to wake up. That's my theory, anyway," she said thoughtfully. "Prior to that, her last complete memory is of her and Danika walking down the road on the outskirts of Strahan. It was on Sunday, two days before we found the body," Lacey added. "They were looking to hitch a ride into Cradle Mountain, where they were going to stay at the local lodge for the next few nights. She said they were only hitching because they'd slept in and missed the bus and the next one wasn't until the following day." Lacey's brow furrowed at the thought of two young women being silly enough to hitchhike. "A brown sedan pulled over and the guy seemed nice, an older gentleman who said he was going to Devonport to visit his son and grandchildren and he could drop them at the turnoff to the national park, so they got in."

Nico gritted his teeth. It was the nice ones you needed to look out for. "Does she remember much of what the guy looked like? Could we get her to work with a sketch artist?"

"Maybe." Lacey didn't sound that convinced. "I'm not sure how much we can trust of her memory, if what the doc says is true. She could be remembering the face of the man who served them their breakfast at the café that morning for all we know. She said the man was drinking from a bottle of water, and he offered them both one. They were thirsty from walking. So..."

"So, they drank from it," Nico finished for her.

"Yep." Lacey's features were as grim as his own. "And that's the last she remembers."

"So, was this a crime of opportunity?" Nico asked. "Was it a sheer coincidence he happened upon them?"

"Don't know," Lacey replied. "But we know he must've been planning something, because he had the spiked water already in his car."

Nico scratched at his three-day growth thoughtfully. Lacey liked him a little on the scruffy side, said it made him look dangerous, and who was he to argue? "Unless it wasn't random. Could he perhaps have been following them? Just biding his time?"

"Perhaps," Lacey conceded. "If it is the same killer, and if he did, we're no closer to understanding why he's switched from killing sex workers, to fresh-faced university students. And why he's now torturing his victims."

"No, we're not." Nico stared into Lacey's face. It was still pale and there were lines of tension around her mouth. He tipped Lacey's chin up with his thumb so that she was looking into his eyes. "But we'll figure it out. He's fucked up majorly by leaving Taylor alive. She's our principal clue to hunting this guy down." It was looking less likely in Nico's mind that Taylor had escaped her tormentor; she surely would've remembered something about a fight to escape a madman if she had. No, the killer had let her go for some reason. They needed to figure out that reason and quickly.

"Yes, you're right." She smiled at him for the first time since they'd found the girl on the farmer's back road, and a little of the tight band squeezing all the air out of his chest eased. "And I'd better get to the station and file that report. I've got a make and model of the car this guy was driving, so we can put out an APB."

Silently, Nico thought it was a long shot. If the killer had an ounce of intelligence, he would've dumped that car like a hot potato as soon as he could. Lacey had dropped her gaze again, but hadn't made any move to stand up to leave, and something in his gut tingled.

"What?" he asked.

She puckered her lips. "There's something else."

That band around his chest tightened a few notches again.

"While Taylor doesn't remember much about the past few days, as soon as she heard my name, she burst into tears."

"Yes," Nico prompted, trying to keep the unease out of his voice, but that tingle was getting stronger.

"When she could finally talk after her tears stopped, she told me that my name was one of the few things she remembered from her time in captivity. She clearly recalls a man's voice telling her to look for a woman called Lacey. That she could trust Lacey. That Lacey would help her."

Nico's blood turned to ice. "What?"

"I know." Lacey laid a hand on his arm. "I didn't show it at the time, but it shocked the hell out of me." She worried at her bottom lip with her teeth, a move Nico usually found sexy as hell, but he couldn't get his mind off this sickening news.

Now he knew why the killer had left the girl alive.

He was sending them a message. Singling out Lacey for some reason. But why? Was he threatening Lacey? Or was the threat aimed at Nico? Because if the killer knew anything about Nico, he'd understand that Nico would protect Lacey to the death. He'd leave no stone unturned to find this guy and nullify the threat. Why was he taunting them? Did this guy actually want to be found?

CHAPTER SEVEN

Lacey would kill for a soak in a really hot bath while holding a glass of ice cold chardonnay. But these were two more of the wonderful things she could no longer do while pregnant. Not that she dared look at a glass of wine after the other night. Argh. She needed a way to unwind from the stress of this harrowing day. How did pregnant women relax when they were denied the fundamental ways to do so? The best she could do was to locate the block of chocolate hidden at the back of the cupboard, tune into some Enya on her music app, and sit back in the comfy armchair with her feet up. Smudge sat below her chair, his warm, dark gaze resting lovingly on her face. At least Smudge was here for her.

She bit into a piece of dark, slightly bitter chocolate as she let the music soothe her. A foot massage would be nice, but she needed Nico here to do that, and he was still at work. Probably would be for hours. And she'd better make the most of the chocolate tonight, because it'd probably all end up in the toilet tomorrow morning. Her morning sickness was showing no signs of abating; in fact, it was getting worse. She'd been able to hide it from Linc this morning by nibbling on dry crackers when he wasn't looking. The small mercy was that she seemed to be okay by lunchtime, and by then she was as hungry as a horse. But she hadn't had the chance to eat lunch today, because she'd spent most of the afternoon with Taylor. Then she'd crammed down some terribly unhealthy "health food bar" from the vending machine in the hospital on the way out.

At the thought of that poor girl, Lacey's woes were suddenly put into sharp perspective. She had nothing to complain about. Taylor's mother had arrived at the hospital late this evening, so at least she was no longer alone.

After they'd found Taylor wandering on that road, Lacey had barely thought about her pregnancy all day. Which was probably a good thing. She'd worked many hours past the official end of her shift today, writing up reports, filing paperwork, and helping Sally-Ann research some of the mountain of things related to the murder case, trying to keep thoughts of Taylor and her absolute heartbreak at the girl's horrific treatment at bay. One thing that kept circling round and round in her head was the way Taylor had cuts to just about every surface of her body. Why had the killer done that? It was another huge break in his well-established routine. He'd never sexually or physically abused them before. Why now? What did it all mean?

It was times like these that Cindi reappeared from the recess of her mind. The little girl never really went away, but as time passed, and with therapy, the horrible images faded. Lacey found hope the little soul was happy somewhere in a place full of pink dresses—her favorite color—where no one could hurt her ever again. Lacey had already booked in to see her wonderful psych tomorrow, knowing that to stay mentally healthy was always an uphill battle, but there were good people like Imran always on her side.

Her stomach growled, reminding her of how little she'd eaten today. She should get out of the chair and find something more suitable for dinner than a bar of chocolate, but her legs refused to budge. It was all she could manage to lock her gun in the safe in the kitchen, change out of her uniform, and dump some dog food in Smudge's bowl when she'd arrived home. The best remedy for her would probably have been a workout at her Judo dojo, but she couldn't even face that. Besides, it was already after nine and she needed an early night more than a training session.

Smudge gave a low growl, then stood and pricked his ears toward the front door. Lacey's fifth piece of chocolate stalled halfway to her mouth as she strained to hear what had caught the dog's attention. After Nico's father had broken into their house right before Christmas, Nico had installed security cameras on every corner and reinforced the old windows with brand new, state-of-the-art security screens. She'd been afraid they'd spoil the colonial look of the cottage, but the screens were so discreet you could hardly see them, as well as being completely unbreakable. Now, no one would get into the house without her knowing about it, and Lacey relaxed as she remembered this.

But she needn't have worried as Smudge's growl turned into a happy waving tail and he bounded off to wait at the back door. Lacey heard the low drone of Nico's motorcycle in that same second, and a wave of relief washed over her.

He was home. Early, considering the big case load, but that was fine by her. She'd be glad of the solace of his arms around her. That'd be just as good as a hot bath and a wine. But it meant she should probably see what they had in the way of food so she could cook them both a healthy meal.

She had her head stuck in the refrigerator when Nico came through the door.

"I've bought Japanese takeaway for dinner," he announced over Smudge's excited whining.

She straightened and looked him in the eye. "You are a god!" she said. "And I love you to the moon and back."

"I know." He took three strides into the kitchen, and kissed her full on the lips, ignoring both Smudge still vying for his attention and the large paper bag dangling in his left hand. "I hope it's still warm, I had it in the side pannier all the way home," he said when he finally came up for air.

"Right at this moment, as long as you got me chicken katsu and some miso soup, I don't care what temperature it is."

"Yes, I did. But no sushi, because I know you can't have raw fish."

Damn, that was right, another thing she wasn't allowed while she was pregnant. This carrying-a-child thing seemed to have more cons than pros right now.

"How did you know I hadn't cooked yet?"

"I wasn't sure, but the way you looked when you left the station tonight, it was a good guess."

Lacey lifted one shoulder in defeat. Nico knew her too well.

He started to set the food on the kitchen table and she put out plates and cutlery, a beer for him and a soda and lime juice for her—she may as well get used to them because she was going to be drinking them for seven more months. They sat down together and silently dished up huge plates of Japanese food. Chicken katsu for her, beef yakitori skewers with special sauce for him.

Lacey fell on her food like she hadn't eaten in a whole week, while silently wondering if she could ask for a foot massage afterward. After eating half of her chicken and slurping great gulps of her miso soup, she finally looked up at him.

"How come you left work early?" she asked through a mouthful of warm, salty, seaweedy liquid.

"I've left Pederson and Saito on the case. I was worried about you, and they understood that." This was an interesting development. Nico wouldn't normally show his partiality toward Lacey openly at work. Neither of them wanted the rest of the team thinking he was giving her any special treatment. But that being said, everyone also realized she and Nico were partners, lovers, committed to each other. And without anything being mentioned, everyone understood innately how anxious he would be about her. Nico would've reported that the killer had put Lacey's name in Taylor's mind by now, and Nico wouldn't be the only one wondering why she'd been singled out. Silently, she thanked the two detectives for their dedication. "I'll do some more work from home later," he added.

"Any new developments since I left?" she asked, not really expecting anything; he'd only been an hour behind her.

"Not really. I organized a local unit in Brisbane to break the news to Danika's family. The father is going to fly down tomorrow to identify the body." Nico scowled at the idea of a father having to identify his own dead daughter. It was horrific.

It wasn't until after Nico had first interviewed Taylor in the hospital that Sally-Ann confirmed through social media posts and photos, that Danika and Taylor were indeed friends, and had been backpacking together around Tasmania. Which meant Danika was almost certainly the murdered girl lying in the ditch.

Nico had known better than to ask if Taylor was up to identifying her dead friend even though it would've given them the definitive answer they needed. Lacey and Mary had already decided that if he had asked, the answer was going to be an emphatic no. They believed the poor girl may have been forced to watch on as the murderer strangled Danika, but as part of the dissociative amnesia, Taylor didn't remember any of that, just echoes of the horror of it all. Taylor was just too fragile, and she was glad Nico could see that.

"Then, I was going around and around in circles, chasing my tail, trying to confirm beyond a doubt that the serial killer's first three victims were all related to the sex trade—which they were. But that made me question if this is the same serial killer, then why would he change his predilection to a certain prey. It's as if he had an appetite for one thing yesterday, and that seemed to have changed overnight. These girls seem to be the furthest thing from a woman in the sex trade. They're almost too sweet and wholesome. It's driving me crazy not knowing why. And I might've answered a little abruptly when one of the junior officers asked me a question," he admitted. "So, I decided it was time to call it quits and come home and be with you instead."

"I'm okay with that," she said, grinning at him through a mouthful of rice. "And thank you for worrying about me. I was a little down," she conceded.

"I could see it in your eyes," he replied, putting down his fork and looking at her from below lowered eyebrows. "You take on too much sometimes, Lace. You absorb too much of other people's pain. I'm not sure it's good for you."

Lacey considered him for a few seconds. He was right; she probably did empathize with some of their victims too deeply. But she couldn't see any other way to do it. It was built into her DNA. And Nico had even told her that it was one of her strengths as a cop, the fact she could be so in tune with them that she could ask exactly the right questions or see to the heart of a matter when he just couldn't. But she could see his point. She shouldn't get so lost in her victim's story that she became biased or forgot to focus on what was important. Catching a killer.

"You're probably right," she agreed, and he raised a skeptical eyebrow; she didn't always agree so readily with him. "But you know what would help enormously to make me feel better?"

"What?"

"A foot massage." She gave a hopeful grin.

"It's a deal," he said with a flourish of his fork.

What a man she had. Not only did he bring her takeaway when she needed it most, but he was prepared to rub her feet to help banish those stress demons sitting on her shoulders. He was as close to perfect as they got.

Ten minutes later, Lacey was ensconced back in the armchair, her feet resting in Nico's lap as he sat beside her on the couch. "Oh, that's heavenly," she moaned, tipping her head against the backrest and closing her eyes. There was almost nothing that could top a good foot massage, not in Lacey's books anyway. Nico's big hands felt exquisite as he wrapped them around her ankle and kneaded the arch of her foot. She groaned again in response.

"Careful," he growled. "Keep making those noises and I'm likely to throw you over my shoulder and drag you to bed."

"We could do that too," she replied. "Later, once you've done the other foot," she added, not opening her eyes.

There was silence for many moments, the soft strains of Enya filling the space in the room. Then she felt Nico shift slightly on his seat.

"I know it's still early days, but maybe we should talk about our plans."

"Hmm?" She didn't really care about anything right now, especially plans, but she opened one eye and lifted her head to give him a questioning look.

"Like when we're going to tell the people at work about the pregnancy. Our friends. That kind of thing."

Oh, that. She'd almost forgotten about that too. She'd been expecting him to want to talk about the current case, so this out of the blue topic surprised her. Opening the other eye, she gave an inward sigh. The scar on Nico's cheek was pronounced as he considered her, a sign he was more worried than he let on. She sat up a little so she could concentrate on his face, and swapped her feet over, letting him massage the other one.

"I think it's usual to wait until twelve weeks. So that gives us a month to come up with the details," she replied patiently.

"Okay, that seems fair. What about our families? Are we going to wait until twelve weeks to tell them, too?"

Lacey screwed up her mouth in thought. "Um, I'm not sure." The doctor had confirmed her pregnancy at her appointment yesterday, so the news was definitely official. But she was only seven weeks along; it all felt a little soon to be broadcasting the announcement.

"We're still coming to terms with the whole baby thing, but I'd like to tell them soon. I think they have a right to know. And my mum will be over the moon. Her first grandchild and all that." Nico's eyes brightened at the idea of his mum being a grandmother.

Shit, that meant if he was going to tell his parents soon, then she'd have to tell hers. The idea scared the hell out of her. Nico's mum, Catarina, would make a wonderful grandmother. Her mother, on the other hand, wouldn't.

Nico caught the fearful look in her eye, and almost as if he could read her mind, he said, "You have to tell them, Lacey. This isn't something you can keep from them." He stopped massaging her foot and laid his hand on her thigh.

"I know," she said miserably. "But I don't think I could cope with my mother demanding to come here and take over everything to do with the baby. It's what she does. It's what she's always done."

"This time will be different," Nico assured her. "We're going to set the ground rules early. And I will be there to enforce them this time. She doesn't get to overstep, or I'll quite happily send her packing."

"Well, you might have to do exactly that," Lacey told him. "Boundaries are there to be broken in her book. She takes being told *no* as her own personal challenge to do the exact opposite."

Lacey hadn't really wanted to consider the ramifications of everything bringing a child into the world would entail. She'd wanted to keep the secret safe just between her and Nico. But of course a baby would make an impact in more than just their lives. There were other people to be considered. It was over six months since she'd talked to either of her parents. Ever since she'd made them aware of how their treatment of her was no longer acceptable, and that something needed to change. But of course, nothing had changed. Lacey was conscious the impasse needed to be stopped soon, otherwise their rift might become irreparable. She knew she would have to be the bigger person and be the one who broke the ice first. But her stomach quivered at the mere idea of talking to her mother. Perhaps she should phone her dad first.

She put a protective hand over her belly. One thing she was certain about was that she wasn't letting her mother's corrosive manner and toxic manipulation touch this baby's life. If she had to cut her mother out of her life for good to protect her child, then that was what she would do.

"I'm sorry to bring it up, Lace, but you need to start thinking about when and how you're going to tell them."

She nodded. "It's just sad. You're so excited, and you can't wait to break the news to your mum and sister and brother. But I'm the complete opposite. Elora is going to find a way to make this all about her, I just know it. And we're going to end up fighting. Again."

"Maybe," Nico acknowledged. "But what about Mathew and Sammy? They'll be happy for us, right?"

She knew her older brother, Matty, would definitely be

happy for them, for her. His own life was hectic and fast-paced and that's the way he liked it. There was no time for a wife, let alone kids. But her younger sister, Sammy, well... Lacey wasn't so sure. Sammy was becoming more like Elora every day. It probably had something to do with the fact she was still living at home in the mansion in Toorak, enjoying all the perks of having rich parents. While Lacey had shunned everything to do with that lifestyle. Except her trust fund, she still had that, but she never used it.

"Matt will," she consented. "But I won't tell them until I'm ready to reveal it all to my parents. The secret might be too much, especially for Sammy."

"Fair enough."

"I'm sorry," Lacey said quietly. She was scared her side of the family were going to spoil any happiness this baby might bring.

"You have nothing to be sorry about. We all have family dramas, no one comes without baggage of some kind, and I went into this relationship with my eyes wide open. Like I said before, we'll get through this together." He pushed her foot out of his lap and grabbed her hand, tugging her to sit on his thighs instead. "This is going to be the best adventure of our lives. We need to stay focussed on that and the rest will fall into place."

Lacey stared into his indigo eyes, his pupils huge and dark. Slowly, Nico leaned in and kissed her. Not with the intent to seduce, but with a sweetness and tenderness that made her heart swell. He was right; nothing mattered more than the two of them—soon to be three—and their life together. No one could touch that. Not now, not ever.

CHAPTER EIGHT

Nico stared out of the window at the busy main street below. It was Friday afternoon and the operations room was fairly quiet, every officer on his team either out on patrol or following up leads and errands of his making, Lacey and Linc included. Which left him alone in ops. He stifled a yawn just as Detective Pederson strode in. Sitting up straighter, he shuffled some of the papers on his desk.

"Anything new to report?" he asked, keeping his tone all business.

Pederson screwed up his face in the closest thing to a scowl Nico had seen on the man. Detective Jay Pederson normally kept his feelings under wraps and played his hand close to his chest. Pederson was one of a very few indigenous detectives in Tasmania, and Nico put his cool reserve down to a sort of self-protection. The life of a detective was hard enough without all the added strain of prejudice and social judgement he would've endured on his way through the ranks. Regardless of how hard the man must've worked to get where he was, and how much Nico respected him for that, he still couldn't find it in his heart to like the other detective; he was blunt and abrasive, and a pain in the ass.

"Perhaps." Pederson leaned down and pulled out a chair,

sitting on the opposite side of the desk. "But I also wanted to pick your brains on a few things that have been bothering me."

"Sure, go ahead." Nico sat back in his chair and watched the other man's dark eyes as they roved over the murder board before coming to rest on his face.

"Just to update you, Saito has spent the day working with Sally-Ann. They're looking at every unsolved cold case going back twenty years, both in Tasmania and on the mainland. Trying to see if they can find any similar murders."

"Mm hm." Nico made a noise wondering where Pederson was going with this. The Hobart police had already looked into cold cases when the serial killer had first come to their attention, but he didn't bother to mention this to Pederson. Hobart PD hadn't uncovered anything of interest, but they'd only gone back ten years, not twenty, which had made Nico highly dubious as to the depth of their research skills. Silently, he applauded the two women's proactive approach. Most cops hated the dull, repetitive job of research, but it was an important part of police work, and Sally-Ann was especially good at it. With the help of Tasman Saito, they'd make a formidable team. He always encouraged his team to follow their intuition on a case, and the two women might have more luck with their superior fact-finding skills than the lackluster Hobart team.

Pederson nodded his head sharply. "It was Saito's idea. We discussed it last night, and I said she should follow it up ASAP as you weren't around this morning when we got in." Nico held back a frown. Of course it was Pederson who'd encouraged Saito to follow her idea. Saito was a stickler for the rules, and Nico knew if she was working alone, she would've waited to get Nico's go-ahead first before taking one of his valuable team members off on a tangent. And just because he was a few minutes late into the station didn't give

Pederson the unspoken right to judge him. Nico and Lacey had driven in to work together this morning. Her shift started at eight, and he was more than happy to wait for her. With a baby on the way, things were going to have to change, including his overzealous, workaholic tendencies, and so this was his first step in hauling it all back a notch or two.

"Right." Nico gave another noncommittal answer, again wondering where this was going.

"But this got me to thinking about our potential serial killer. About his pattern. The way he kills women. And where he kills them. The majority of serial killers have a pattern, right?"

"Agreed." Most people, both civilians and police, recognized that for a murderer to be called a serial killer there needed to be at least three homicides and those were usually in some form of pattern in the type of victim selected—until now, ours had been sex workers—as well as their methods of killing, in this case it was strangulation. They often also worked within the certain confines of a particular area, in a state or city.

"Looking at patterns, let's start with the killer's sense of place." Pederson tapped his notes with a pen thoughtfully and Nico wondered if the other man had just read his mind. "We can safely say, that to our knowledge, the state of Tasmania is his hunting ground."

Nico nodded. "He started in Hobart, but he moved quickly to Zeehan on the northwest coast, and now we've got one in Burnie." The only part of Tasmania the killer had yet to appear in was the small pocket of the northeast. They'd been over this in all of their morning meetings so far, and Nico wanted to know why the detective was rehashing it.

"Which means he's either a traveling killer from somewhere else in Australia, or a local from somewhere in Tasmania who's moving around the state to commit his crimes." Nico merely raised an eyebrow. All Pederson was doing was outlining just how little they knew about this guy because they were no closer to answering that one.

But he decided to play the game. "If he's a local, then he'd be stupid to kill in his hometown," Nico replied. If Pederson was thinking out loud, Nico could also join in this brainstorming. It was the first time he and Pederson had really sat down and talked one-on-one. Pederson and Saito seemed to be joined at the hip most of the time and they made an almost impenetrable team, so he decided to make the most of it.

"Yup. That would rule out Hobart, Zeehan and Burnie as places where this guy might live." Pederson stood and made his way over to the whiteboard at the front of the room, tapping the large map of Tasmania they had taped to the wall next to it. "But killers often return to the scene of a crime," Pederson added thoughtfully.

"Yes, they do. But we have no evidence this killer has done that, so far," Nico reminded him.

"No, but we should keep it in the back of our minds," Pederson continued. Nico had already considered this possibility, but if the killer had come back to gloat over his kills or relive his crimes, he'd been very careful about not revealing himself. Pederson's reminder tickled a thought at the back of Nico's mind, however, and he tried to catch that elusive idea.

But Pederson was on a roll now and Nico's thought trail was interrupted when he said, "Most killers have a *type*. And we thought our serial killer had a definite one when he murdered three sex workers in a row."

Nico nodded. When a murderer targeted prostitutes, it could often have something to do with either religious beliefs, or the social stigma of their profession that then became a killer's justification.

"But this killer also never raped or sexually assaulted these women," Pederson continued. This was an anomaly when it came to prostitute killers, as it was usually about sex, or the control of sex for these men. "So, our profilers were looking at a male perp, with a pathological dislike of sex and or women, perhaps from the military because of his pedantic need to clean a scene. But we need to review this profile now, because he seems to be happy to change his *type*. And his preference for inflicting pain. And that could also mean he's changed his motivation."

"Okay," Nico drawled, also standing now, so he could pace in front of the whiteboard. Was Pederson onto something here? They'd discussed the possible motivations for this killer earlier on in the investigation, but not since Danika's body had been found. And then Taylor had been found alive. Danika and Taylor changed everything they thought they knew about this perp. Especially Taylor. The killer had never left a mark on a victim before her. So why had he tortured her in particular? Perhaps Saito was right to think about reviewing cold cases. When the Hobart cops had done it, they'd been looking for cases involving sex workers. But maybe this killer had started off with a different victim and evolved over time to prostitutes. And now the pendulum was swinging back again. Which might explain why they hadn't found any matches.

Nico reviewed what he understood about the pathology of serial killers. They were often broken into four loose categories when it came to motivation. Some killers were on a mission, those were the ones who were trying to eliminate a certain group of people and were often radicalized and killed because of racial or religious reasons. Then there was the hedonistic killer, who sought thrills or pleasure from taking another life. This type of murder often involved rape, however, so it probably ruled out their serial killer. Visionary killers usually said that voices in their head told them to commit the crime, which didn't seem to fit this killer either, as he was too efficient and controlled. Which led to the last category. Someone who killed for power. These types usually didn't kill for sexual reasons, but rather because of their ability to exert power—or control—over their victim. The pleasure in the kill for these types probably came from forcing the victim to beg for mercy, the most extreme form of power over another person. And their killer had exhibited this drive when he'd forced Taylor to watch him murder her best friend. But was it also a power trip to inflict suffering on his victim as well? Torture belonged more in the sadistic group, than in the power and control group. And while the small cuts all over Taylor's body would have been painful, they weren't life-threatening, and on the scale of torturous injury, fairly mild in comparison to some killers' tactics he could name.

"This guy kills for the power it gives him," Nico said, turning to stare at Pederson.

"Yes, that's the conclusion I also came to," Pederson confirmed.

Nico took a marker pen and wrote the words *Power/Control* on the whiteboard in the box that represented their perp. There were other words in the list of things they knew about him. *Organized. Military style. Ritualistic*—which referred to the way he set out the body postmortem—*Careful. Male.* Nico had added this one when Taylor had given them the description of the man driving the car who'd picked them up in Strahan. They'd been pretty sure their killer was male, but this almost set it in concrete.

Pederson pointed at the word *Organized.* "He could be stalking his victims. I don't think this was a crime of opportunity. That would be too disorganized for this killer."

"I agree. The way he leaves his crime scenes clean and

sterile. But he's also bold—or stupid—not bothering to bury any of the bodies, instead leaving them in remote places, but out in the open, where they will eventually be found. Why is he doing that?"

Why indeed? Nico felt his frustration mounting. He was glad to be bouncing ideas off Pederson, but they seemed to be going around and around in circles.

That niggling thought at the back of his mind came back, stronger this time. What had Pederson said that'd first set off that itch in his gut. Something about how they should remember that a killer often revisited the scene of his crimes. And if he had been stalking those two girls, then where had he picked up their trail? They'd started their trek in Launceston and traveled most of the way around the island in the past three weeks. Surely, he couldn't have tracked them all the way from Launceston? Or maybe he'd picked them up in Hobart. He clearly knew Hobart well, as that was the location of at least two of his murders. Or had he noticed them somewhere closer to Strahan? By Taylor's admission, they'd spent three nights in the tiny town, because they loved the little backpackers accommodation down there: a suite of old wooden A-frame huts that'd been turned into shared dorms or couples accommodation, set along one of the back roads of the small town.

"I think we need to concentrate more of our energy on Strahan," Nico said, staring thoughtfully at the whiteboard.

"We've already canvassed the locals and swept the area where the girls were abducted." Pederson directed his dark stare at Nico, his deep frown indicating this wasn't the direction he'd been anticipating their conversation would take them. "And haven't you requested the local units to step up their patrols?"

"Yes, I have." A larger police presence in the area would hopefully make the killer think twice before he struck again.

Either that, or it might just drive him to do his hunting elsewhere. But for some reason, Nico didn't think so. And for some other reason, he had a growing confidence that what he was contemplating was a good idea. "But I think we need an undercover presence as well. Do a bit of investigation under the radar. Talk to the locals as a worried citizen. They might tell me things they'd never tell a cop in uniform." While Nico had directed his team down in Strahan, he'd never actually visited there during this investigation, so he was a good choice to go undercover, as he wouldn't be recognized.

"That's true," Pederson agreed hesitantly.

"I'm going to spend a night or two in Strahan. Stay at the same hostel where the two girls spent their time. If this guy was stalking them, he must've been in the town, and he might've left a clue." Nico's thoughts were racing now with hundreds of possibilities, the idea cementing itself in his mind.

"I want you to talk to Taylor and see if you can pinpoint the girls' exact movements while they were in Hobart. Then liaise with Hobart police to track down CCTV and local witnesses to corroborate all that." Of course, they'd confirmed Taylor's statement regarding dates of travel, times and places while they'd been in Hobart, but that was it so far. Now, he wanted a deep dive into everything the girls had got up to in the past two weeks. "You're right," Nico conceded. "I believe this guy stalked them, and if that's the case, we need to find out exactly where and when he targeted them. We need an exact timeline of how and where this guy first came into contact with his targets."

This was good. At last Nico had an angle from which to attack this investigation. And it was all thanks to Pederson.

"Thanks," Nico said, meaning it. "You've helped to clarify a few things here." He wasn't sure if Pederson felt the same way. He'd started this line of questioning to help explain a few things he was unsure of, but had helped Nico solidify an objective instead.

"That's what I'm here for," Pederson said magnanimously, and for once, Nico caught a glimpse of the man beneath the solemn façade. But he didn't have time to explore the fact Pederson might actually have human emotions, he had a trip to plan. As well as figuring out a way to tell Lacey what he was planning on doing without her hitting the roof.

* * *

"I want to go with you." Lacey's green-eyed gaze fixed on him like twin jade gemstones as she slowly laid her fork on the table. They were halfway through a late dinner, and looking at Lacey's face, Nico decided with a flash of insight that perhaps he should've waited to spring the news of his trip to Strahan until later. Like maybe ten minutes before he was due to leave tomorrow morning.

"I want to go with you," she repeated. "You need me on this op."

No, he didn't. Which was why he was kicking himself that he'd let the words slip out. He blamed the glass of red wine and the delicious steak Lacey had cooked them for dinner—she seemed to be eating a lot more meat now she was pregnant.

"Nico, look at me," Lacey purred, changing tack and putting on her sultry voice. Shit. It was so much harder to resist the seductive Lacey than it was the logical Lacey. "You really do need me. I think we'd work much better as a team on this one."

It was déjà vu. Lacey's words took Nico back to the time standing in Sandra Brown's kitchen when he'd discovered that Sandra's next target was walking the Overland Track and Lacey had demanded he take her on that mission too. In the end, it'd turned out to be a good decision, because Lacey had saved his life. Back then, he'd known Lacey was a headstrong, determined woman, and that hadn't changed in the past few months. Something *had* changed since then, however. Because she was pregnant, although he dare not even say that out loud, let alone use it as an excuse. But it was true. And sometimes her stubbornness was a thorn in his side. Like now. She'd be safer here at home, with Linc keeping an eye on her at work and the security system keeping an eye on her at home.

Besides, he'd already decided it'd be much simpler if he went alone. He and Pederson had hashed out a plan where he'd take accommodation at the same backpackers the girls had stayed in and start his undercover investigation from there. Shadbolt had given the go-ahead for the plan, but had given Nico a stern warning to play things by the book. There could be no reports of evidence improperly obtained. He wanted this killer brought to justice as much as Nico, but they needed to do it correctly so there were no legal loopholes for the slime bag to squeeze through. But Shadbolt hadn't given the okay for Lacey to accompany him.

He laid his own fork down and gave the half-eaten food one crestfallen glance, knowing his fine steak was going to end up cold and congealed on his plate.

"Look, Lace, I've talked this over with Jay, and he agrees with me." Nico hoped that Pederson's endorsement might lend this plan the validation he needed to get it past Lacey. "I need to go and play an undercover tourist. I'll be in Strahan to see the sights for a few days. I'll ask a few questions, you know, a concerned citizen that's heard all the terrible things on the news about murdered girls and abductions. That way the locals might drop their defenses and tell me things they wouldn't tell the cops. Gossip is rife in those small country towns, you just have to know how to get them to talk."

"Yes, I agree. And the way to get them to talk is to have a couple of newlyweds, spending their honeymoon in town.

We can tell them we're expecting our first baby soon, and this is our last trip away before our lives change forever. It works even better than the single male theory. Everybody loves a newly married twosome besotted with each other, don't they?"

Lacey's comment knocked the wind out of his sails for so many reasons. That story cut so close to the truth it wasn't funny. Apart from the fact he had yet to ask Lacey to marry him.

"Newlyweds?" he repeated dumbly.

"Yes. Why do you seem so surprised by that? It's a great undercover story."

"Newlyweds, expecting our first baby?"

"Yes," she replied patiently. "Because we are expecting our first baby, that bit won't be hard to fake. And all the women in the town will want to talk to me if they know I'm pregnant. I'll be like a magnet, especially to the older generations. The ones who like to gossip the most."

She had a point, but Nico still couldn't move past the newlyweds thing. Yes, he'd been working up to asking Lacey to be his wife, but the whole pregnancy had thrown that for a loop. And now he didn't know where he stood on it. Or where she stood on it. And pretending to be married while on an undercover op felt like he'd let her down somehow. Because maybe they should be getting married.

"You need me on this, Nico," she said triumphantly, mistaking the look on his face for one of capitulation.

Damnit to hell. Now what was he going to do?

CHAPTER NINE

They strolled arm in arm down the pathway, looking for all the world like the happily married newlyweds Lacey had been talking about when she'd convinced Nico to take her on this op. Perusing the few little boutique souvenir shops on the main street and enjoying the sunshine. And perhaps the reason they looked the part was that Lacey was also feeling the part. She'd eased into this role like it was made for her, even if the idea seemed to take a little getting used to for Nico. She *had* been going to ask him to marry her just a few days ago. But the bigger news of her pregnancy had put that on the back burner. And now they were going to have a baby together she didn't want him to feel like he was being pushed into marriage. She wanted him to *want* to do it for love, for them to move forward as a couple.

Being arm in arm, happy and content, felt so natural she could almost forget the real reason they were here. To find out more about their so-called serial killer. It wasn't a relaxing weekend away, even though that was how it felt, she needed to keep her mind on work and not romance. Lacey had won the battle of wills between her and Nico, just as she knew she would. She was right to convince him to take her along, and he knew it too, he was just a sore loser and wasn't prepared to admit it yet. They'd had to leave Smudge under the tender care of Margie and Herb for the next few days. You couldn't take a dog on an undercover police op. But she was sure Smudge was now fat and happy, relaxing on the couch next to Herb and chewing on the treats Margie swore she never fed him. Yesterday had been a bust when it came to finding any new information, but they'd used their time to ingratiate themselves with some of the locals, get their bearings around the town, and put weight to their story of being a couple of tourists in the area for a few days.

Nico stopped walking beside her and tapped his chest pocket where his phone normally sat. "Damn. I think I left my phone in the café." He looked stricken. "I must've left it on the counter when I paid."

"Quick, go back and see," she told him. "I'll wait here." She was just starting to feel normal now, after a careful meal of toast and Vegemite—while watching Nico devour a huge plate of eggs Benedict, which almost had her dry retching— and found herself not wanting to tempt fate by rushing back up the winding street to the Coffee Shack with him. The morning sickness was still a bugbear, but at least she was learning to live with it. She made sensible food choices in the morning and didn't rush herself. There wasn't a lot of choices for cafés here in Strahan, especially on a Sunday morning, but Maureen, the owner of the Strahan Backpackers where they were staying, had recommended the Coffee Shack. The coffee had been good as they'd sat outside on the wooden picnic tables and enjoyed the bright morning sunshine. Thank God she could still stomach her coffee in the morning, she'd heard of women who went off that staple beverage because it made them throw up. She couldn't even imagine how she'd cope without her morning heart-starter.

"I'll be right back." Nico took off on his long legs, jogging up the wide street back the way they'd come.

Lacey turned to survey the view across the road. Strahan sat on the edge of Macquarie Harbour, but this little bay at the end of the broad expanse of water sheltered the town from most of the weather. Sunlight reflected off the small wavelets, while a few wooden boats moored close to the edge of the harbor. To the left, a large industrial building perched on the brink of an even larger jetty, a sign announcing it as the headquarters of a large cruise company, running boats up the famous Gordon River. On her side of the road, the local pub sat a little farther up the hill, a big old colonial building done up to show off its glorious heritage.

Cute little town, she thought absently. If Nico didn't already have the best cottage anyone could hope for, she might consider asking him if he wanted to move down here. Only problem was that the police station in Strahan was a two-person job, and the odds of getting a position down here were nil, at least until old Joe retired, and he still had a few years on the beat left in him yet. When she really thought about it, perhaps this town was a bit on the small side for her liking. Not enough coffee shops.

And while their accommodation at the backpackers was rustic and interesting, it certainly couldn't be called luxurious. They had a cute little wooden A-frame cottage all to themselves, nestled on a patch of grass and encircled by tall forest on three sides. The best part of the hut was the small, covered front veranda, where they could sit in the two deck chairs and commune with the surrounding wilderness.

Maureen had been a treasure trove of information this morning when Lacey had gone into the reception office, in her undercover guise of honeymooner, ostensibly to ask about the best place to eat breakfast. Her actual plan was to ply her for the details of all of her guests over the past few weeks, to see if anyone might fit the bill of the killer. A team had already interviewed Maureen extensively, and asked the same questions Lacey was asking now. But they'd done it with a lot more aggression and a much less feminine bonding.

In between giving out the best advice for how to treat cracked nipples while breast feeding—Lacey was still coming to terms with that actually being a thing—Maureen had been happy to prattle on about *those poor girls* and how, *these types of things never happened in Strahan*. Maureen became teary as she told Lacey that she'd started having nightmares after she'd heard what'd happened to those sweet girls on the news. She could hardly believe that she might've been one of the last people to see Danika alive, after the two of them checked out of the backpackers that morning, all happy and excited about the next leg of their adventure. Cradle Mountain was on the top of both girls' bucket lists, and one of the main reasons they'd wanted to do this trip in the first place. The whole thing had made her nervous, *jumping at shadows*, the older woman put it, and now she found herself studying every new guest who came in with renewed suspicion. Lacey made the appropriate noises of commiseration and then asked, eyes wide with trepidation, if Maureen thought the killer had actually stayed at the backpackers. Maybe that was where he first saw them, she theorized. Maureen had gone to great pains to let Lacey know there was no way that *monster* had stayed in her establishment. The cops admitted to only having a very vague description of their person of interest, but Maureen was sure no one like that had been near here.

This news had disheartened Lacey a little, but then Maureen had leaned across the reception desk and touched Lacey's arm. "Just between you and me," she'd whispered conspiratorially. "Most of the locals have been saying that if someone wanted to stay in the area undetected, they wouldn't be stupid enough to pay for accommodation. There are plenty of out-of-the-way campsites hidden up along the trails in these forests where someone could stay for weeks without being noticed. And I agree with them," Maureen stated, her double chin wobbling with assuredness. "So, if I was you, I'd stay away from any isolated hiking trails, my dear. Stick to the town proper, and you'll be fine."

Nico and his team had already considered the idea of the killer hiding out in the bush. But the logistics of searching every secluded trail and backwater was a mammoth task and Nico had decided to shelve it, especially as they couldn't even be sure the killer had stayed in the area. "Thank you," Lacey had replied. "I must admit, I was a little worried about coming here after what we heard on the news." Lacey decided to push her luck and ask a direct question. "But do you really think this murderer guy might still be hanging around?"

Maureen leaned in even closer and waggled her slightly bushy eyebrows at Lacey. "The cops keep trying to tell us that we're safe in our own homes, and we shouldn't become overwrought, and they're going to catch this guy. They're sure he's already moved on, and they're going to protect us." Maureen gave a loud snort at this last statement. Lacey doubted that was exactly the line Joe and his right-hander, Constable Stacy McCloud, were actually using, but she held her tongue. "How are they going to protect us, if they can't even protect those two poor girls?" Maureen went on.

Lacey was stung at Maureen's lack of faith. She wanted to argue that police work wasn't an exact science; they didn't have a crystal ball that could tell them where and when a crime was going to be committed. But they always did their best, and most officers she knew would put their life on the line to protect innocent citizens.

"So some of us locals have got together and formed a concerned community group. We don't need the coppers to protect us, we can protect ourselves." Maureen's pale-blue eyes lit up.

Sounded more like a vigilante group, Lacey thought. It was sad, how one horrible deed could corrupt the inhabitants of a small town like this.

"Old Mal, he's got a property on the edge of town." Maureen waved an arm in some vague direction. "He's organizing it all. We're all going to meet at his place tonight. He's talking about groups of us making patrols around the town, especially at night. We don't want to be scared in our own homes. And we don't want people like you, tourists and travelers, to be scared off either. This town relies on visitors to keep us going."

Lacey could see Maureen's point, and she answered with the sort of meaningful nod a worried young newlywed might give as Maureen kept on telling her details of how they were going to keep their little town safe. While at the same time, she mentally catalogued the danger this *community-minded group* posed and weighed up the risks of letting the meeting tonight continue.

"So, you and your handsome hubby don't need to worry," Maureen had concluded. Then she'd tapped the side of her nose and artfully raised one eyebrow. "I've got my own protection, right here, behind the counter, if you know what I mean?" Maureen raised her thumb and pointed her finger in the air, simulating a gun. Lacey hadn't needed to fake her shock at the woman's revelation. "And I'm not the only one who's not afraid to protect myself, either. Mal and me and a few others are in complete agreement on that." Lacey shouldn't have been surprised, a lot of country people owned firearms, mainly to help keep vermin populations such as rabbits down. And most of these firearms were legal. But what wasn't legal, was carrying them around in public, certainly not using them as some kind of vigilante group, even if it was well-intentioned.

When she'd relayed all this new information to Nico back in their hut, she'd raised her own eyebrows, but had managed to hold back the words, *Now do you see why I'm such an asset on this case?* Instead letting him process that thought on his own time. It sounded like at least a few of them had weapons and were prepared to carry them on this nightly watch, and this was too dangerous to be allowed to happen. She'd leave that call to Nico, but if she were in his shoes, she'd have the local guy, Joe, go and have a quiet chat to Mal about the *rumors* he'd heard around town and try and nip it in the bud that way.

As she stood lost in her rumination, staring across the road at the vista of sparkling water with forest-covered hills rising behind it, a movement caught her eye. A man stepped up to the edge of the road on the opposite side. He said nothing, merely stared broodingly at her. Where had he come from? She could've sworn he wasn't there a few seconds ago.

The man raised a hand and crooked his finger at her, beckoning her over. She frowned and stood straighter. What did this guy want? Was he a local? Something about his careworn face was familiar. He was handsome in a silver fox type of way. But when she looked into his eyes, alarm bells sounded loud and clear in her head. Something was off about this guy. He motioned to her with his whole hand now, a sly smile sliding onto his face. Blindly, she reached for her weapon on a duty belt that she wasn't wearing. Shit. She needed to remember she was merely a young woman on holiday with her husband.

How would sightseer Lacey react? Should she go over there? Nico wasn't here to make the call, and she was suddenly unsure what to do. A chill ran down her spine as the man continued to stare at her, and she suddenly felt vulnerable on this side of the street where she was completely alone.

No. She was a cop. There was no feeling vulnerable. She was tough, could handle anything this man could throw her way. He was an older white male, and she knew she could take him if the need arose. Which it wouldn't, because he probably just wanted to talk to her. Perhaps he was an out-of-towner too, lost and confused and had mistaken her for a local who could offer him directions. Although those eyes didn't belong to a tourist.

Duty drew her forward. They were in Strahan to try and unearth a lead to a murder case. It looked as if he wanted to tell her something. Something important. This could be a lead, and she needed to follow it. And if he were merely a lost traveler, they could joke about being lost together and she could recross the road and wait for Nico to return.

Focussed completely on the man, she took one step off the curb. Then as her other foot landed on the road, a horn blared and she jumped back, shocked. She'd been so fixated on the man she hadn't even checked for traffic. Not that there was much traffic in this one-horse town. It was just her luck for a car to come down the empty main street at that particular moment.

"Lacey." Nico's panicked voice had her turning her head to see him jogging down the path toward her. He must've seen her near miss, and she suddenly felt foolish. But by the time she turned back to look across the road, the man was gone. As if he'd never been there in the first place.

"You nearly got hit by that car," Nico said as he reached her side, puffing with exertion, alarm showing clearly in his wide, blue eyes. "What were you doing?" He pulled her protectively into his chest. "God, don't do that to me."

"I'm fine," she replied vaguely, foolishness turning to guilt that she'd scared him. That she'd been so thoughtless. But he needed to know. "There was a man." She turned and shaded her eyes against the increasingly bright rays of the morning sun. "Over there." But he was definitely gone now. So strange. Because there weren't a lot of places to hide on the other side of the road. Unless he'd melted around the side of the boat cruise building.

Now she was beginning to doubt herself.

"What do you mean, a man?" Alarm was quickly replaced by his seasoned detective persona.

"A guy over there on the other side of the road. He was signaling me to come over to him. But I'd never seen him before, and I didn't know what he wanted. He made me feel… I don't know, it was all a little uncanny."

"What did he look like?" Nico demanded, and she loved him a little more for not brushing her story aside, instead, believing her straight away. Nico didn't question her, didn't state the obvious, that there was no one there now. He trusted that she had seen someone. And it'd freaked her out enough to make her forget all her police training for those few costly seconds.

"It was a little hard to tell, he had a baseball cap drawn down low over his face and a short beard and mustache." Lacey drew on her police training on how to take a quick physical sketch of a perp in one or two seconds. "He was tall. The top of his head almost came up to that stop sign over there." She pointed to the traffic sign on the corner. "That'd make him six-three or six-four," she said quickly. "A lean build, like he was physically active, you know." She drew on those few seconds the man had been in her sight. "Perhaps late fifties, early sixties, although it was hard to tell with the grayish beard and the hat, wearing all black."

"Good. Anything else?"

"Gray sideburns and a long, crooked nose, like it was broken in his youth and never fixed properly."

Nico went completely still beside her. "And?" he said, but

this time there was something unsettled in his voice.

"And dark-brown eyes, almost black." That was the one feature she remembered clearly. The way his dark eyes had pierced her, chilling her to the bone. "I didn't like the way he looked at me," she admitted.

"Stay here. I'm going to check it out." Nico put a hand on her shoulder and forcibly pushed her back toward the safety of the shopfront.

"I'm not staying here," she replied, brushing his hand off her shoulder. Now it seemed that it was Nico who was mistaking their undercover status with reality. She was here as a cop. His partner. Equals. Not some fragile woman he could force to stay behind while he went off to investigate. Even if he was technically her commanding officer, there was no sensible reason for her not to follow. She'd been the one to see the man in the first place, she was best suited to identify him again.

"No, you don't understand..." he began. "The way you described this guy, I think he might—"

"Oh, I understand all right," she interrupted tersely. "You don't get to tell me what to do, Nico." Her blood pressure was rising. She knew why he'd automatically told her to stay behind, but she was having none of it. "I'm not some meek woman you can keep barefoot and pregnant in the home."

He stepped back and nearly stumbled off the curb at the ferocity of her words. She was seething now. The look in his eyes told her he suddenly understood he'd gone too far. His knee-jerk reaction was definitely the wrong one.

"I didn't mean—"

"Yes, you did. You need to remember that I'm a trained police officer with a job to do. And I will decide when and how to do my job."

A petulant pout turned his mouth down at the corners, and she just knew he was about to say something like, *It's my baby too*, but she wasn't having it. Now wasn't the time for this pregnancy conversation. And it wasn't the time for him to go all ninja protective warrior on her either. They had a good chance to catch this guy. Her gut told her he had something to do with their case, and now they were letting him get away while they stood here and argued.

"Get moving, or get out of my way." She pushed past him, heading toward the spot where she'd last seen the man standing. "We have a POI to apprehend, we can talk about this"—she waved her hand in his direction, indicating his obstinate refusal to let her do her job—"another time."

She jogged across the road, and he followed. The cruise ship headquarters was big, running the entire length of the esplanade for at least a couple of hundred yards, and there was no way he could've run the full length of the metal building along the road without them seeing him. Had he ducked inside? The only other option was that he'd sprinted around behind the building to where Lacey could just make out a couple of the boats tied up at the dock. Either that, or he'd dived into the water, but that seemed unlikely. That water was freezing, even in the middle of summer. And there was no splashing, not even any ripples to suggest someone had jumped off the jetty.

Nico came alongside her, his jaw clenched tight with the things he wasn't saying. But he kept his words to himself and they moved forward as one. The cruise ship welcome area was paved with polished concrete, a glass and metal atrium beckoning them toward the front entrance of the building.

"Let's check inside first," he commanded. Lacey almost spat back at him that if they separated, they'd cover a lot more ground. But something held her back, and she conceded to Nico's authority by swinging right at the same time he did. They pushed through the door in a hurry, and were brought up short by a young woman leaning against a large reception desk scrolling through her phone. Her expression changed from bored to startled as they both appeared through the door, and she stopped chewing her gum and stared at them.

"Ah, hi," Nico said. "We're, ah… Looking for someone. Our friend. We were supposed to meet him here. Has anyone come in here in the last few minutes?" Ten out of ten for thinking on his feet. Nico had managed to remain in character.

"No, sorry." The girl shook her head and went back to leaning on the countertop and noisily chewing her gum now that it was clear they weren't here to purchase tickets for a cruise.

"Thanks," Nico said, but he needn't have bothered, the girl never looked up from her phone.

Trying not to look like she was rushing, Lacey backtracked through the door, leading Nico onto the esplanade. Walking as quickly as they dared, they darted around the side of the building, past a covered waiting area, and along a short pathway that led to a narrow parking lot at the rear of the warehouse and the small jetty where two boats were moored. Lacey stood on tiptoe and peered down the length of the building, but it morphed into an industrial area farther down, with a couple of rusting shipping containers and a pile of old rope and red buoys.

"Could he have climbed onto one of the boats?" she asked, eyeing the sleek cruise ship with trepidation; she wasn't good with boats.

"Maybe. But then he would've cornered himself, and I don't think he's that stupid."

Carefully, they stalked along the length of the jetty, checking behind a stack of metal bins and then down to the shipping containers. Nothing. It was like he'd disappeared in a puff of smoke. After another ten minutes of fruitless hunting, they turned and retraced their steps around to the front entrance.

As the adrenaline began to fade from her body and her blood cooled, she realized she probably owed Nico an apology. He'd reacted on instinct when he'd tried to stop her chasing their perp, and he was only looking out for their unborn baby. She'd overreacted, and she knew it.

"Look, Nico." She stopped and took him by the arm, pulling him to a halt beside her. "I shouldn't have yelled at you like that."

"No, you shouldn't," he growled back, but there was little heat in his words as he stifled a sigh. "Because I had a good reason to want you to stay where you were," he continued. "I was trying to tell you…" He took a deep breath, and she felt his arm go rigid beneath her fingers. "Your description sounded an awful lot like the man I remember from my youth. My father."

"Oh. My. God," she said slowly as sudden realization dawned on her. This was what Nico had been trying to tell her and she'd shouted him down. "That was Serge?" Nico had shown her an old photo of his father, back when they'd still been a family, as dysfunctional as that was. Was that why he'd looked strangely familiar?

"Maybe." His shoulders were still rigid. "But without seeing him with my own eyes…" He shrugged. "We know he broke into our house, and I was afraid he might still be in the area."

"But why?" Lacey could hardly get her mind around the revelation. "Why is he here in Strahan? And why show himself now?"

"I don't know," Nico replied absently. "But we should probably get back to the main street and start acting like our undercover personas, just in case anyone is watching."

"Good idea." Lacey had forgotten in her rush that a normal citizen—especially a pregnant one—wasn't supposed to be chasing people.

As they walked quickly back alongside the cruise boat building, Nico pulled out his phone. "I missed a message from Sally-Ann when I left my phone at the café," he explained. "I was just about to open it when I saw you nearly get hit by that car."

Lacey scowled up at him. How long was he going to hold that against her? She was just coming up with a smart retort when Nico's face blanched and he stopped mid-stride.

"What?" she asked. Something about the information Sally-Ann had sent him wasn't good.

He didn't answer; instead, he turned his phone around so Lacey could see the photo Sally-Ann had forwarded. Lacey leaned in to study the image. It was a hand drawn depiction of a male portrait. "We sent a police sketch artist to visit Taylor yesterday. This is the composite drawing of the man she remembered as having picked them up on the side of the road on the day of the abduction," he said. "Of course Taylor's memory is hazy, and we were worried that with the amnesia, she might not remember anything correctly, but..." Nico's voice faded out. But Lacey needed no explanation. Her blood ran cold, and she lifted dazed eyes to Nico's. It couldn't be, could it? This looked a lot like the man she'd just seen across the road. The beard was much longer and scraggly in the drawing, but the crooked nose and the piercing eyes were the same. It seemed like Taylor's memory had still been working because...

"I think that's him. The man I just saw," Lacey confirmed, even as her palms began to sweat. The sketch was light on detail, but she could interpret the pieces that were missing and fill them in to come up with the man across the road.

"Yeah, well, it's also a pretty good likeness of my father," Nico added through gritted teeth.

"Holy Fuck." Lacey could barely believe it. Could barely

form the words. But they needed to be said. "Are you suggesting this serial killer and your father are one and the same?"

"Yes," Nico sucked air in over his lips. "That's exactly what I'm saying."

"Oh. Shit!" Comprehension suddenly hit. Not only had she been about to walk over and put herself within reach of Nico's long-lost father, she'd also nearly allowed herself to be lured into range of the serial killer they were hunting. One and the same man. As the ramifications of what she'd nearly done sank in, her legs began to feel like jelly, and Nico's arm came around her for support.

"What have I done?" she asked in a whisper.

CHAPTER TEN

What had she done indeed? Nico was still reeling from everything that'd just happened. Almost losing Lacey to a speeding car had turned his mind blank for a few moments. Long enough to blind him to the fact that she'd also just spotted the very person they were hunting. And nearly been abducted by him.

His father.

The killer.

Nico still couldn't reconcile the two things in his head. It was as if both possibilities couldn't coexist in his mind at the same time. It was inconceivable that his father was a murderer. And yet...

"Oh, God, Nico, I'm so sorry. This is terrible." Lacey's jade-green eyes filled with empathy and she took his hand. She, of all people, would understand how this would be turning his guts inside out.

But there was no time for empathy now. They were still standing at the side of the cruise ship greeting area, like two sitting ducks. He suddenly felt extremely vulnerable. His hip ached, almost as if trying to remind him of a time when he had felt helpless.

"We need to get back to our accommodation," he said,

letting his cop brain take over, because his emotions were so conflicted right now he could barely make a decision. "We're not safe out here in the open." His father could be anywhere, watching them right this second, and the back of Nico's neck tingled.

Tugging Lacey by the hand, he crossed the road and then lengthened his stride. It was a ten-minute walk back to their hut, and they did it in silence, both of them super vigilant, watching for any movement or sign that someone was following them. Nico had a dreadful feeling that their hut was no longer safe either; Serge probably already knew where they were staying. Perhaps he'd been following them from the second they'd arrived in town yesterday. The thought made him feel physically sick. But he said none of this to Lacey, not wanting to scare her any more than she already was.

Their little A-frame cottage came into view, but Nico no longer saw it as cute and bucolic. Now he saw how easily the place could be breached; how hard it would be to defend if the need arose. The windows were low to the ground and didn't even have security screens, and while the doors were solid wood, the locks were simple latches that any thief with half a brain could pick with their eyes closed. The thick circle of trees surrounding the structure made a great place to hide and watch without ever being seen.

Setting his jaw, he marched up the stairs and in through the front door, shutting and locking it carefully as soon as Lacey was safely inside.

"Stay here," he said in a low voice, moving quietly through the small, three-room hut to make sure it was empty. After he'd checked all the windows were still untouched, he bent down and retrieved both his and Lacey's guns from the lockbox under the bed.

"We wear these from now on," he said, handing her the

pistol and watching as she tucked it into the waistband of her shorts without comment.

"Right. Good." Lacey let out a sigh of relief and sat heavily in one of the two flowery armchairs, pulling out her phone. "We have to call this in," she said without looking up.

"Wait." His hand on hers stilled her fingers right before she hit the dial button.

"Wait? Why?"

"You know Shadbolt will take me off the case the second he finds out, don't you?" He could see the cogs of her mind whirring behind her eyes, still dark with fear and shock. He didn't think that she'd processed their predicament as thoroughly as he had yet, and he watched as understanding arrived on her face.

"Oh, shit," she said quietly.

"Yeah, shit," he repeated. "This is a huge conflict of interest. Even Shadbolt won't be able to turn a blind eye to this one."

"But you need to work on this case. We need to work on this together," she said, rising part way to her feet. "You understand your da—this perp better than anyone. You're lead on this case, they can't remove you." Indignation made her pretty mouth pucker into a tight line.

"They can, and they will." He took the armchair next to hers and tugged on her hand until she sat down with him. "Can we just take a few minutes to talk this through first before we call it in?" He needed to get his head on straight, to banish this terrible fuzzy numbness that'd overtaken his head, his soul.

"Sure." Her thumb traced soothing circles over his knuckles. "Take as long as you need. I agree, we should figure out where we stand before we let the team know." He loved her for saying *we*. Even though this was *his* father, and this was *his* problem, it never even occurred to her that they weren't in this together. A grim silence settled over them as they sat, hand in hand and considered their options. All sorts of dire scenarios formed in his mind. So many unanswered questions he didn't know where to start.

It wasn't thoughts about how he was going to capture Serge that clamored the loudest for recognition, however. It was the much deeper emotions that rose to the surface like lava bubbling, hot and fiery. "How am I going to tell my mother?" His voice hitched on the word *mother*, and his heart broke just a little at how his passionate, determined mother would shatter under this news. She might even blame herself. Wondering if there was some manner in which she should've foreseen this in her twelve years of marriage to the man. Unaccountably, his hands began to shake. "This is going to kill her."

"No, it won't," Lacey replied softly. "She's a strong woman, she'll deal with it the same way she dealt with his disappearance the first time." Her hand tightened around his to stop the shaking. "You and your family will get through this together. You have to, you have no other choice, especially if we're to stop him." He lifted his gaze from where it rested on their hands linked together and sought her eyes. "I know this is terribly personal, Nico, and it's hard to separate this intimate disaster from the unbiased cop you are normally. But you need to focus." Her answer surprised him. He'd been expecting more compassion, more understanding; this was by far the hardest thing he'd ever had to deal with as an adult. Lacey wasn't prepared to let him wallow in his own self-pity, but she also didn't appreciate the depth of his guilt and shame, not just for his family.

"The blood of those women feels like it's on my hands," he whispered. Now that he knew it was his father who was the murderer, it changed things. Changed his perspective. Without being told, he knew his mother would absorb some of the blame upon herself. But he too, felt culpable. As if he should've known somehow. Should've been able to stop him somehow. It was illogical, but nonetheless, his self-reproach was enormous. People would look at him differently when they found out. And they had every right to. How ironic was it for a homicide detective to not even realize his own father was a serial killer. He gave a low groan of misery and hung his head, his hair falling down around his eyes.

"Don't," she whispered back, getting down on her knees in front of him, both hands on his thighs. "Don't do this to yourself. These are the sins of your father. They're his, and his alone. These murders have nothing to do with you. You couldn't have stopped them no matter what you did."

"I wish it were true," he replied.

"It is true," she insisted. "But you want to know the best way to redeem yourself?" He knew what was coming, even before she said it. "To catch him and put him in jail for the rest of his life."

Part of him wanted to follow that continuous spiral down to the depths of hell, where recriminations were the name of the game, but Lacey's warm grip on his thighs, and her pleading, green eyes kept tugging him away from the vortex. She was right. Now wasn't the time to fall to the ground and curl into the fetal position, wailing like a little child. He could do that later. Now was the time to act like the cop he was supposed to be. He gritted his teeth and nodded his head, not trusting himself to speak.

"At least now you know your hunch was correct. Coming to Strahan helped us to stumble across the killer," she said, a hint of a smile tugging at the corners of her mouth.

That much was true. His gut hadn't let him down on that count at least. He nodded his assent, beginning to feel a little more in control.

"Let's work this out logically," Lacey offered, her gaze still fixed on his, almost as if by sheer will she could pull him out of that dark place he'd been headed. "Try and work out a timeline of his movements. Okay?"

"Yep." He sat a little straighter, brushing his hair back into some semblance of order. He decided the most pressing question centered around the time Serge had first come back into his life. "Let's start when Serge broke into our house," he said. It made no sense as to why Serge would try to rekindle contact after so long, even if it was in a completely random way. His skin crawled at the idea that his father had been slinking through his house in the dead of night, pawing through his things.

"Right. We need to know why he did that." Lacey sat back on her haunches, narrowing her eyes and staring out the window, but leaving one hand comfortingly on his knee.

Why indeed? At first, Nico hadn't been sure the burglar was even his father, it'd just been an intuition. But then Serge had made that disturbing phone call, giving details that cemented the fact it had been him in the house that night. Nico had been quick to update his security afterward, not wanting a repeat event. But neither he nor Lacey could come up with a reason why, apart from Lacey deciding that his father was lonely and wanted to have a peek into Nico's life, no matter how small or insignificant.

But after Serge's attempt to make contact with Lacey this morning, that break-in took on a more sinister feel. He'd made veiled threats against Lacey in his call. Had Serge been after Lacey all along, and Nico had been slow to see it?

"What if his presence in our house was something more than just voyeurism?" he asked slowly. "What if he had a more nefarious goal?"

"Like what?" Lacey questioned.

"Like, what if he'd found you asleep in the house alone when he'd broken in?" Lacey had been late arriving home that night. Had Serge been hoping to catch her unawares? Or had he actually been lying in wait for her?

"But we know..." Lacey tapered off, considering his question.

Smudge had alerted as soon as she had entered the house, telling her someone had recently been inside. And then when she'd looked out the front door, Serge had been standing a little way down the road staring back at her. The part that scared him the most was how she'd taken off after him in only her bare feet.

"And what if I hadn't come home at that particular moment?"

"You think he was after me?" she asked. Getting to her feet, she began to pace across the small living room, and his gaze snagged for a second on her shapely, long legs, beneath the hems of her rather brief jean shorts.

Nico's mind was buzzing now, pulling together everything he knew about his father's interactions with them over the past few months. "Then there's the way he left his recent kill so close to Burnie, where we'd be sure to find her; to be the first on the scene. Add to that, the fact that Taylor knew your name. She'd been told to look out for you. Serge was sending us another message."

"Why?"

"As a way to get to you. And by getting to you, he'd get back at me."

"But again, why?" It was a valid question. Why would Serge want to get back at him? He had no idea if his father held some kind of twisted grudge against him, and if he did, what the reasons behind it were. And why had Serge chosen Nico to be the target? Why not Brice or Gaëlle?

"Because of what you do for a living?" Lacey theorized. "You're a homicide detective. He's a serial killer." It made a certain kind of perverted sense. And Serge was nothing if not perverted.

"Maybe it's his way of warning me to stay away. He's threatening you to make sure I back off."

"Or pull you in closer," Lacey said darkly. "You know the saying, keep your friends close and your enemies closer."

"That would be suicide," Nico snorted. "Even Serge isn't that crazy." But one thing was becoming crystal clear. Serge was targeting Lacey. For whatever debased reason his sick mind had come up with. Nico thought back to how Lacey had described Serge as beckoning her over to him from across the road. Had his intention been to abduct her in broad daylight? Nico licked his suddenly dry lips.

One thing Nico knew with absolute clarity. If Serge so much as harmed one hair on Lacey's head, he wouldn't stop until he'd hunted him down. Killed him, if that's what it took. A son should never have to consider taking the life of his own father. But Nico was prepared to do it, if it came to that.

"We need to keep you safe," he said, surging to his feet and heading for the bedroom. "We're going back to Burnie right now."

"What? We can't leave. We're so close to him. He might still be in town." Lacey put her hands on her hips in a now-familiar stance. But he was having none of her stubborn denial. Not now.

"Don't worry. I'm going to make a few phone calls and the full force of the law will descend on this place in a few hours. I'm prepared to let them do the hard work. My job now is to get you—us—to safety."

"But we could lose him. He's a serial killer, Nico. And this is the closest any of us have been to catching him."

"I know. And I don't care." There were some things in this world more important than doing his job. Lacey's logic wasn't going to sway him, not this time. He'd been wrong to let her convince him into bringing her on this mission and he was cursing himself not to have seen the danger before.

But Lacey wasn't taking this news docilely, and she stepped in front of him, her blonde ponytail swinging from side to side in agitation.

"And what if Shadbolt takes you off the case? Are you prepared for the consequences of that?" She raised an inquiring eyebrow, and he knew where she was going with this conversation.

It wouldn't be *if*, it'd be *when*. There was no way Shadbolt would let a conflict as big as this continue, not even for his star detective. But again, he was prepared to take the hit if he was to keep Lacey safe. A small voice—a very small voice— argued that if they didn't call it in straight away, they could have a few hours leeway where they might get lucky and apprehend Serge on their own. How he'd love to be the one who brought Serge in. His fingers itched with the need to find that dirtbag father, take him down, cuff him, and drag him to the station. It would be his biggest triumph yet if he achieved the capture. To put Lacey in that much danger was unacceptable, however, and so he discarded the idea before it was even fully formed.

"Don't argue with me on this one." He stood his ground. "Or I'll be forced to pull rank as your commanding officer." He was also prepared to throw her over his shoulder, caveman style, if she refused to go, but he kept that bit to himself.

"But he is your father," she tried once more. "I know you haven't seen him in seventeen years. But don't you want to... I don't know, see him with your own eyes? Meet him face to face? Ask him why? I know I would."

"No, I don't," Nico lied. God, yes, he wanted to confront his father. But not at the sake of putting her in more danger than she was already in.

She gave him an icy stare, and they locked gazes as they

silently battled wills. Finally, her lips twitched up. Whether in agitation or amusement, he wasn't sure, but she took a step back.

"All right. Back to Burnie it is. But you should at least get the local cops out hunting for him right now."

He could hardly believe that Lacey was conceding defeat; stubborn was her middle name. But maybe she could see the fear he couldn't quite hide in his eyes. Fear of what might happen to her or their baby if they didn't play this one strictly by the book.

"I'm on it now," he said pulling his phone out of his pocket.

"I'll go and pack," she said, skirting around him toward the bedroom.

But he snagged her elbow and pulled her into his chest. "Thank you, Lace. Thank you for being here for me. For being strong when I couldn't."

The lines around her mouth softened, and she melted into him for a moment. "You're the best man I know, Nico Favreau. A lesser man wouldn't have been able to get past this at all, never mind so quickly. I'm aware how soul destroying this must be, and I want you to know that I'm here for you. Whenever and wherever you need me. We'll get through this together."

Now he knew why she'd capitulated so quickly; she was concerned for his mental and emotional wellbeing. But right now, he'd take whatever he could get.

"I love you" was all he could think of to say. But the words just couldn't convey how deeply he needed her. How much she affected him, right down to the core of his soul. And how madly he wanted to protect her. Because if something happened to her, he knew he'd never recover.

CHAPTER ELEVEN

The two-hour trip back to Burnie was mainly spent with Nico filling Shadbolt in on the events of the day, and then directing his team via phone, while Lacey listened from the passenger seat. Shadbolt was yet to officially remove Nico from the investigation, and so he took as much advantage as he could of these precious few hours while he was still in charge.

They went straight to the station, not bothering to stop at home first, and when they arrived the place was buzzing like a human wasp nest. More units had been pulled in from Davenport and Launceston as Nico assembled a task force to flood Strahan with armed police officers. Two teams from Burnie, consisting of Gorman and Hickey, Tyrell and Linc, as well as Detective Saito, had already been dispatched to Strahan to help the local Sergeant Joe Jackson and his offsider.

As Nico skillfully maneuvered their car into a spot in the underground parking lot, Lacey let her hand rest on top of his. "How are you doing?" she asked. It was the first chance she'd had to ask this since their hurried departure from their accommodation.

He flashed her a look of surprise as if he'd been so caught up in the machinations of organizing a manhunt, he'd almost forgotten his own emotional pain.

"I'm okay," he replied. "I just need to get through the next few hours. And then…"

"I know," she replied, squeezing his hand. And then he could break apart, if that's what he needed. "One more thing." Her words stopped him just as he opened the car door. "Are we revealing my pregnancy yet?" She laid a protective hand over her abdomen. They'd agreed to tell their families this weekend. But she didn't want the news escaping before they'd made those important phone calls.

After a moment's hesitation, Nico replied, "No. Not unless we absolutely have to."

"Good." Her pregnancy should have no impact on this current investigation as far as she could tell, but she wanted confirmation from Nico. They walked hand in hand up the stairs leading from the parking lot to the main level. No words were required; they both knew they'd be walking into a shitstorm and this final few seconds of peace was welcome. They unlinked their hands as they passed through the door.

Jay Pederson stood waiting for Nico in the hallway outside the operations room, and Lacey held her breath, even though she knew what was coming. "Shadbolt's appointed me as lead on this case." His words weren't spiteful or aggressive, but there was a certain authoritative ring that told everyone he wasn't to be messed with. "You're officially off the case," he added, even though that point was already clear.

Nico merely nodded.

"But I could still use your input," Pederson continued. "After all, you know this perp intimately. I'll need everything you've got on him." His tone was concise and to the point. There was no sympathy there. If he had any inkling of what Nico was going through, then he either wasn't showing it, or wasn't concerned. "And also to hear your account firsthand." His gaze slid to Lacey, dark-brown eyes filled with what could only be called intense curiosity. And what good detective wouldn't want the eyewitness account? "Come inside." The tall indigenous man gestured with his arm, indicating they precede him into the room.

"Two units from Davenport are mobilizing to Strahan as we speak and the other two units coming from Launceston will be here in twenty minutes. So that gives us time to talk." Pederson spoke as if Nico wasn't already completely aware of the procedures he himself had set in motion in the car on the way home, and Lacey glanced at Nico, but he carefully kept all emotion off his face. The other detective took a seat at the front of the room, watching as Lacey and Nico took the two chairs to his left. They were still dressed in their casual clothes they'd been wearing to blend in, her in jean shorts and a tank top, and Nico also in shorts, a tee, and loafers, his shoulder-length hair which was normally tied up, was loose but slicked back. Pederson, however, was wearing his detective uniform of a dark suit, white shirt and tie. For some reason, this made Lacey feel at a disadvantage, and she knew Nico would feel it too. It clearly outlined the fact he was still working the case, and they had now been demoted to… She wasn't sure what they were now. Witnesses at best, civilians at worst.

Lacey had to admit, it looked like Pederson was taking to being a lead investigator like a duck to water. He was cool, organized, and prepared. That arrogance was still there, but sometimes it was needed if you had a large team to keep under control. Respect was often hard-earned in the police fraternity, and a strong ego never hurt to maintain authority. Nico had already earned the respect of his peers by hard work and producing great results, and Lacey was thankful he was one of the least conceited men she knew. Nico would have also shown some compassion for a man who'd just found out his father was a killer, rather than the icy coolness of Pederson's requests. Another point in Nico's favor.

"Let's start at the beginning, with your impressions of this guy." Pederson turned to face Lacey. "Tell me about the very first few moments after you spotted him." He wasted no time in getting directly to the point.

Lacey recounted her interaction with Serge with clinical detail, leaving nothing out. But when she came to the part where they'd given up the chase and decided to head back to the hut, Pederson stopped her.

"That's all good stuff," he said. "But I'm looking for more. Your gut instincts about him. How did it make you feel when he first caught your eye? I want to know what your intuition told you about him, before you actually suspected who he was. Before that knowledge colored your story."

Lacey looked into Pederson's face. He was good-looking in an unconventional manner, with a large, slightly flat nose and an equally big mouth with plump lips and white teeth which lit up a room when he deigned to smile—which wasn't often. There was also a sharp intelligence behind his dark eyes, and he was using that acumen right now by diving to the heart of her interaction with Nico's father. When Nico had asked her about him, she'd skillfully avoided the part where the other man had made her skin crawl. But he was going to hear it now, whether he liked it or not.

"Something was off about him right from the start," Lacey admitted. "He made me feel…weak? No, that's not it. Maybe ineffectual. Like he had all the power, and he knew it. As if we were playing a game of cat and mouse, and he was most definitely the cat." A small shiver ran down her spine at the memory. "I looked directly into his eyes, and it was as if they were dead. Like he had no compassion left; maybe he never had any."

As she spoke, she glanced at Nico. She was most probably reaffirming in his mind that he'd made the right decision to pull out of Strahan when they had. He'd done it for her. Her and the baby. Lacey knew that if she hadn't been there, Nico would've been the first one to be out there hunting down his father. And if he'd found him, perhaps he'd have obtained the answers he deserved. And perhaps that's what Serge wanted all along. To goad his son into doing something stupid. To pull him in, like she'd theorized earlier. Maybe Nico had it wrong, and it wasn't Lacey he was after. Maybe the father was out to kill his son all along.

"So, the eyes of a killer? Is that what you're saying?" Pederson asked curtly.

"I guess so," Lacey said with a shrug, leaning back in her chair.

"And what's your take on all of this?" Pederson turned to Nico, finally bringing him in on the conversation. Shadbolt might've taken Nico off the case, but Pederson was right, his input on his father's motivation and weaknesses might just make the difference in capturing him. One thing neither Pederson nor Shadbolt knew, however, was how little Nico truly understood his father. Which was a good thing in Lacey's eyes, because it meant Nico was absolutely nothing like Serge. Even though that was one of Nico's worst fears, that he'd turn out like his father, she knew it was groundless. Nico was a good man. A kind man. And a courageous man. All things Serge wasn't.

"I have a theory," Nico said, and Lacey tensed. Even though they'd discussed this, she still wasn't happy he was exploring it with Pederson. "Nobody but Shadbolt knows this yet, but I believe it's now pertinent to the case. We had a burglar break into our house during the Sandra Brown case, I'm not sure if you remember?"

Pederson tilted his chin to confirm he did.

"I had a phone call about a week after the break-in from my father, and among other things, he validated my suspicions that it was him in our house that night. He also threatened Lacey. I don't think that him turning up on that corner in the split second Lacey was alone was coincidence. I think he's been trying to get to her all along."

"Hmm." Pederson tapped his pen against his chin. "Interesting theory. Especially when you add into the mix the fact that the second victim, Taylor, knew to ask for Lacey specifically. Which seemed odd at the time. But if you include those other facts, it's more than a coincidence."

"Exactly," Nico slapped his knee in endorsement.

"Why? What's his interest in her?" Pederson asked brusquely.

"That's what we're still trying to figure out. But it's the main reason I got out of Strahan as fast as possible." Nico was practically bristling with indignation now. He wasn't used to not being in charge, and Pederson questioning him was frustrating him like nothing else.

"So you think all of this could be directly related to Lacey somehow?" Pederson asked.

Nico stiffened even more, but inclined his head.

"Sometimes a killer's motive is a lot less personal than we like to think," Pederson said slowly.

"And sometimes it's not," Nico barked back.

"What does he mean by that?" Lacey butted in, suddenly intrigued, but also wanting to calm the situation, wondering if Nico might've missed the point.

"Sometimes they kill just for the sake of killing. It's almost as if they're hardwired to kill. Just like you and I are hardwired to smile at a puppy," Pederson added.

"If my father just wanted to kill people, he could've easily stayed on the mainland to do it. That doesn't explain why he's here. He knows I live here. He knows I'm in love with Lacey. Maybe he sees killing Lacey as his ultimate triumph, as a way to hurt me, I don't know. But there's a whole lot more to it than him being a simple serial killer." A deep red was creeping slowly up Nico's neck and Lacey was suddenly nervous for Pederson's well-being. Nico didn't like being lectured to, and he certainly wouldn't like Pederson suggesting that Nico had it all wrong. It was one thing to take the lead on this case away from him, but a whole other level to try to throw it back in his face.

"Hmm," Pederson said calmly, not rising to the bait. "We also have to consider that it might be you he's after. Even though you don't seem to fit his archetypal victim." Lacey sent up a silent cheer. Nico might not listen to her fears, but he'd certainly take more stock if Pederson said it too. "I'm wondering if I need to put you both under guard?"

Nico rocked back in his chair as if Pederson had struck a physical blow. "No," he said roughly. "I'm not the target here, she is. And I can take care of her. I can take care of both of us." This time, he stood up, hands clenched by his sides. Oops, looked like Pederson had gone a step too far. It was one thing to question his lack of knowledge about his own father, but to question Nico's ability to protect Lacey, that was sacrilege.

Time for her to step in. Standing up, she positioned herself between Nico and the other detective. "We'll definitely consider your advice," she said to Pederson. Nico took a tiny step forward, as if he meant to move her out of the way, eyes blazing, and she put a warning hand on his chest. "But we'll decline your offer of protection. For now." She didn't take her eyes off Pederson's face, but she could feel Nico's rage vibrating through his ribcage. She needed to get him out of here before he became violent and got himself arrested for assaulting another officer. "You can call either one of us if you need any more info. I think it's best if we both go home."

Pederson studied her for a few moments. There was no fear in his eyes, merely cool regard. But he was underestimating Nico if he thought he'd take these veiled insults lying down. And he also severely underestimated her own abilities as a black belt to set him on the floor if need be. Together, she and Nico could incapacitate the other detective in a heartbeat, but that wasn't the point. Violence wasn't going to solve anything here.

"I think that's a good idea," Pederson finally acknowledged, taking a step away from them and straightening his tie.

She sucked in a lungful of much needed oxygen, and was surprised to note her heartbeat thudding loudly in her ears. The air around the trio was still humming with tension, and she never took her gaze off Pederson, even as she pushed hard against Nico's chest, forcing him backward. Now there was breathing space between them, she turned to Nico and gave him a warning scowl that Pederson couldn't see. He scowled back at her, but she continued to narrow her eyes at him until his face changed and she could see a semblance of sanity return. His hands slowly unclenched and he finally ran a hand through his hair.

"Can we go now?" she asked him quietly, feeling the weight of Pederson's stare boring into her back but choosing to ignore it.

"Yep, let's get outta here," he growled in reply.

"Oh, I've got one more bit of interesting news before you go," Pederson said and Lacey hated the smugness in his voice. She was quickly reevaluating Pederson's motives in this whole interview. At first she'd thought he was unbiased, merely wanting the best outcome for this case. But now, she wasn't so sure. There was definitely resentment brewing under that cool façade. "Remember how Saito and Sally-Ann were working together on the unsolved cold cases?" he said leisurely.

Lacey snapped all the way around to face him. What was

Pederson up to now?

"Sally-Ann only put the pieces together a few hours ago once we found out the link with your father. They think they might've found something. A murder in Canberra with many similarities to our serial killer's case, except that the girl wasn't a prostitute. She was like Danika, young, a university student, who'd been strangled to death, seventeen years ago. Right before Serge faked his death."

She felt Nico go as rigid as a statue behind her. Oh, shit. This wasn't what they needed to hear. This meant that Serge had been a killer right back when he'd still been a family man. It changed everything. Including Nico's memories of the father he thought he'd known back then. Not only had he been an unsatisfactory father figure, but Nico's family had been living with a murderer in their house without even realizing it. But this news would also change the way they ran this investigation. Because if there was one linked murder, there were probably more cold cases that might be attributed to Serge.

"Why didn't you tell us this earlier?" Lacey couldn't keep the accusation out of her voice.

"I wanted to get your accounts of this morning unimpeded by any prejudice or sentiment first. We certainly didn't need to add any more melodrama to your story."

Ooh, how could he have been so duplicitous? Coldly withholding that information until he decided it was the right time to tell them. Lacey pulled her lips back in a snarl. Now she was sure Pederson was enjoying this. Enjoying Nico's pain. She wanted to smack him, feel her palm hit his face with satisfying force so that it left a red welt. But she couldn't be the one to lose her cool. Not with Nico so close to the edge. She took Nico by the hand and led him out the doorway without so much as a backward glance.

CHAPTER TWELVE

Nico was still seeing red forty-five minutes later as he drove up the driveway and parked his Jeep in the shed. "That little twerp. Who does he think he is?" he growled to himself under his breath. Lacey gave a quiet sigh from the passenger seat beside him, letting him know that she'd heard him for the umpteenth time. But keeping up his rage at Pederson was better than the alternative—thinking about the bombshell news he'd dropped on them just as they were leaving.

His father was most likely a killer even before he chose to leave his family behind.

Perhaps that was why he'd abandoned his family. To keep them safe from the homicidal maniac he was becoming, or more likely, to keep them from discovering his secret proclivity. But either way it was a small comfort to Nico at the moment.

He was taking no chances. Not this time. He was going to make sure everything was safe and secure. Although it was highly unlikely Serge had discovered yet that they'd fled back to Burnie, followed them here, and was now lying in wait. Highly unlikely, but not impossible.

"Got your weapon?" he asked, slipping out his door and taking his gun out of its shoulder holster. "We need to make sure the grounds and house are clear."

He had to hand it to her, she simply nodded and followed his lead without comment. Humoring him. At least he knew how to handle this kind of threat. Using hand signals, he directed her to flow right as they exited the shed through the large garage door, while he slipped around the corner to the left. There was no welcoming bark from Smudge as he was still happily ensconced at Margie and Herb's place. Which also meant someone could've broken into their house unimpeded. Nico focussed on the fence line that surrounded the orchard at the rear of the property, trying to peer through the low-hanging branches of the apple trees into what lay beyond. His flock of geese were happily dust bathing in a bare patch to the far right, and their total lack of concern gave him grounds to think there was no need for his heightened security. The guard geese, as Lacey now called them, would alert if there was a stranger on the property, or if they felt threatened in any way.

Lacey appeared around the other side of the shed, gun raised and indicated everything was clear. He signaled her to take one side of the orchard, while he took the other, and they diligently checked the area. Nico stopped at the farthest fence line, narrowing his eyes and glaring into the dense forest at the back of his property. It was too much to expect to search the entire forest, but Nico wanted to. Lacey glanced at him and shook her head, and he begrudgingly turned around.

They didn't speak until after they'd searched down each side of the house before entering the house and painstakingly clearing each room.

"Right, can I get my bag out of the car now?" Lacey asked, tucking her gun back into her shoulder holster. "And we should let Margie know we'll come and collect Smudge soon."

Nico's guts were still roiling, but he had no other choice

than to acquiesce. All he wanted was her safely locked inside this house until Serge was caught, however long it took, impractical as that might be. Instead, he followed her out to the car and helped her carry their luggage back to the house.

"I'll make a cuppa," Lacey announced after they'd stowed their bags and put away their guns. "I just called Margie, and she said that Herb has taken Smudge for a walk, and he'll bring him by in about half an hour. She was surprised we'd returned so early."

"Yeah," Nico grunted in reply. They were supposed to have been gone two nights minimum and it was only Sunday afternoon. Normally, they'd be taking it easy, relaxing and getting ready for the coming week ahead. Instead, he was wound tighter than a loaded spring.

He forced himself to sit at the small kitchen table while Lacey busied herself making tea. When she placed a mug in front of him and took her seat opposite, he took her free hand in his. "I hate all this," he said forcefully. Everything about this situation sucked. From him finding out about his father, to being taken off the team, to having to hide out in his house, afraid of everything that moved.

"I know," she said, entwining her fingers in his. "Nothing about this is ideal. But we have to stay confident that they'll catch him quickly, then this will all be over."

It wouldn't be over for him. Just because his father was in jail wouldn't necessarily mean he'd be any closer to answering the million and one questions he had.

"Shadbolt is assembling a huge task force. He's even pulling in units from Hobart to help us catch him. He doesn't want Serge getting away."

Nico nodded at Lacey's words. Even though Pederson hadn't mentioned it, the junior officer on the front desk had been all too keen to tell them they were preparing for even more officers to arrive shortly, not only from Launceston but all the way from Hobart.

"I think he wants Serge almost as much as you do," she added.

That wasn't possible, but Nico merely gave a wan smile. No one could want to catch that dirtbag of a father more than him. It was his right as the maligned son to stop Serge in his tracks. To gain some form of retribution from this game his father was playing with him.

They both sipped their tea in silence for a few moments. "I think it's time," Lacey said into the quiet kitchen. "It's not going to get any easier the longer you leave it. Better to get it out of the way."

He knew exactly what she meant. Time to make the inevitable phone call to his mother. To his family. To let them know their husband and father was an alleged murderer.

The tension ramped up inside his chest. He really didn't want to do this. But there was one small ray of sunshine amongst all the darkness. "I'm going to tell her about the baby too," he announced. It was probably the worst time to declare that Catarina was going to be a grandmother, but he hoped the news would soften the blow of finding out her ex-husband was the worst kind of liar and a cheat.

"Okay," she replied simply. "I'll call my family at the same time. At least then my mother can't accuse me of playing favorites by breaking the baby news to her second," Lacey added with a sigh. Why did everything connected with Elora have to be so fraught with heightened emotion and drama? He hated that she affected Lacey this way. "And I guess it's time they knew about your family dramas too."

Up till now, Lacey hadn't mentioned anything about the mystery surrounding Serge's disappearance, or his re-emergence from the grave. Mainly due to the fact she hadn't spoken to her family since Christmas. But also partly because it'd only give Elora ammunition with which to attack both

Lacey and Nico. She'd have to tell them eventually, and with events unfolding so quickly today, it was time they knew. "Wish me luck," she said, rising to her feet.

He understood how hard this phone call was going to be for Lacey, he could detect the slight tremble in her voice. It'd be almost as hard as the phone call he was about to make. But it was time to break the icy wall that'd formed between Lacey and her family. This news was too important to withhold.

"I'll do better than that." He swung around the table and pulled her into an embrace. The feeling of her body held against his eased a little of his own tension. She was warm and supple and alive. Her presence grounded him. It was exactly what he needed. To reconnect. To remember there was more to life than this singular moment in time. They would get through this and joy and gratitude would feature again somewhere in their future. He hoped he could offer her the same comfort. The same support.

Twenty minutes later, he returned to the kitchen feeling completely drained, like a dried-up husk of a man. That phone call had been even worse than he'd imagined. He'd made a group call, bringing in Brice and Gaëlle as well, so they all heard the news together, and he didn't have to repeat himself over and over. He could hear Lacey's muffled voice behind the closed living room door and knew not to interrupt her. He hoped her call was going better than his, but knew it was probably a vain hope.

Busying himself, he pulled open a cupboard to see what they had by way of foodstuffs that might inspire him to cook something. A packet of dried pasta, two tins of kidney beans, rice, a jar of pesto, and—

A knock at the front door almost made him jump out of his skin and he unconsciously reached for his gun, grabbing only air, as it was still locked in the safe. "It's only me," came Herb's voice from the other side of the door. "And me mate

Smudge." Nico smiled at that. Herb loved Smudge's visits, and Nico wondered why the elderly couple didn't just get themselves a canine friend. Herb said it was because they traveled too much, and Nico couldn't really disagree. Owning a pet was a constant commitment.

Careful to check the peephole before opening the door just in case, Nico was confronted with a very happy dog bouncing all over him as well as a foil-covered dish being thrust toward him. "Margie made a whole batch of casseroles this morning. Told me to bring one up to you youngins, because you probably didn't have time to cook anything."

"Thank you, Herb. And tell Margie I'll bring her down a basket of apples soon, they're nearly ripe."

"Will do, Detective." Herb used the term loosely, more because he secretly liked the fact they had a real-life homicide detective living in their midst, than as a form of respect.

Smudge pushed his way past Nico's knees, intent on getting inside, and Herb let go of his leash. "We've just had a lovely long walk, so he shouldn't need any more exercise tonight," Herb said, staring wistfully after the dog who'd disappeared down the hallway.

"Thank you so much. You can walk him anytime you like," Nico said, balancing the warm dish in one hand and holding the door with the other. Normally, he'd invite the older man in, but today he and Lacey needed their space.

As if sensing his mood, Herb snapped his heels together and said, "Better be off. Got a bent spoke in my front wheel on this morning's ride. Need to fix that quick smart."

"Thanks again, Herb." Nico watched the spritely old man practically skip down his front stairs and waved as he made his way down the long dirt driveway.

At least that solved the problem of what they were going to eat tonight.

The door to the living room was yanked open just as Nico

passed by in the hallway, and Lacey stalked through it. "Thank God that's over," she huffed.

"Bad?" Nico questioned.

"Yep. Worse than I imagined." Lacey threw up her hands in exasperation. "How dare I? How dare I keep such vital information about your father from them." She put on a high-pitched imitation of Elora's tone. "They could've been murdered in their sleep by a serial killer because they hadn't known to take precautions," Lacey parodied, then gave a snort of derision. "As if your father cares one whit about *my* family. And you and I both know that if we thought there was any danger to them, we would've made sure they had protection," she added. Lacey's eyes were flashing, but she wasn't nearly finished. "Oh, and she's also not ready to become a grandmother, and how dare I get pregnant without any warning. She accused me of doing it on purpose, just so I could hold it over her." He could see the tight lines around her mouth, the slight tremble in her lips, and the dark shadow in her eyes, and he silently cursed Elora. The woman was a narcissistic bitch, but she never owned her actions, her manipulations, or her lies. Instead, she always put the blame squarely back on the people around her. Nico wondered what it'd be like to live in an artificial world of your own creation. In a bubble of conceit where everything was always someone else's fault. Wanting everything and everyone to dance to your tune and never the other way around.

He dropped one arm around her shoulders, still holding the casserole with the other. "If she's going to be like that, I don't have a problem with not inviting her down to see the grandchild she isn't ready to have," he said in a low rumble. He desperately wanted to protect Lacey from her mother's emotional entanglement, but he knew not to overstep where family was concerned. Lacey wouldn't thank him for being overbearing; she'd always wanted to solve the problem herself. But secretly, Nico thought Elora was an unsolvable problem, and he had no issue with passing a decree banning that woman from their home forever, even though he knew Lacey would never agree. Families were complicated at the best of times, blood ties the hardest of all to break.

"I have half a mind to agree with you," Lacey grumbled. "But let's just do this in little steps. The worst part is over. Now they know about Serge, and they know I'm pregnant. Two birds with one stone." She gave a long, drawn-out sigh. "The ball is now in their court."

"Hmm." Nico's reply echoed his doubt. But not wanting to bring Lacey down any more, he held up the still-warm casserole as he guided her into the kitchen. "We have one ray of sunshine. No need to cook tonight. Herb brought up a freshly cooked casserole from Margie."

Lacey's eyes brightened as she lifted her gaze to take in the foil-covered dish. "Nice." But they soon darkened again as her thoughts slipped back to her conversation with her parents. "God, it just makes me so mad," she blurted. "Why can't she ever just be happy for me? Why does everything have to be such a trial?"

"I know," Nico soothed, placing the dish on the table and turning to wrap his arms around her.

"Thank you," she murmured into his T-shirt. "I don't know what I'd do without you." She tilted her head and their lips met in a chaste kiss. "Talking to my mother always makes me feel drained, and…I don't know…dirty. I need to feel clean again. Need to wash that woman out of my soul," Lacey stated.

"Hmm," he murmured agreement, his lips pressed against the silken hair on the top of her head.

"Oh, God. I haven't even asked you about how your family took the news. I'm so sorry." She looked up and shook her head as if ridding it of all her own bad thoughts. "Tell me," she requested. "Tell me how is Catarina?" Her green eyes filled with compassion, so deep and so profound all he wanted to do was take her and kiss her. Kiss the bad thoughts away. Bury them under an avalanche of lust and wanting. To be blameless for a few moments in time. To obliterate everything with the heat of his desire for her. His cock stirred at the idea of sex with Lacey. She must've felt the length of him hardening against her stomach because she took his lips with hers again, their kiss deepening as she ground her hips into his.

"Can we talk about it later?" he asked and then reclaimed her mouth.

"Okay," she mumbled as his tongue swept across her bottom lip, then delved deep, taking and claiming. Without speaking, she led him straight to the shower. There was no grace in the way they disrobed; all they wanted was to be naked as soon as possible. Nico guided her under the hot water and held her, with her back to his front, letting the hot water soothe, letting the skin to skin contact comfort. Letting their hunger build. Letting their carnal lust replace all the pain and distress of the past few hours, even for just a few moments. One hand wandered down over the curve of her breast, brushing the nipple and then cupping the fullness. His cock grew as hard as granite. God, she was so beautiful, and she was all his. He wanted to give her everything, all the pleasure he was capable of.

Then he was turning her, on his knees in front of her, ignoring the cold tiles beneath. Steam rose up around them, but he barely noticed as he used his tongue to trace down her stomach to the cleft between her thighs. Her head thumped softly against the wall as she let out a long, low groan. He licked and sucked, as if he were worshiping at her altar, concentrating on her pleasure. Concentrating on building her desire. Taking her closer and closer to the edge.

"Nico, please," she finally gasped, gripping his head in her hands, forcing him to look up into her eyes. "I need…"

He knew exactly what she needed. He spun her around to face the wall, his cock so hot and hard he could barely contain it. His hands took hold of her hips and she arched backward into him. Resting his mouth against the curve of her neck, he could feel the pulse of her erratic heartbeat on his lips, the thump echoing his own longing. Then he was inside her and she welcomed him in as they moved together, the water running down their bodies, making them slick like seals. Dropping an open-mouthed kiss to her shoulder, he nipped at the skin, urging her on. Faster. Every muscle tightening, becoming rigid and begging for release.

He was close. So close. And so was she. They climaxed in unison, shaking and panting as they each tumbled over the edge, wave after wave of rapture taking them. Their cries mingled together with the hot water, bouncing off the tiles, loud and ecstatic. His knees felt like jelly and he could barely hold himself up as he leaned his weight into his hands on the wall on either side of Lacey's head.

"Good," she panted, her forehead resting against the wall. "So good." Then she turned in his arms, her hands resting languidly on his shoulders as she gazed up at him.

He could see his future in her eyes. And that was all that mattered.

CHAPTER THIRTEEN

Tuesday mornings were sometimes hard, but this Tuesday was extra challenging, knowing that she was no longer involved in the murder case. Both she and Nico had taken the day off work yesterday, on orders from Shadbolt, who said they needed a day or two to get their heads on straight. But Nico especially, needed to be doing something to stop him from going bonkers, as he put it. So Shadbolt had relented and let them both come back to the station, as long as they didn't work on the serial killer case.

Lacey sat at her desk staring at the pile of paperwork, but not really seeing it, brooding and thoughtful. The shared office normally had at least one other person skulking behind one of the four available desks, but today it was conspicuously empty. Linc remained a part of the serial killer task force, and was currently down in Strahan engaged in the search, which left her without a partner for the near future. And left her handling the paperwork for him and the others like Hickey and Gorman, who were staked out down in Strahan.

They hadn't managed to find Serge—it was like he'd vanished in a puff of magician's smoke—but they had made an interesting discovery late yesterday afternoon. One of the search teams had found an abandoned campsite, deep in the forest. It'd been a tip-off from one of the locals, Mal, who'd been the instigator of the vigilante group, which had been summarily shut down by Sergeant Jackson. Mal's property bordered the national park, and he said he'd heard unusual noises late one night. The campsite was hard to spot, but the tracker they'd employed had detected the subtle signs Lacey could never dream of learning how to discern. By all reports it'd been cleaned up so that hardly a trace remained. A forensic team was going over the site this morning, and Pederson had also called in a sniffer dog to see if they could uncover anything else of interest. Nico had already decided that the campsite had probably belonged to Serge, the marks of him were all over it. Pederson tended to agree, although he wanted to wait for concrete evidence before he was certain. The search teams must've spooked Serge, or whoever was using the camp, however, and he'd moved on; was now like a whisper on the wind. Lacey wondered where he'd turn up next. One thing was for certain, Nico was convinced that Serge was long gone from Strahan. Pederson was harder to persuade on that fact, and Nico's mouth had twisted bitterly when he refused to stop the search for Serge.

Her stomach roiled, and she snatched another dry biscuit from the packet on her desk. Nibbling on it until the queasiness settled once more, she stared morosely out the window. At least their Sunday night hadn't been a complete fail. The casserole had remained uneaten in the refrigerator that night, because after their epic shower sex, they'd gone to bed and made love again rather than eat. Almost as if proving to themselves that no one could truly hurt them when they were together. Then they'd lain in bed, hands entwined, heads together on one pillow as they talked through their problems and tried to come up with solutions.

It was good to see Nico finally relax; he'd been like a

tightly coiled spring when it came to his father. His greatest fear being that Serge was even then, standing outside their window, waiting to trap them. And Lacey had to admit that this time she wasn't so sure he was wrong.

Constable Dawn Lawson entered the office, a stack of more files under her arm. She gave Lacey a sympathetic glance as she placed them carefully on the corner of her desk. "Sorry." Lawson grimaced in commiseration. "Pederson has seconded me full-time onto the murder case. He said you could handle all this now." She waved a hand over the pile of paper. Lawson was highly organized with great computer skills, and as such was very good at research, and so had—willingly— taken on fact-finding missions for a couple of current investigations being carried out at the station. One was a suspected drug ring from Hobart trying to set up a new trade in the Burnie region. The other was surveilling a militia-style biker gang suspected of shipping guns and other illegal weapons through the area and using their compound as a storage facility. Both required digging into names, places, identities, shipping manifests, trucking companies, company dealings, and even shell companies. All of which had Lacey shuddering at the mere idea of spending hours poring over a computer screen.

"Great," Lacey replied, suddenly feeling small. Was this what she was reduced to now? Shuffling paperwork while the others did the hard work. It felt like she was being punished for something she hadn't done. But if she was feeling this way, it must be worse for Nico. He'd been sent to Devonport for the day to take witness statements from an old couple who'd had their jewelry shop broken into overnight. Their safe had been raided and a stack of cut and uncut diamonds stolen. It'd clearly been a targeted attack, the thieves knowing exactly what they were looking for. Nico's dark frown as he'd come to tell her he'd be back later that afternoon had been so foreboding she hadn't dared ask any more questions. So she felt even more alone today than ever.

"I'll be in the ops room, if you need me," Dawn said.

Lacey felt a tiny shred of pity for Dawn. While still on the serial killer team, she'd been left behind at the station to handle logistics from this end, while most of them were down in Strahan. Someone had to do it, but it always sucked to be the one, and Lacey silently commiserated with the constable. Pederson had driven down to oversee the search in Strahan early this morning, but was due to return later this afternoon, deciding Saito could run the team down there, while he continued to pore over witnesses' statements and strategize the search as new information came in.

Lacey had wanted to go and see Taylor; she'd heard the girl had been discharged from the hospital last night and was staying in a hotel with her mother. But Pederson had advised her against it, citing the fact it'd be another one of those *conflicts of interest*. Pederson was being pedantic if you asked her. All she wanted was to say goodbye to Taylor before she went home. To find out if her body and her mind were healing. She'd formed such a strong bond earlier, and it felt like she owed Taylor that last farewell. Lacey also needed to see her one last time for her own peace of mind. Mary would probably call it closure. To know that Taylor was safe and on the road to recovery. But she would hate to jeopardize anything regarding this case, so she sat and stewed on Pederson's words, trying to decide if she was going to heed them or not. She could always go tonight, after her shift was finished, in a completely non-official capacity. Maybe that was the answer.

Taylor still couldn't remember anything about her time under Serge's control, her dissociative amnesia not lifting at all. But those few small moments of memory that'd remained intact before she'd drunk the water and the drugs had kicked in had been crucial in helping them identify the killer. Without that artist's sketch of the killer's likeness, they may not have been able to prove the man Lacey had seen had in fact been the same as the man who'd abducted Taylor—Serge. She had given them that vital link. And Lacey wanted Taylor to know how much she'd helped.

Three hours later, Lacey was thinking it was well past time for lunch, and now that her morning sickness had subsided, she might pop down to the bakery to get her favorite sandwich. Just then Constable Lawson walked back into the office, a small frown marring her features.

"A message just came in for you. A phone call." Dawn looked down at the piece of paper in her fingers.

"Why didn't you just put it through?" Lacey asked, slightly irritated that Dawn had chosen to write the message down instead.

"The caller was very calm, but he said I had to write this down exactly as he said it and give it to you. He kept saying it was urgent, but when I asked if I could transfer him to you, he refused. I had to ask him to repeat his name three times, because I wasn't sure I heard him right."

"Okay." Lacey's interest was piqued now. "Show me."

Dawn handed the paper over, and Lacey read her neatly printed words.

You need to come out to the farm. I have something to show you. It has to be you, not anyone else. Pacca.

Lacey felt a chill of foreboding slide down her spine.

"Is that the man who owned the farm where the girls were found?" Dawn asked.

"Yep," Lacey replied, only half concentrating on the constable's question.

"What do you think it means? Is it something to do with the serial killer case?"

"I have absolutely no idea." Lacey turned the paper over in

her hands as she considered the words. But that gut feeling of hers was yelling that this had everything to do with the serial killer case. What did Pacca want to show her? They'd searched the area where Danika was dumped with a fine-toothed comb. If there'd been something, the police would've found it. What did it mean? Unless he was more intimately linked to the case than Nico believed.

"You're not thinking of going out there, are you?" Dawn's dark-brown eyes went wide. "If this is related to the murder, you're not allowed to—" Lacey held up her hand to stop the other woman.

"I know what I am and am not allowed to do." Of course she knew the rules. But if Pacca had some new information, then surely they had to make an exception. "He did specifically ask for me, though, didn't he?"

"Yes," Dawn replied thoughtfully.

What to do? Nico would most likely caution her against this, but he wasn't here to tell her not to do this. But she also knew she couldn't go rogue and do this without the proper authority, because if she did uncover some vital evidence, then it might be rendered inadmissible later on if a court case ensued.

"I'm taking this to Pederson," she said at last. Pederson would look at this with an unbiased eye. Unlike Nico, who'd veto her going anywhere near the old farmer because of personal fear for her safety; just in case Serge was using Pacca to get to her somehow. If the newly in charge detective deemed it important enough to bend the rules—and she knew he might well be hungry enough for glory that he may just do it—then it was a possibility she'd be able to go. Strictly speaking, it was Nico who had the conflict of interest on this case, not her. Technically, she could still work on the case. Technically Serge wasn't her relative, either by blood or marriage. Yet. But Shadbolt had removed them both to appease Nico. And at the time, she hadn't argued. But now…?

Fifteen minutes later, after a sometimes heated conversation with Pederson, she and Constable Lawson were on their way to the farm in a police cruiser. It hadn't been that hard to convince the detective to let them go, his gung-ho attitude made him eager for an outcome, and if Lacey was the one the farmer wanted, then Pederson wasn't going to argue. Neither of them mentioned Nico or how he would react to this news. By tacit agreement they both decided that the potential of gaining a break in this case was too important, and weathering the storm afterward was a price they were willing to pay. The whole farm had been searched from top to bottom and there was nothing whatsoever to point to Pacca being involved in the killings. Pederson had surmised Pacca was just a victim of circumstance and the killer had chosen his property at random to dump the body. But he warned her not to enter the house alone; Lawson was always to be by her side.

"Yeah? Whaddaya want?" The old man stared at them from behind the closed fly screen door.

"I thought you might tell us that," Lacey said, straightening up to her full height, as she and Lawson presented a united front, standing side by side at the door. "You rang us."

"I don't know what you're talking about." Pacca glowered at them belligerently. Lacey could smell the old guy from where she was standing; it was like he hadn't washed in the few days since they'd last seen him. "I told you blokes everything I know. You've been hounding me forever since that girl was found dead. I've had enough of yous, I tells ya."

"You rang the police station half an hour ago and asked to speak to me, and me alone," Lacey repeated patiently, wondering why the old man was suddenly rambling.

"Not me. I never rang," Pacca replied obstinately.

"Constable Carmichael, may I speak with you a moment?" Lawson tugged insistently on Lacey's sleeve. Lacey allowed herself to be pulled down to the other end of the veranda, where Dawn leaned in and spoke softly into her ear. "That wasn't the man on the phone. The guy I spoke to was younger. His voice was deep and…kind of confidant."

"Are you sure?"

"Absolutely."

Then if it wasn't Pacca who'd rung… The alternative sent a quake of fear through Lacey. Could it possibly have been Serge?

Lawson gazed fixedly at Lacey, but she clearly had no more answers. Lacey needed to get to the bottom of this so she strode back down the old wooden floorboards, hoping this hadn't been just a hoax call.

"Mr. Mcmillan," Lacey started, hoping the use of his formal name might prompt him into action. "We received a call from someone stating they were you and specifically requesting me to come out to your farm."

The old man stared at her through rheumy eyes, his mouth set in a pugnacious line. Suddenly, a noise erupted from the cruiser parked ten yards or so away at the bottom of the front steps. Both constables turned toward the interruption. It was the police radio; the dispatcher saying something in urgent tones, but they were too far away to hear the details. Lacey decided to ignore it for now; she needed to sort this out and then they could be on their way. But Dawn took a step toward the vehicle, trying to decipher what dispatch was saying.

"The caller said, and I quote,"—Lacey said holding up the slip of paper with Dawn's scrawled message,—"You need to come out to the farm. I have something to show you." She folded the piece of paper and glared at him, her patience running thin. She was staring directly at the old man and she saw the second that his face changed. He blanched, his lips pulling back in a rictus of fear.

Dawn had taken another step away as the radio continued its urgent calls, flicking Lacey a worried glance. "I'm just going to see what's going on," she said, pointing at the car. "I won't be a sec."

Lacey didn't answer as the other constable went down the steps, keeping her gaze trained on Pacca. He knew something.

"He promised me I'd never see him again." Pacca spoke as if he'd forgotten she was there, his voice a low whisper as he wrung his arthritic hands together, the dry skin rasping.

She lifted her chin sharply. "What do you mean?" Lacey asked. "Who promised you? Tell me what you know. Do you know who the killer is?"

Pacca looked at her, startled. "What? No. No. That's not what I meant. I don't know nothin'." But Lacey didn't believe him.

A quick glance behind told her that Dawn had opened the cruiser door and was leaning in to listen. She tried a different tack. She took a step closer and whispered conspiratorially, "What's this all about? You've got about ten seconds before the other constable returns. It's now or never."

Pacca hesitated. "If I give it to you, will you leave me alone? For good this time?"

"I can't promise that unless I know what you've got."

He grumbled and shuffled his feet for a few seconds, then finally said, "Wait here."

Lacey turned to watch Dawn, whose face was changing from puzzlement to concern. But before she could ask her what was going on, Pacca was back.

"Here." He thrust a small package into her hands. It was wrapped like a present, in birthday paper. A square box, small enough to fit in the palm of her hand. "I don't know what's in there, and I don't know nothin' about that girl's murder either. He said you'd know what to do with this, but to keep it to yourself. Please, just go away now," he pleaded.

She studied the package, noticed the words printed in bold handwriting on the front.

DON'T TELL ANYONE OR HER LIFE WILL BE FORFEIT

What did that mean? Who's life? Lacey's? She was about to ask who gave him this box, what did these words mean, and how long he'd had it, when Lawson's voice echoed across the dirt, loud and insistent.

"Lacey, we've got to go." She was beckoning her over, arm waving wildly in the air, already halfway into the driver's seat. "It's important," she called again when Lacey hesitated. Lacey could see the young constable holding back, not wanting to say what'd whipped the police radio into such a frenzy in front of the old man.

Before she could question the sanity of her actions, Lacey glanced once more at the box, then quickly tucked it into a pocket on her vest and turned on her heel. She didn't know who the statement was referring to, but the words—a clear warning—sent a chill down her spine. She'd play along and keep this to herself. For now. The words *her life will be forfeit* had her worried that the killer—Serge—may have yet another victim. And if he did, her safety may depend on Lacey's silence.

"You stay away from me from now on, you hear," Pacca whined at her as she took the steps two at a time. "You got what you came for, now leave me alone." Lacey tuned out the old man's words as she jumped into the passenger seat. Dawn already had the engine started and was headed down the dirt driveway almost before Lacey had her seat belt fastened.

"What's going on?" she inquired above the chatter still

coming over the radio.

"Taylor has been reported missing. They want all units on it ASAP." Dawn came to the junction of the driveway and the main highway and flicked on the police lights, then took off at speed back toward town.

"What?" Lacey was almost too stunned to speak.

"She and her mother checked in to a hotel last night before they were supposed to take the ferry home this afternoon. But Taylor was gone when the mother checked on her this morning."

"Oh, shit." Was it too much of a coincidence that the girl who'd got away once from the serial killer was now missing again? Lacey didn't think so. And now she thought she knew who those words on the box were referring to. A cold sweat broke out along her backbone, and her hands became clammy. Shit, what was she doing? Should she keep the box a secret? Or not?

"They want us searching down along The Esplanade, near the hotel where they were staying. Just in case she went out for a walk and didn't tell her mother."

"That seems unlikely," Lacey muttered, her mind a jumble of racing thoughts.

"I agree. We also need to be on the lookout for our POI, in case he's no longer in Strahan."

"Oh, shit," Lacey repeated. Had Serge managed to evade the cordon of police searching for him, made it undetected to Burnie, then taken Taylor? To what end? To finish the job he'd started? But why? The police were crawling all over the place. It was only a matter of time before they caught him. Why was he staying in the area, rather than beating a hasty retreat?

"Did the old man have anything to show you?" Lawson asked, taking a corner at high speed that had Lacey grabbing for the bar above her head.

"What?"

"The guy on the phone said he had something to show you. The whole reason we went out there in the first place." Dawn didn't take her eyes off the road, but Lacey could hear the irritation in her voice.

"Oh, no. There was nothing." Lacey pretended nonchalance, her heart racing like she was running the hundred-meter sprint. Whatever was in that box weighed like a heavy stone in the chest pocket of her vest. Why she didn't reveal that Pacca had given her a parcel, she couldn't rightly say. But something about the clandestine way it'd been delivered and the fact those words warned her not to tell anyone, made her hesitate. She wanted a peek at what was inside. Just one little peek. Once she knew for certain what it contained and if it were relevant to the case, then she'd disclose the truth.

This was a breach of protocol. She was required to divulge any clue or piece of evidence she found, even if she was unsure it related to a case. There was a resonance about the package, however; a tickle that swam in her gut. Backed up by those ominous words. This was meant for her eyes only. There was danger if she revealed its existence. To her and to Taylor. And it was this that kept her mouth shut, even though her cop brain was telling her in no uncertain terms that she needed to come clean with Constable Lawson, sooner rather than later.

All she needed was a few moments alone with the parcel to divulge its secrets. That was all. Then she'd tell her.

CHAPTER FOURTEEN

"How did you let this happen? She was supposed to be under police guard," Nico roared, throwing his hands in the air. Pederson merely lifted his chin an inch higher and eyed Nico coldly. "How did you let the star witness disappear?" Nico asked, this time getting right up in Pederson's face. "She was a poor traumatized girl who escaped the clutches of a killer and you were supposed to be taking care of her. It's our duty to take care of her."

"I'd like to remind you that this is no longer your case," Pederson replied calmly, not backing down an inch, and not letting his hard gaze leave Nico's face.

A certain grudging respect blossomed in Nico's chest. Most people wouldn't stand their ground under one of his heated tirades. This man must have an ego the size of an elephant. And balls of steel. But Nico wasn't backing down either. "They took me off this case because I was too close to the POI, and they said it might impair my decision making. But I tell you what, my decision making would've been a hell of a lot better than yours today. How could you take away her guard?"

The young detective glowered at him for a second. "She was due to head home today. She's told us everything she knows. I needed the manpower down in Strahan, hunting the killer," Pederson explained.

"Yeah, well, now you need to recall all that bloody manpower to find the missing girl you were supposed to be protecting," Nico spat. And bloody Serge wasn't in Strahan any longer, why wouldn't Pederson accept that fact? The abandoned campsite pointed to the fact he had been there, perhaps for a while, but he wasn't stupid enough to hang around once the police had swarmed the place. If they hadn't found him by now, nearly forty-eight hours after Lacey had spotted him, then they weren't going to find him at all. Serge might even have something to do with why Taylor was missing, which was the scariest part. Nico assumed Pederson had taken that into account, but he was done arguing with this man.

Pederson gave a one-shoulder shrug, but Nico was already out the door on his way to give Shadbolt a piece of his mind. He needed to take himself out of that room; otherwise he was likely to do Pederson a permanent injury. If that girl was harmed in any way because of Pederson's incompetence... Nico tensed his shoulders and rolled his neck trying to stem his rising anger.

The second he'd heard about Taylor going missing over the radio, he'd dropped everything and raced back to Burnie, even though he knew he was off the case and wouldn't be allowed to help in the search. Nico knocked roughly on Shadbolt's door, barely waiting for permission to enter before bursting through.

"Pederson can't handle this case, you need to take him off it," he said, not waiting for Shadbolt to speak. This wasn't about Nico wanting to take the lead on the investigation again; he understood the conflict of interest rules were there for a good reason. This was about needing someone more senior on this case. Someone with better judgement, able to look outside the box instead of concentrating wholly on the facts.

"That's not for you to decide." The chief inspector glared at him over the rim of his glasses, then motioned for him to close the door behind him. Shadbolt was looking a little disheveled, mouth set in a grim line and Nico suddenly remembered seeing the crowd of journalists camped out on the front steps of the station as he returned from Devonport. The media would be lapping up this new twist in the murder case, ready to sensationalize it with their embellishments and drama. Shadbolt was probably preparing to talk to the media, make sure they had their facts straight before they sent the rest of the population into a panic. He felt a twinge of pity for the chief, but not enough to divert him from his objective.

"He admits he didn't reassign a guard for Taylor once she left the hospital. He fucked up, Charles. Big time," Nico continued, barely able to contain his indignation.

"Take a seat, Detective," Shadbolt said by way of answer. But Nico was too wound up to sit, so he shook his head.

Shadbolt kept his steady gaze fixed on Nico. "Even if I agreed with you, that doesn't change the facts. That girl is gone and we need to find her. Quickly." It was the closest Nico was going to get of an admission of agreement from his boss. And it took some of the steam out of Nico's rage. "Pederson made the best call he could using the information at hand. He decided the girl was no longer in danger and he needed to redistribute his resources," Shadbolt continued.

Spoken like a true administrator, Nico thought. Possibly an unfair judgement, because Shadbolt usually still thought like a cop on the beat, but in this instance, it was true.

"He's a good detective," Shadbolt said, but Nico didn't understand why his boss was so keen to defend him. "You were young and green once." The words were soft, not chiding, but matter-of-fact.

The tone in his voice made Nico look at his chief inspector, really look at him. And then do a quick reevaluation. Yes, the chief was looking out for Pederson, but he'd done the same thing for Nico when he'd been new and untried. Nico hadn't been nearly as gung ho as Pederson, didn't have as big an ego or as much to prove. But then he also hadn't come from an underprivileged, indigenous background. Nico couldn't forgive Pederson for his oversight, but he could see why Shadbolt was giving him a long leash. Nico let out a long sigh.

"Yep, all right," he acknowledged.

Shadbolt nodded slowly and relaxed back into his chair a little. "Pederson's a very determined man. And his determination just uncovered something really interesting today." The chief fixed his pale blue gaze on Nico over the rims of his glasses. Nico lifted his chin in curiosity, realizing that Shadbolt had been holding back, waiting to see if Nico calmed down first before he offered this new tidbit. A small pang of regret ran through his gut. He'd let his temper get away with him, which didn't happen very often.

"What did he find?" he finally asked, reining in the hint of resentment in his tone.

"A black plastic bag buried at the campsite containing clothes and other items, as well as some charred documents that look like they've come out of a campfire." There was a slight hesitation before Shadbolt continued. "Pederson's pretty sure the clothes belong to Danika."

"Wow. Okay." If that were true, it'd be a big find indeed. It'd definitely link the campsite to Serge. And might even provide them with more solid proof to help put Serge away— if they ever caught him. "That's a good find," Nico said, this time not begrudging Pederson his unorthodox methods.

"Yes, it is. And if he hadn't pushed to bring in the sniffer dogs, they might never have unearthed that evidence,"

Shadbolt continued.

"Right," Nico answered absently, but his mind was still on the bag of clothing. Something was bugging him about it, but he couldn't put his finger on what exactly.

"Ser—the POI, did a good job of trying to conceal the evidence."

Nico noted the chief's slight hesitation over using his father's name, but ignored it.

"Pederson is hoping to find more, now that he knows where to look. If the POI was using that campsite long term, they might even find traces from the other girls he murdered. He's got Tyrell and Saito working on it down on Strahan as we speak."

"Good. I'd probably have done the same thing," Nico replied. But the more he thought about it, the odder it felt. Then suddenly he knew what'd been bugging him. Finding that bag was too convenient. It was almost like putting a red flashing light outside of a hooker joint. Too bright and lurid. He was about to say something to the chief inspector when his boss changed the subject.

"In any case, I've got a job for you. Pederson and his team are stretched to the limit right now, so I'd like you to go and have another chat with Taylor's mother, see if you can glean any more details. Where did they have dinner? Did she notice anyone suspicious hanging around last night? Was Taylor acting normal—well, as normal as you can get after the trauma she suffered. That kind of thing."

"Will do." Had Shadbolt just given him an opening back into the case? Albeit a minor one. Nico knew protocol wouldn't allow him to work on this case with his father as the alleged killer. But while asking Taylor's mother a few questions might help them find the missing girl, it wasn't going to interfere with any important evidential boundaries. If Shadbolt was prepared to give him this minor access to one of the individuals involved, then who was he to argue?

"And then, can you go and chat to the psych, what was her name?"

"Mary," Nico confirmed.

"Right. Yes. You know the drill." Shadbolt reached out a hand and repositioned one of the piles of paperwork on his desk, the only sign of his slight discomfort.

"You mean, ask her if Taylor might've been suicidal?"

"Yes, that." Shadbolt nodded, and Nico grimaced. It was a sad fact that victims subjected to that amount of trauma often couldn't bear to face the repercussions of their attacker's actions. Couldn't bear to live with what they thought of as their own shame. Thought themselves to blame for some reason. Nico didn't need to qualify with an answer. That poor, poor girl. He hoped with all his heart that she was safe, had just needed some time to herself and wandered off somewhere, because the other two options—either Serge had recaptured her, or she'd taken her own life—were unthinkable. It made him so mad, that someone's twisted mind could ruin someone else's life forever.

But it wasn't just someone with a twisted mind. It was his own flesh and blood causing this devastation. He could barely contain his revulsion. The nerve of his father. And now he was trying to target Lacey. It made him feel physically sick. Which reminded him…

"Where's Lacey?" he demanded, not able to keep the heat out of his voice. He suddenly needed to know she was safe, especially if it turned out that Serge was in the near vicinity. They'd agreed last night that returning to work was the best way to stay sane, even if they had to deal with mundane tasks while the rest of the force concentrated on tracking down Serge. Nico also secretly thought that work was the safest place Lacey could be right now. There was no way Serge could possibly get to Lacey while she was locked inside a fully manned police station. And if she was out on patrol, she'd always have a partner to back her up. She was definitely safer here than sitting alone at home. But he still worried.

Shadbolt ignored the subtle disrespect in Nico's tone, and said, "I believe she and Constable Lawson are patrolling The Esplanade, out looking for the girl, just like everyone else."

"Good." Nico let out a breath. "Thank you," he added belatedly.

Shadbolt tapped a finger thoughtfully on the tabletop. "Lacey seemed to have a connection with Taylor. It's another reason Pederson assigned her that duty. If anyone can find her, maybe she can."

"Hmm." Nico wasn't sure he agreed. Lacey had first formed a connection because Serge had made it so. It was true that Lacey had gone on to forge a strong bond with Taylor on her own, but Nico often wondered if her connection would've been that strong if the girl hadn't reacted so strongly to her name when they first met. And it also made him wonder why his father was so interested in Lacey. Not knowing made his insides twist in a million knots. But the sooner he got out there and helped capture Serge, the sooner he could ask those questions. He stood, getting ready to exit the office, already intent on his task.

"Oh, and, Nico?" He turned at the reproach in his boss's voice. "I'm only letting you take part in this because most of our people are stuck down in Strahan. But if you find Taylor, or any clue to where she might be, I want you reporting straight back to me. Do you understand?"

"Yes, sir." Nico met Shadbolt's gaze, knowing that he'd overstepped earlier and probably needed to make amends. "I understand the stakes here, sir," he replied evenly.

"Good. Off you go then." Shadbolt dismissed him with a wave of his hand. "I've got a media interview to prepare for."

"Good luck, sir." Nico threw his boss a wry grin as he exited the door, glad he didn't have to walk in Shadbolt's shoes today. As lead investigator on a case, it was often Nico's job to stand at Shadbolt's shoulder during one of these shit-shows and answer any tricky questions thrown their way. But today, that honor would go to Pederson, and Nico gave a roguish smile as he strode down the hallway, knowing the upcoming interview could well be a baptism of fire.

CHAPTER FIFTEEN

Lacey sat at the kitchen table, watching the phone on the countertop charge up. She knew a burner phone when she saw one, and her first instinct when she'd unwrapped the box had been to take it straight to the station. Let Pederson deal with it. But curiosity, along with a sense of urgency had got the better of her and she'd plugged it in to charge instead.

This was the first chance Lacey had to investigate the box, as she and Lawson had driven straight from Pacca's farm to the foreshore as directed by dispatch. On the way, she'd called Pederson over the radio, reporting the interview with Pacca had produced no new information, all the time hoping he didn't detect the slight wobble in her voice. But Pederson was so caught up with the search for Taylor—because he was the lead on the case, this would be seen as his gigantic stuff up—he'd just grunted a few unintelligible words at Lacey and rang off. Lacey silently hoped that Pederson forgot all about their little visit to the old farmer.

The two female officers then spent a fruitless afternoon out searching for the missing girl. Walking the streets of Burnie near the harbor, probing every disgusting, dead-end alley, searching through the parkland along the foreshore, lifting the lids on all the dumpsters to check inside, and showing

Taylor's photo to passersby. But even while she did this, her gut told her they weren't going to find Taylor just wandering aimlessly, like they had before. It was different this time.

More than once, Lacey had drawn the box out of her pocket when she found herself alone down the end of an alley or standing on a quiet corner, but then Dawn had called to her from the other side of the street, or someone had walked close by, forcing her to replace it until she had the proper time and space to inspect it.

Finally, the order had come over their radios that they were to report back to the station. They'd already worked way past the end of their shift, but both female officers would've kept going all night if they could've. There was no arguing with a direct command, however. She and Lawson were to go home and get some sleep, while other officers continued the search through the night, and then they could recommence the hunt at first light if need be.

Possibly, the only reason that Lacey complied with the order to go home was the tug of the little birthday-wrapped box still resting in her pocket, screaming at her that this might be important, and she needed to find out what it was. The whole time she'd been searching, her mind kept returning to the box, wondering what was in it and if it had any relation to this case. She was taking a huge risk by not telling anyone about its existence—not even Nico. Especially not Nico. But the instructions had been explicit. And if there was the slightest glimmer of hope that this phone might help her find Taylor, then she was willing to take that risk.

Nico was going to kill her when he found out. He'd called an hour ago as she was driving home, checking up on her and saying he might not be finished until late. It was good to hear his voice, but Lacey found it hard to concentrate on his words as the guilt of her huge secret ate away at the corners of her mind. It was a betrayal, and she knew it. Their relationship was firmly based on trust, but it was hard won, and they'd weathered a few storms regarding matters of trust in the past. She didn't want this to become a wedge between them. Would he ever forgive her? Even if it meant saving the life of an innocent girl?

And now it wasn't just her she had to think about. There was a new life forming in her belly, a life she was wholly responsible for. Was the life of an innocent girl worth putting her unborn baby at risk?

Shit. She was so conflicted; she really didn't know what to do. Even the idea of opening that box had been ridiculous. She should just disconnect the charger and take the whole thing back to the station. There would be consequences for withholding evidence, but that'd be better than keeping it a secret. But then her mind seesawed again. Taylor's survival could depend on her following those instructions. When she thought of what that poor girl had been through. And how terrified she must be now, confronted with the same man who'd abducted her days before. She couldn't even bear to think about it. Lacey might be her only hope, and it was that thought more than anything that kept her from calling Nico right now and telling him everything.

Smudge got up from where he'd been lying in the doorway to the kitchen and came over to sit at her feet, as if sensing her distress, those intelligent ears pricked in her direction. "I know," she said, patting his head. But this time, the dog could do nothing to ease her torment, because even though those brown eyes were full of compassion, he couldn't give her the answers she needed.

Impatient, she stood and walked over to the countertop, staring down at the small, incongruous thing. It was a simple, generic brand, android phone, small and compact with a full screen display, probably available in most big retail stores. The phone was only forty percent charged. But it didn't need to be fully charged for her to use it, so she pushed the on button, then worried at her bottom lip as the phone lit up and went through its startup sequence. What if it was password protected? But she needn't have worried. When the screen finally glowed blue it showed a single phone number saved into the contacts. A way to correspond with whoever was on the other end of this phone.

What to do? Running her thumb around the edge of the screen she weighed up her options. Make a phone call? Send a message? She had more control over a message. Wouldn't be so easily swayed if she didn't have to listen to that man's compelling voice. Hand hovering over the phone, she wavered, half tempted to place it back in the box and close the lid. No, she needed to do this for Taylor's sake.

Her fingers trembled slightly as she typed out the words.

Who's there? What do you want?

The reply came back almost immediately, as if he'd been waiting for this exact moment.

You know who this is. Nice to finally hear from you, Lacey.

Her skin crawled as she read the words. It was Serge, she just knew it.

What do you want?

Are you alone? Is Nicolas there?

Again, she hesitated, her forensic mind working through the minute details of everything he said. Serge must not be watching the house if he was asking where Nico was. Perhaps he didn't even know where she was right now? Could she use that to her advantage somehow?

I'm alone.

It was simple and to the point.

Good. I have the girl, Taylor.

Lacey froze as she read the words. It was confirmation that he had her. *Holy Fuck!*

I won't hurt her if you do what I ask, he typed, and her chest tightened at his words.

What do you want from me?

I just want to talk to you. I'm not going to hurt you.

What if I refuse?

Then the girl will die, and Nico will be next.

Her whole body shuddered as she stared at the message. Not only was Serge threatening Taylor, he was also threatening Nico. But why? She already knew she was dealing with a mentally unstable, psychopathic killer, and maybe that was reason enough to want to kill his own son. But what had Nico ever done to Serge? All he'd ever wanted was to please his aloof, discontented father.

Why would you want to kill your son?

All will be revealed, if only you'll come and talk to me. I promise I will not hurt you.

Lacey gave out a snort of disbelief. He was prepared to kill his own son, but she was supposed to believe he wasn't going to hurt her? What could Serge possibly hope to gain by talking to her? What answers did she have that he needed? If he wanted answers, then he should be talking to Nico.

You promise you won't hurt me?

Yes, I promise on my fallen comrades' lives. I will not harm you.

Lacey knew Serge had fought in the French Foreign Legion, and Nico had told her that he'd lost two good friends while fighting in the Gulf War. Serge had lived with military precision, even after he left the FFL; it was the one thing that remained important to him, and he'd tried to instill those rules and regulations on his family. But he also deeply respected the other men he'd fought alongside, and Nico surmised that his connection with his soldier mates went deeper than even his relationship with his family. The loss of his friends—if you could call them that—affected Serge profoundly. So this promise on his friends' lives could hold merit.

"I'm sorry, Nico," she whispered as she typed the words with shaking fingers.

All right, I'll come. Then she quickly typed something else. *But only if you release Taylor in exchange for me.*

There was no immediate response, as if she'd caught him off guard. But she needed something out of this, he couldn't be allowed to hold all the aces. The three little dots appeared as he began to type a reply.

Agreed. Come to this address, ALONE, and I will release Taylor. No one else. No cops. No Nicolas. If you bring anyone else, I'll kill the girl.

She could understand why he didn't want any cops, but wasn't so sure why he would stipulate she didn't bring Nico. She still firmly believed that Serge wanted to see his son, not kill him, but for what reason, she wasn't so sure. Perhaps he wanted to seek retribution for some unknown misdeed, or even closure, to see his son's face one last time. Was Serge deranged enough to kill his own son? Maybe. But Lacey knew the real question she should be asking herself; was Serge deranged enough to kill her as a kind of fuck you to Nico?

She waited as the three dots told her he was typing in the address.

Then Lacey's hand flew to her mouth, as the address appeared.

He was here! In Boat Harbour Beach. He was literally in the next street, just around the corner.

What the fuck? Had he been here all along? So close they could almost reach out and touch him. So close that he could keep tabs on them. Perhaps he'd been watching them all this time. Lacey's gaze shot to the window and the encroaching darkness outside. Was he outside right now, looking in at her? Watching her? They'd thought he'd been down in Strahan, but what if he'd been here and picked those girls up in Strahan on a whim? All just happenstance?

Calm down, she told herself. If he was out there looking in, he would've known she was here alone, but he'd specifically asked her in the message if Nico was here. The address was for a place closer to the beach and on the outskirts of the small township. She could walk there.

Smudge bumped her knee with his nose, concern in his lovely brown eyes. Staring down at him, a sudden idea formed in her head. Serge hadn't said anything about not bringing a dog. But what possible help could Smudge be to her? If she took him with her at least he'd provide some sort of security in the dark night. She didn't think Serge meant to ambush her on the way over, but anything might be possible. Would Smudge attack on command? He was very protective of her and Nico, but they'd never had to test the dog that far before. Would he attack Serge if she told him to? Perhaps she could let him go once they reached the address, tell him to run back home as fast as he could. Tell him to bring Nico back to save her.

She laughed, startling the dog as she leaned down to pat his head. "You might be the best dog in the world, but this isn't a Lassie movie. What was I thinking?" He might be smart, but not that smart. The dog wasn't going to be her savior. Not tonight. Tonight, she'd have to do this alone.

She pulled herself up short. Had she actually decided to go through with this? To give herself over in exchange for Taylor? Become his hostage. A small part of her had refused to believe this was real. Even when she'd typed the message agreeing to go to him, her cop brain had been looking for an angle, some option where she could turn this around so she didn't have to go. But there wasn't one. Taylor was in a house less than a block away, probably scared and terrified. The only way to save her was to hand herself over to Nico's father. Thereby giving him the ace of hearts.

Once Serge had her in his clutches, she was hoping like hell that she might be able to sway him around to letting her go again. Talk him out of whatever he had planned. She could appeal to that side of him which still had some paternal feelings for Nico perhaps. But that idea depended heavily on the fact that Serge still had human emotions. He'd already killed four women that they knew of, and perhaps more over on the mainland over the years. Did serial killers have feelings? Or more to the point, did this particular serial killer still have feelings?

Her pregnancy was a secret that Serge couldn't possibly know yet. And she was going to make sure it stayed that way. It could be terribly dangerous to reveal she was carrying Nico's baby. If Serge wanted Nico dead for some as yet unrevealed crime against him, then he might be more than happy to take the life of his unborn child as well. Unless she thought the news might be used to sway Serge around to her thinking. By telling him he was going to be a grandfather, appealing to his mortal soul and telling him that his legacy would live on in a better way.

Lacey touched her belly with her fingertips. Was she prepared to gamble with the life of their baby? Serge promised he wouldn't hurt her, but could she believe him?

The burner phone dinged with an incoming message.

Are you coming? Taylor is waiting for an answer.

God this man was calculating.

Yes, I'm coming. Will be there in ten minutes.

She'd probably better get going, before Nico came home and found her dithering and then her chance to save Taylor's life—and possibly his as well—would be gone. Lacey thought about her police service weapon stored in the safe in the kitchen cupboard. Should she take that along? After weighing up her options, she unlocked the safe and tucked it into the waistband of her shorts. If she got any opportunity to use it, she wouldn't hesitate. But she also needed to make sure Taylor was safe, and she'd only use it if the circumstances allowed.

Then she scanned the kitchen… Searching for what? There was nothing else she needed to take. Her wits were going to be her most important weapon this time. The jean shorts, T-shirt, and runners she'd donned when she'd arrived home while she was waiting for the phone to charge were both practical and no-nonsense, and it wasn't cold enough to require a sweater.

At the last moment, she turned back to the kitchen and grabbed the notepad and pen they used to make their shopping lists stuck to the refrigerator. She owed Nico something. He'd probably never forgive her anyway, but she couldn't leave him completely in the dark.

By the time you read this, Taylor should be safe.

She wavered over her next few words. How much should she tell him? If he came home too soon and read this, then he might ruin everything, especially if she gave him the exact address and he rushed over and busted the door down and then ended up dead with a bullet through the chest, shot by his own father. But she wanted him to know she was close.

He's in Boat Harbour.

She touched the tip of the pen to her chin as she considered her next words.

Talk to Pacca, he knows more than he's letting on.

That last part was true. The old man had practically confessed that he knew Serge somehow when he'd given her the box. Pacca was tied up in this by fair means or foul, she just wasn't sure what the connection was.

Her last line said, *He promised he wouldn't hurt me.*

It would probably be of little comfort to Nico, but she needed to give him something. Some hope. Something to keep him from going crazy. And she also hoped that he trusted her enough to know what she was doing. Yes, it might be foolhardy and rash, but she was doing this to save his life. To save Taylor's life.

She laid the pen on the table next to the note, picked up the burner phone, patted Smudge on the head and told him to stay, then walked out through the back door.

CHAPTER SIXTEEN

Nico drove his motorbike up the driveway and into the shared garage. The Jeep was parked up in its normal spot next to Dotti and the kitchen light was on in the house, so he knew Lacey was home. Removing his helmet, he released the tie holding back his hair and shook it free. Hopefully, the Chinese takeout in his side pannier was still warm enough to eat when he got inside. He'd stopped at their favorite place on the way home to pick it up on the off chance that Lacey probably wouldn't feel like cooking. He knew her; she'd be too consumed with worry about Taylor.

Lacey had a connection with the girl, an unhealthy one, if you asked him. She had a habit of getting too close to some of the victims in the cases she encountered. And this one had really drawn Lacey in; she'd become attached to Taylor more than anyone before her. Perhaps it had something to do with pregnancy hormones, although he dare not mention that around her. Compassion was always a strong emotion in Lacey, but maybe she was feeling extra solicitous toward anyone who needed mothering right now. And Taylor had been through a harrowing experience, it was only natural for Lacey to want to protect her, offer her comfort.

He unpacked the Chinese food from the pannier and then

closed up the garage, making sure to check his surroundings first. As part of the new security system, he'd also installed a series of bright floodlights that were motion sensitive; he'd be able to see a gnat flying at twenty paces, it was that bright. All clear. So he strode across the lawn toward the house, his mind turning to the interesting events of this afternoon at the station.

His interview with Taylor's mother hadn't turned up any more pertinent information; the poor woman was almost hysterical, and he didn't blame her. Neither she nor Taylor had noticed anything or anyone untoward, either last night or this morning. Although she had questioned that young detective as to why he thought they no longer required a police guard, but she'd taken him at his word that Taylor was no longer in danger. Now she wished she'd demanded the guard stay. Poor woman swore black and blue that after this nightmare, when Taylor came home, she was never letting her daughter out of her sight again. Nico assured her they were doing everything in their power to locate Taylor and kept his dark thoughts on whether she would be alive or dead when they eventually found her firmly to himself.

His chat with Mary hadn't revealed much more of interest either. Mary was adamant that Taylor wasn't suicidal. Confused and traumatized, yes, but not so much so that she'd take her own life. Mary divulged that Taylor had mentioned in one of her many sessions that she owed it to Danika to keep on living. She was immensely conflicted that she'd survived and her friend hadn't—survivor's guilt, Mary called it. Danika's life had been cut so terribly short, and Taylor wanted to honor her best friend by keeping her memory alive, and by doing all that she could with this future she'd been given.

Nico had gone back and reported all this to Shadbolt, and then, begrudgingly, and under Shadbolt's direction, to

Pederson as well. The other detective hadn't seemed to have taken umbrage to anything they'd said earlier; it was like he had the thick hide of an elephant. He'd received the news with the cool detachment Nico was becoming used to. But Nico couldn't bring himself to sit and chat with the other man, just filing his report and then getting out of the ops room as fast as he could.

On his way back to his office, Nico decided to call in on Sally-Ann, and it was a damn good thing he had. Because she had some mammoth news. Instead of joining the task force in Strahan, Sally-Ann had stayed behind to continue to investigate the cold case murder in Canberra that was possibly linked to Serge.

But even better—or worse, depending on your point of view—she'd found another case in Aireys Inlet, a small town only half an hour's drive from Lorne in Victoria that seemed to match their serial killer's MO. Young, pretty, hitchhiking out of town. She'd been strangled to death too. Lorne was where his father had supposedly spent years hiding out, using a different alias before he finally got spooked and moved to Tasmania. If his mother's old friends Marco and Priscilla Normandy hadn't spotted him and then passed on the information, they may never have known where he'd been all this time, let alone that he was still alive.

Sally-Anne told him that more things about the case in Canberra were starting to match up. The girl had been found lying in a shallow grave, hands crossed over her heart in a ritual position, the crime scene cleaned and left sterile. Police had been stumped right from the beginning, unable to even find a single POI on which to concentrate their efforts, and the case had been shelved after less than a year, with no new leads or clues. The homicide detective in charge of the case seventeen years ago had since been promoted to detective inspector, but when Sally-Ann had contacted him he was astounded to learn there might be fresh leads, and keen to reopen the cold case file as soon as possible.

It wasn't concrete proof that Serge had been the killer, but Nico's gut told him it was true. He wondered if they'd find any more bodies that matched his style in Canberra. Or perhaps that was his first kill and then he'd quashed his urges until he'd made his escape to Victoria, where he'd started again.

Sally-Ann was yet to hear back from the cops in Lorne, but Nico had no doubt that when she did, the details would be chillingly familiar.

One question that still stumped him—one of the many—was why his father had moved on from fresh young girls to killing sex workers. What did he have against them? From all accounts, as much as his mother would talk to him about *that*, anyway, his father had normal sexual urges and appetites. If anything, he may have had a slightly lower libido if he was reading his mother's hints and innuendos correctly. Men often chose women in that profession because of their own failures in the bedroom. Either that or to fulfill some sort of sick fantasy. It could be either of these or something completely different driving Serge, and it bugged Nico to no end that he knew so little about his father that he couldn't even guess at his motivation. And now he seemed to have digressed back to his old fondness for sweet young things. But why? Was it simply that his tastes had changed? Or was it because he wanted to send Nico some sort of particular message? One that he currently had no idea how to decipher.

Serge had come back damaged when he returned from the Gulf. Looking at it now, he probably had some form of PTSD. But Nico didn't know enough about that to guess at how or why it might have changed him, and even if it was the reason he'd become a killer. Or had Serge always had the capacity to be a killer, and that's why he'd joined the military? So he could kill and maim with impunity in the name of his country. Their usual police psych, Imran, might be able to shed some light on that subject, and Nico made a mental note to ask him if he had time to pop down to the station tomorrow for a chat.

As Nico got closer to the house, he could hear Smudge barking inside. A little odd, Smudge would normally know it was his master coming home and be waiting at the door with a wagging tail and a doggy smile, but not barking. Vaguely, he wondered why Lacey didn't hush the dog.

Greeting Smudge at the door, he pushed past his eager dog, wondering where Lacey had got to. He dumped the Chinese takeout on the countertop and called out that he was home. But there was no answer. That's when he noticed a handwritten note on the kitchen table underneath the bag of food. He was just about to read it when a loud banging alerted him to someone at the front door. Smudge began to bark frenetically.

Immediately on alert, Nico touched his gun, which was still in its holster on his hip.

"Detective Favreau, it's me, Detective Jay Pederson." Nico could barely hear the deep voice from the other side of the door over Smudge's barking. He tried to hush the dog as he made his way down the hallway.

What the hell? Why was Pederson here? When Nico had left the station, Pederson had still been in the ops room, taking phone calls and poring over the whiteboard. He opened the door—there was no mistaking it was Pederson outside, that voice couldn't belong to anyone else—and stood staring at the tall man standing on his front door mat.

"We have Taylor Longbrook in the car. She's safe and unharmed," Pederson said without preamble, almost as if he expected Nico to know. But he didn't, and he was left gaping like a stranded fish.

"What?" Try as hard as he might, he couldn't get his mind to function properly. "I don't understand." How could that have happened in the short time it'd taken him to drive home? He would've seen Pederson drive past him in the cruiser, especially if he had lights and sirens on. Nico had only stopped for ten minutes on the way to get his takeout. Which must've been when Pederson passed him. The takeout joint was in Wynyard, a small township halfway between Burnie and home, a few minutes off the main highway.

"The call came in a minute after you left the station," Pederson spoke slowly, as if explaining something to a child. "A citizen found her wandering a few streets from here and called it in."

"Okay. That's good. Isn't it?" Nico leaned around the other detective and saw the figure of the young woman, long hair pushed behind her ears, staring at him from out of the cruiser window, and he let out a sigh of relief. Thank God. An image of her distraught mother came back to him, and he was so glad they wouldn't have to make that terrible, soul-destroying knock on the door that every parent dreaded.

"The POI had her, but he let her go again without hurting her," Pederson continued slowly.

So they'd been right all along, Serge had taken her. But why? And why let her go again, for a second time? But no matter, the outcome was a good one. For Taylor at least.

"That's good," Nico echoed his previous sentiment. "That's a great outcome. Even better than we hoped for."

But Pederson didn't seem happy. In fact, the detective looked at him with what could only be called pity in his eyes. Pity? It was unlike Pederson to show any soft emotion let alone empathy or sadness. What was going on? Why was the detective staring at him as if he was about to lose his marbles?

"You don't know then?" Pederson said in that annoyingly

calm voice.

"Know what?" Nico's elation at the girl being found alive and well was quickly turning to irritation. Then he remembered Lacey's note on the bench, and he stilled as a frisson of fear ran down his spine.

"I had Sally-Ann try to call you. Did you have your phone turned off?" Nico shook his head. Of course his phone had been on. But he'd forgotten to charge the battery on his helmet's headpiece yesterday and so he couldn't receive or make any calls while riding the motorbike. He hadn't yet had a chance to check if he had any missed calls.

"The suspect—your father—let her go because he now has Lacey instead. Lacey swapped herself to make sure Taylor could go free."

Nico merely stared at the other detective. It took many, many seconds for Pederson's words to sink in. Then the world spun on its axis, and his body went suddenly numb.

"No!" This wasn't right. Pederson was lying. No! No, no, no, no, no. Not Lacey. This couldn't be happening.

"Serge doesn't have Lacey," he snarled at Pederson. "You're lying to me."

"I wish I were," Pederson replied, hand outstretched, watching him carefully, much as you would an unstable person, teetering on the very edge of a precipice.

"Oh, God." Nico could barely believe it. How could she have done this? Why…

Then a second, even more devastating thought hit him.

The baby. What about the baby? Surely, she wouldn't put the baby at risk?

Nico dropped to his knees, a primal roar echoing in his chest, an animalistic howl of pain and anguish ripping up his throat.

CHAPTER SEVENTEEN

Lacey stood in the corner of the empty room, eyeing her nemesis warily. This was the same man who'd beckoned to her from across the road in Strahan all right. Except now the beard and mustache were gone, his face shaved clean to reveal a strong jawline and a shallow cleft in his chin. Lacey absently documented the fact that Nico had not inherited that cleft chin, but he *had* inherited the high, dark eyebrows. And where this man's eyes were dark, almost black, Nico's were a brilliant blue, bright and clear, but just as piercing.

Lacey had described Serge as handsome, in a silver fox type of way, and that was even more evident now she was up close. She could see that Nico's good looks weren't only from Catarina. The slightly crooked nose gave Serge the air of a viking warrior, as did his outfit—black long pants and a black tee—stretched over an impressive chest and biceps. The man might be in his early sixties, but he'd stayed extremely fit, perhaps a hangover from his military days. Which would make it harder for Lacey to overpower him, if it came down to it. But she wouldn't let his physical prowess intimidate her; she'd taken down bigger men than him before.

Serge's gaze had chilled her to the bone back in Strahan, and even now that she was prepared for it, a shiver of trepidation shook her as he stared at her intently. *Don't show fear. Don't show weakness.* Lacey stood a little straighter and glared back at him.

At least Taylor was safe. Serge had been a man of his word on that front.

It was dark by the time she'd arrived at his hideout, but the warm glow of a streetlight illuminated her surroundings. He was waiting for her in the front garden, holding Taylor by the neck of her shirt, like he was holding a puppy by the scruff of its neck. It wasn't until she'd got closer that she'd been able to see the gun he had jammed up against Taylor's ribs. The girl was quietly sobbing, big, silent tears streaking her face. Lacey's heart had flipped over at the sight, and right then, she knew she'd do just about anything to get the girl out of this situation. She walked slowly up the driveway, stopping around ten feet in front of them.

"I'm glad you could make it," Serge said in his deep voice, so reminiscent of Nico Lacey almost did a double take. "Now, let's get business out of the way first. Throw your gun over there." He lifted his chin and indicated she throw it on the edge of the driveway opposite him. That stopped her for a second. This man was no dummy. But he couldn't know for sure she was carrying, it was just a guess. Could she bluff her way through? As she hesitated, Serge added quietly, but with enough menace to make Lacey know he was serious, "I know you're armed, so don't try to deceive me. No cop worth their salt would put themselves in this situation without arming themselves. Do it now, or I will follow through with my promise." His eyes tracked down to Taylor, and Lacey knew he meant that he'd kill her. And he'd do it without remorse, the same way he'd killed those other women.

Holding one hand in the air, she reached slowly around her back to take her gun out of her waistband, her mind still turning scenarios over frantically in her head. Could she risk taking a shot, try to wing him without harming Taylor? Like she'd done up in the mountains when she'd taken down Sandra Brown?

But Serge was too smart for that, he was using Taylor as a shield, tucking himself behind her, the gun still jammed tight up into her ribs. It was too chancy for her to even try, and so she threw the weapon on the ground where he'd indicated with a grimace of displeasure.

"Good," Serge said, a feral smile lighting up his face. The next thing Lacey knew, he'd released Taylor, sent her stumbling down the driveway with a little push to the back. "Get out of here, girl," he commanded.

"What?" Taylor stopped, staring at Lacey, confusion and hope warring in her features.

"You're free to go," Serge growled. "Now scram, before I change my mind." Serge had then pointed his gun at Lacey, putting paid to any ideas of her trying to escape. But Lacey had no intention of running. She'd come here with one aim, and that was to see Taylor set free.

"Go," she said, shooing Taylor with her hands, willing the girl to get moving.

Taylor turned away, but then turned back again. "But what about you?" she asked, the tears coming again, her sobs resuming.

"I'll be fine," Lacey encouraged. "He promised he wouldn't hurt me. Besides, I'm a cop, I can look after myself." She cast a sidelong glance at Serge, but his face remained impassive. "Now go," she said more urgently.

Taylor turned slowly, uncertainty in her blue eyes. But then she saw the open driveway and the street beyond and began to run toward freedom. Lacey watched as Taylor jogged around a large bush at the edge of the property and disappeared out of sight.

Lacey let out a sigh. Thank God. At least if everything else went to shit, Taylor was now safe.

"Inside," Serge commanded, the gun remained trained on her, but he waved her in the direction of the house behind him with his other hand. She couldn't see any other option, so she did as she was told, walking silently up the stairs of the little cottage, Serge close behind, stopping to pick up her gun as they went. The front door was slightly ajar, and she let herself in. She heard Serge lock the door behind her, and her heart sank. What had she been thinking? Being locked in this house with a madman?

And that's how she found herself backed up into a corner of the living room, staring Serge down. The room was empty, lit with one bare bulb in the ceiling, and Lacey guessed he was renting this cottage. Short-term and tourist rentals were usually furnished with everything a visitor might need. But it was rare to find a furnished long-term rental in this area, and perhaps that was the way Serge wanted it. She'd glimpsed a black bag and a folded camp bed in a room off to the left as she entered; Serge's bedroom, perhaps. His military background clearly evident in the spartan but spotless house. But he was packed up, as if getting ready to move on.

"Put your hands behind your back and turn around," Serge commanded.

Oh, no, she wasn't going to put herself in any more of a vulnerable position, not if she could help it. She needed her hands and feet free if she were to have a hope of overpowering him.

"You told me you just wanted to talk. That you wouldn't hurt me," she said, edging farther away.

"And that is true," he replied, lowering the gun, and fishing around in his shirt pocket for something. "But you don't honestly think I'd be stupid enough to stay here where that girl can lead the cops straight back to me, do you? I'm moving you to another location, where we can talk in peace."

"About what? What's so important that you couldn't ask me over the phone?" she hedged. The last thing she needed was for Serge to move them around; it'd make it so much harder for Nico to track her. Stall for more time. That's what she needed to do. Time enough for her team to come and find her.

Serge just gave a gentle laugh. "Everything is so black and white with you. Is Nico the same? Or does he see the gray mixed in between? Not everything is so cut and dried, you know."

She wanted to say, *Yes it was*, especially when she was the one putting her life on the line. And she also wanted to shout that Nico was a cop, so of course he saw things in black and white, good and evil, but she didn't want to give Serge anything. He didn't deserve to know even that much about Nico. This man had forfeited any parental rights long ago.

"Come on now, we don't have much time. I've got a car parked up in the garage, we need to get out of here."

Lacey shook her head, feeling her way along the wall, getting as far away from him as she could. But even as she did, she was judging distances, measuring his height, working out how many ways she could take him down. The gun was held loosely in his right hand but pointed at the floor, and his left hand was still prying something loose from his shirt.

"Come on now, Lacey," he said reproachfully. "Don't get all coy on me now. We can do this one of two ways," he added blandly. "If you want to fight me, I can drug you and then do as I wish with you." He held up a large syringe that he'd plucked from his pocket. "Or you can agree to come quietly and I won't have to use this." He waved the syringe in the air.

Lacey glared daggers at him, but her first thought was for the baby. Any kind of drugs could be harmful to the fetus, and she would fight him tooth and nail before she let him get anywhere near her with that thing. Taylor had been drugged with a cocktail of ketamine and GHB, both commonly used date-rape drugs. And Lacey guessed it was the same brew Serge wanted to pump into her.

"I know all about your judo prowess, young lady. You have quite the ability, but I'm not going to give you a chance to use your hands as weapons on me." Serge cocked a dark eyebrow in her direction.

Shit. How did he know all that about her? Had he perhaps been watching her and Nico for months? Following them, studying them, finding out their every move, their likes and dislikes? They already knew Serge was meticulous and calculating, so learning that he'd researched her and Nico shouldn't come as any surprise. But one thing he couldn't know was that she was pregnant. And she needed to keep that knowledge from him at all costs.

"Fine. I'll come with you," she finally agreed.

"Good girl. Put your hands behind your back and turn around."

She did as she was told and felt the hard rasp of plastic ties wrap around her wrist.

CHAPTER EIGHTEEN

Sally-Ann knocked on Nico's office door and held up a mug of coffee and a pastry. "I bet you haven't eaten anything yet, have you?"

It was midmorning already but his stomach roiled at the thought of food. How could he think about eating when Lacey had been missing for over fifteen hours and they were still no closer to finding her? He was about to shake his head and send her away, but caught a whiff of the coffee and it smelled so good, so familiar, he changed his mind. A caffeine hit would be welcome, help him to stay awake, so, he beckoned her in.

"Rough night?" she asked, plonking herself down in the chair in front of his desk. But it wasn't so much of a question as a statement, and Nico could see by her rumpled hair and over-bright eyes, that she'd been awake all night too. They all had. Almost everyone had been recalled from Strahan to concentrate on finding Lacey, finding Serge. The station had been buzzing with people and energy all night as everyone did what they did best to help. Even Detective Saito had been recalled, only Tyrell and Gorman were left in Strahan to oversee the campsite search.

But no one, not one single other person, was going through

what Nico was going through right now. They couldn't begin to guess. Even Sally-Ann with her sympathetic gaze and motherly quality couldn't hope to understand. His barely healed bullet wound had throbbed all night long, as if it were a physical reminder of what had been stolen from him. But he'd take ten bullets to the chest, if only it meant Lacey was found safe and sound.

All night long, the same thoughts had clattered around in his head. He'd lost her. She'd gone off and put herself in danger to save another person. And he couldn't do a damn thing about it. And it was killing him. He wanted to rage at her, yell at her, ask her how she could do something so foolhardy. Brave but completely bullheaded, that was Lacey. And thoughtless. No, not thoughtless. Lacey would've considered all angles. Then gone and done it anyway.

Had she even considered their baby? What might happen to their unborn child? Of course she must've, but Nico was finding it almost impossible to understand why she'd patently disregarded that fact and gone to Serge regardless. Not only might he lose the one woman who meant more to him than anything—the glue that kept his world together, the person who owned his heart—but he might lose his unborn child as well. He hadn't truly had time to come to terms with the fact he was going to be a father. But the thought of losing that tiny being still growing in her womb, of having the chance to make amends for the sins of his own father by being the best dad he could possibly be ripped away from him, hurt like nothing else. And the worst part was, he dared not tell anyone of that particular secret pain. No one knew Lacey was pregnant apart from their families. He'd considered telling Shadbolt, but couldn't see any advantage in providing that news. They were throwing everything they had at finding her and knowing she was carrying a baby wouldn't change that.

He was such a mess that he hadn't really been much help to anyone, and had eventually retired to his office to be alone with his thoughts. But it was better than being at home, waiting and hoping and praying. At one stage he'd wanted to hop into a car and just drive, hoping to find something, anything, that'd lead him to her. Hoping his famous gut instinct would guide him straight to her. But he'd left his Jeep at home at the behest of Pederson, who said he shouldn't drive because he was too worked up. So, he'd jumped in the cruiser with Pederson and Taylor, and let himself be chauffeured back to the station. Pederson had vetoed Nico's demands that he be allowed to search Serge's bolt-hole in Boat Harbour, telling him there were four officers already there, with a forensics team on the way. Pederson didn't say the words *conflict of interest*, but he didn't have to. Because once Nico had calmed down, he knew his presence in that house might nullify any evidence they uncovered if it went to trial.

Pederson had been right about one thing, however, Nico probably would've driven himself or someone else off the road in his distraught state of mind. But the ride had given him a chance to talk to Taylor, find out everything she knew first-hand, and that information had been priceless. Hearing that Lacey had handed herself over willingly in exchange for Taylor hadn't made him any calmer, but she'd been able to tell him the layout of the house Serge had been renting, and exactly what it contained. She'd also revealed he had a gun, which was new information, but not completely unexpected. Serge was nothing if not efficient.

They'd delivered Taylor into the arms of her near-hysterical mother, and Nico finally had an inkling as to why Lacey had given herself to a killer. Taylor was the innocent party in all this, and she didn't deserve anything Serge had done to her. That thought had made Nico even madder, raging silently at his father, who was clearly using Taylor as a pawn in his own sick plans.

"Eat something, Nico." Sally-Ann's soft voice broke through his veil of dark thoughts.

"I can't," he croaked through a throat that felt like it was being constricted by a vice.

"Yes, you can," she coaxed. "You need to keep up your strength, for… Well, you know."

Nico leaned back in his chair, ready to snarl at Sally-Ann that she didn't know what she was talking about. But a tiny voice of reason told him she was right. When they finally got the break they needed—and they would get it, he couldn't believe anything else—then he didn't want to be unable to focus because of lack of energy. So, he took a small bite of the pastry. It was like ash in his mouth, but he forced himself to follow it with a big swig of coffee.

Taking a bite of her own pastry, she eyed him watchfully. "By the looks of you, I'm assuming you haven't heard the latest news yet?"

Nico lifted his head, eyes sharp and suddenly focussed. "What news?" Had they had a breakthrough? Why hadn't they told him?

"You know how they found Danika's clothes along with some burned documents buried at that campsite yesterday?" Sally-Ann said, barely waiting for Nico's nod of agreement before she continued. "Well, Saito sent those scorched papers to be forensically analyzed last night, asked them to do a rush job, and they got the results back this morning. It seems that just enough of those pieces of paper were left unburned for them to make out some details."

He sat forward, pastry and coffee forgotten. "And," he prompted, when Sally-Ann went suddenly quiet in the face of his burning intensity.

"One of the pieces of paper had an address on it, from a

realtor. They think the killer was renting an apartment in Hobart. Under an alias, of course," she added hurriedly.

"In Hobart?" Nico said the words out loud, but really he was evaluating the validity of such a lead. It was entirely feasible, McTernan had confirmed that Serge had gone to Hobart when he'd first arrived on the island two years ago. Serge would've needed a place to stay, after all. Could he have been renting a place in Hobart all along? His heart rate had doubled at Sally-Ann's revelation, but something didn't feel right.

"Yes." Sally-Ann gave a satisfied nod. "Pederson and Saito are making plans to travel to Hobart right now to check it out." Nico stared at her, assimilating this new detail. His heart gave a tiny leap of hope. Sally-Ann had been very careful not to say anything that might get his hopes up, but he knew there might be a small possibility they'd find Lacey there. It was feasible that Serge could've driven her down there overnight.

"So, Pederson wasn't going to tell me about this amazing breakthrough? He was just going to head to Hobart and leave me hanging?"

"I… I don't know. I assumed he was going to alert you eventually." Sally-Ann put her hands on the table.

"When? After he got back from Hobart? After he's made sure he's the hero of the hour?" Nico said bitterly, leaning forward in his chair to glare at his friend. He stood, no longer able to contain his growing anger. "And everyone else is keeping this from me why? To protect me? Are you all afraid I'm going to break, dissolve into a puddle of uselessness? Well, I'm not. I'm as strong as a fucking ox and I'm going to keep going until I find her. I'll search to the ends of the earth if I need to. I want to go to Hobart with them." Nico knew he was losing it, could see himself from across the room, a raving, ranting lunatic, but he couldn't seem to stop himself.

"Some fucking friends you are. I don't need to be wrapped in cotton wool, Sally-Ann, and I don't need you to—"

She held up her hand right in his face, pushing back her chair. "Don't you dare take this out on me." Sally-Ann stood up, glaring at him from across the table. "We're not keeping this from you. I came to you as soon as I heard. And I told you as your *friend*, not as a work colleague. Nico, you need to dial it back a little. I know you're hurting, but we're all one hundred percent invested in this. We all want to find Lacey. I want to find her nearly as much as you do."

Not possible. Nico kept that to himself. But he had no right to shoot the messenger, and Sally-Ann was right; everyone wanted the best for Lacey.

Nico gritted his teeth and looked down at the table, suddenly having to fight the urge to cover his eyes and give into the tears of frustration that hovered behind his eyelids.

"I'm sorry," he finally said, when he could finally trust his voice. "I know everyone is doing their best to find her." Probably even Pederson, though Nico didn't agree with his methods. "I shouldn't have yelled at you."

He retook his seat and motioned Sally-Ann to do the same. She laid a comforting hand over his. "You can yell at me as much as you like, as long as it's constructive and helps us to find Lacey," she replied. "I know this must be terribly hard, but I for one am not trying to protect you from any of this. I just want you to focus on the right things, so we can find her quickly."

She was correct. He was letting his fury overcome his rational, left-brain thinking that usually stood him in such good stead. So instead of continuing to rage, he reigned in his temper and dissected this new information. Sally-Ann watched him for a few seconds before going back to her pastry. If Pederson was going to Hobart, then Nico needed to find a way to convince the other man to let him go too. But as he contemplated his half-eaten pastry, his gut began to roil every time he thought about Hobart. Why did it feel wrong? He needed to pay attention to this feeling, because it might be important.

"Something feels off about this," he finally said. When he'd first heard the news of the find at the campsite, he'd had the same feeling, but hadn't had time to analyze it. Now he focussed his full attention on the matter.

"Why do you say that?" Sally-Ann prompted, wiping pastry crumbs from the uniform stretched across her amble bosom.

"I'm not sure," Nico mused. "It's almost like this has come too easy."

"I wouldn't say that," Sally-Ann huffed. "That campsite wasn't easy to find. It was sheer coincidence that guy tipped us off to those noises at the edge of his property. And if Pederson hadn't chosen to call in sniffer dogs to check it out, then they might never have found the buried stash."

It was all true. Sniffer dogs weren't routinely used on this kind of search. Police work was sometimes a catalog of unrelated coincidences added to some lucky breaks that helped to solve a case. But something was still bugging him.

"How long have we been hunting Serge?" he asked.

"Over six months now."

"And in that whole time, we've not had one clue, not one tip-off or even a single lucky break to give us a lead. Serge has been meticulous at hiding himself and everything else to do with his crimes. But now, all of a sudden, we find a hideout and concrete evidence linking him to the crimes? It seems too... I don't know. Too blatantly obvious."

"Are you saying you think Serge made it easy to find his campsite? Put those items there on purpose? That would be ridiculous."

"Unless he wanted to point us in that particular direction."

The more he thought about it, the more it made sense. "This is wrong. I need to stop Pederson from going."

"I don't think—" But Sally-Ann's words were cut off as Nico burst past her and out of his office. That was it. He had to warn Pederson that he was going off on a wild goose chase.

Nico surged into the ops room, heedless of who else occupied the room; his focus was on Pederson, who was standing at the whiteboard talking to Detective Saito. This was going to sound a little unhinged, but Pederson needed to listen to him.

"Pederson, I'm glad you're still here," Nico said, stepping between the two detectives and the whiteboard, so he had their full attention.

"You've heard then?" was all that Pederson said, his face devoid of emotion.

"Yes. And I don't think you should go to Hobart. I think you need to concentrate all your efforts here, in Burnie."

"Hmm." Pederson merely regarded him with dark, unreadable eyes, not even asking Nico for an explanation. He was going to disregard anything Nico had to say, he could just feel it.

"I believe the killer wants you to go to Hobart for some reason. And I think for that exact reason, you shouldn't go." Nico could feel his blood pressure rising in the face of Pederson's disregard.

"Hmm," Pederson said again in that noncommittal way. Saito was staring at Nico as if he might've gone a little crazy, but she said nothing.

Nico drew in a calming breath. "You're not listening to me. Serge wouldn't be careless enough to leave that evidence at the campsite," he said slowly and succinctly. "You asked for my knowledge on the subject of Serge's motivations, the rationale behind this spate of serial killings."

"Yes, and you've been distinctly unhelpful with that up until now," Pederson ground out from between clenched teeth, and Nico knew he was referring to the fact that his own girlfriend was now in the hands of the killer and Nico had been none the wiser it was going to happen.

He decided to ignore all the million and one reasons he hadn't been able to pinpoint Serge's motivations more clearly before, and went on to say, "Maybe so, but on this fact, I'm very sure. Serge's profile shows a perfectionist, someone with ultimate precision. And now we know he has a military background it all makes sense. He wouldn't just have left Danika's stuff buried at the site for anyone to find. And he wouldn't have burned incriminating paperwork and left it there either. He did it because he wanted you to find it. I think that paperwork was burned intentionally. He was hoping you'd dig it up."

Pederson shook his head, an incredulous look on his face, then opened his mouth to argue, but seemed to change his mind at the last moment; instead forming his lips into a thin line as he regarded Nico. "Okay," he sighed. "I'll take that under advisement and note it in the reports."

That wasn't at all what Nico was hoping to hear. "But you're still going to Hobart, aren't you?" he asked grimly.

"Yes, I am. This lead is too big to ignore." Pederson had already turned his back, packing up his laptop and wrangling his pile of notes into some sort of order so he could put them in his briefcase.

You're playing right into Serge's hands, Nico wanted to yell. But Pederson was like a terrier when he got a whiff of a juicy bone, and there was no getting through to him.

Saito had said nothing during the whole argument, but now she stared at him with a contemplative gaze. Perhaps she might be more receptive to his rationalization, but even if she was, he knew she wouldn't be able to change Pederson's mind. In one way, the other detective was accurate, this was a big lead. And it might even turn out to be accurate; Serge could well have been renting an apartment down in Hobart. But Nico could feel it in his bones. This was a ruse, a machination to get the cops to focus on Hobart for some reason. But why?

Without another word, Nico turned on his heel and exited the ops room. Taking his bruised ego back to his office, he shut the door behind him. He needed to think this through. Go through all the permutations and see which one fit the best.

His gaze fell on Lacey's handwritten note in a plastic evidence bag on his desk. He must've read her words a thousand times over, but every time he did, he found himself getting so angry he could hardly think.

Now, it was time to read this letter like a detective and not a distraught lover. Time to put his forensic skills to the test.

He's in Boat Harbour.

Talk to Pacca, he knows more than he's letting on.

He promised he wouldn't hurt me.

Back when they'd been profiling the killer, he and Pederson had decided that even if the suspect had been a local, he'd never have been stupid enough to carry out the murders in the same town where he lived. It was like shitting in your own nest. They'd decided it was more likely the killer was a drifter, moving around from place to place. And while they'd been correct on part of their analysis, they'd been so very, very wrong about his not lingering in the vicinity of his murderous spree. Serge had been here all along, right under their noses.

Earlier, Nico had been so blinded by the idea that Serge had been in the neighborhood all along and they'd been completely unaware that he'd barely concentrated on any of the other words in her note. Apart from her last sentence, where he promised he wouldn't hurt her. The mere idea of what his father could be doing to Lacey right now made his chest ache, like someone had stabbed him with a butcher's knife. How stupid could she be to believe that? What had Serge said to her to make her think he'd keep his word?

Pushing those thoughts aside, he concentrated on her second sentence. *Talk to Pacca*, it said. Another interview with the old farmer had always been on his list, at least back when he'd been in charge of the investigation. Now, he had no idea what Pederson was planning to do.

Police had already thoroughly searched the farmhouse and all the outbuildings. Pacca couldn't possibly be hiding anything out there. And Serge would've known the place would be searched, and that they'd be keeping an eye on it, so there was no way he'd be stupid enough to want to use it as a base, or even take Lacey there now. Would he?

With Pederson and Saito probably already gone, there was no way Shadbolt would allow Nico to go out and interview Pacca again on his own. So how was he supposed to find out what else the old man knew? He could ask Linc to do him a favor and drive out there for him. Linc was off duty right now, after spending all night out searching for Lacey, but he would do it, especially if he thought it might help to find her. But would Linc know what to look for? What questions to ask? Nico barely knew himself, and if he were to go, he'd work the questions out as he went, using Pacca's answers to drive him forward.

As he pondered this question, his phone rang, shocking him out of his reverie. He almost didn't answer, but then saw the caller ID and swiped with a grimace. "McTernan," he said roughly. The private investigator hadn't contacted him in over a week. McTernan was supposed to be tracking down Serge. Fat lot of good that'd done, the fucker had kidnapped two girls, killed one of them and now had Lacey in his clutches. So, with everything that'd happened, Nico was no longer in need of his services.

The guy was a failure in Nico's eyes and he was about to give him a piece of his mind, when the investigator exclaimed, "I know, I know. You don't need to say anything. Your father got the drop on me, and I lost the trail. I'm sorry."

"No shit," Nico growled, low and dangerous. He conveniently forgot that his father was a smart fucker and had got the drop on him as well, because he needed something to take his frustration out on, and this guy was gonna be it. Just as he opened his mouth to give McTernan an earful, the other man spoke down the phone.

"But I just heard something real interesting from a mate down in Canberra." That stopped Nico midway through drawing in breath. "They got an ID on the body they exhumed from your father's grave."

"Who was it?" he asked, forgetting his anger in a heartbeat. If they could find out who had been buried instead of Serge, it might give them a tenuous link, another clue to follow.

"A guy by the name of Alexander Gillies," McTernan said, his tone tinged with excitement.

Nico's mind raced, but he came up blank. "Doesn't mean anything to me," he replied.

"It didn't to me either," McTernan admitted. "Until I did a little digging. This guy owned property in the Burnie area."

Nico sat up straighter, his gut clenching, suddenly knowing this might be something big.

"And his property was adjacent to Vincent Mcmillan's."

It took a few seconds for Nico to dredge the name up from the dungeons of his mind. That was Pacca's given name. The tingling in Nico's belly became gut clenching pains. Of anticipation or dread, he wasn't sure which.

"He was Vincent's son, but he took the mother's last name. Owned a house just down the road. But as far as I can tell, that house has been empty for a very long time. In fact, the guy seems to have dropped off the face of the earth around seventeen years ago."

What the fuck… Nico could hardly believe what he was hearing.

"But he was never reported missing," McTernan continued. "And as far as I know, his property is still sitting vacant and decaying. Alexander was Vincent's only child, and the wife died twenty years ago, so he would've stood to inherit everything."

So old Pacca had a son. Now that Nico thought about it, he remembered the man mentioning a son in passing, but the reference had been vague and Nico had never followed it up. How had this guy, Alexander, got from Burnie to end up dead in a fiery car crash in Canberra? And what was the possible connection between Serge and Pacca?

"How come the Canberra office hasn't alerted us?" Nico barked, wondering what those guys were doing up there— sitting on their hands by the sounds of it.

"The results only came through yesterday. I don't think they've made the connection yet," McTernan said simply.

"How do you know all this?" Nico quizzed the investigator.

"I have my contacts," McTernan replied simply. "And I wanted to make up for letting you down this week." Of course McTernan would be up to date on all the pertinent information on the murder case so far; it was his job to stay abreast of everything that happened on this and every other case he was being paid to look into. Nico just wished he'd had the peace of mind to do the same.

"Right. Thanks." Nico's mind was already off on a tangent, analyzing and sorting through the tiny details in his head. When McTernan cleared his throat on the other end of the line, Nico said. "You've done good. Anything else I need to know?"

"Not yet, but I'm still working on it. Trying to find the connection between Alexander and Serge."

"Great. Let me know if you do." He rang off without another word, too busy with the roller coaster in his mind to worry about formalities. McTernan had just redeemed himself. More than redeemed, he might just have given Nico the clue he needed. The man would get an extra fat pay packet at the end of this month.

Nico wasn't going to wait for McTernan to come up with the answers. He was going straight out to the horse's mouth and ask the old guy directly. But he needed to tread carefully.

Nico did what he always did when trying to solve a problem. He got up and paced. The office was small, so he did laps around his desk. Should he take this new information to Shadbolt? Someone needed to go back out and reinterview Pacca. The old farmer knew something; it was clear he wasn't telling them everything. Perhaps withholding information that could be vital to finding Lacey. Pederson and Saito had just left to catch a plane to Hobart. The only other person he truly trusted was Tyrell, who was still down in Strahan, wrapping up the investigation into the abandoned campsite. Linc would be here in a heartbeat if Nico called him in, and he would be out there shaking down the old farmer if Nico asked him to, but even though Linc was a good cop, he wasn't as experienced as Tyrell or Nico. If Linc got it wrong and the old man clammed up, he could risk screwing this whole thing up.

This was too important, this was more than a hunch, more than just a gut feeling. Nico *knew* this was the answer they'd been looking for. But he was banned from the case. Pacca was linked to Serge somehow. And Serge had been pointing the finger at him all along, by dumping the girls on his property.

He needed to do this himself. Lacey was missing. Lacey,

his heart, his soul. His whole world would crumble without her. His bastard of a father had her, and Nico could only feel one emotion. Pure rage. When he found his father, he would rescue Lacey; then he'd make Serge pay. In every way possible.

Nico was out the door before he had time to second-guess himself. He'd need to take a police vehicle; his own was still at home. But he could make up some bullshit story about having to go back and talk to Mary, the psych at the hospital. He assuaged some of the guilt by telling himself that if he found anything of import, he'd call it in.

The midday sun beat down hot and hard on Nico's shoulders by the time he climbed the stairs to the old homestead. When Pacca answered his front door, there was an empty bottle in his hand and he already reeked of alcohol, was already slurring his words. The old man had taken to drinking in the middle of the day now. Nico swore loudly, knowing this was going to make it harder to interrogate him. Nevertheless, he pushed his way past Pacca, towing him inside and forcing him to sit down in one of the battered armchairs in the front living room. He was already breaking so many rules by coming here against orders and without a warrant and no permission to interrogate this suspect, manhandling a witness was a minor infraction by comparison.

"You're going to tell me everything about your son, and what he has to do with the man who abducted my partner," Nico demanded, taking the seat opposite the old man and staring directly into his face.

Pacca's features crumpled into lines of fear and despair. "You know about my son?" he asked, tears springing to his eyes.

"Yes. And I know you're withholding information. I know you have a connection to these murders. It's time to come clean, old man."

Surprisingly, Pacca nodded his head. "I've been waiting for this day for a long time," he admitted.

CHAPTER NINETEEN

Bright sunshine glimmered outside but inside, it was dim and eerily silent. Through the corner of the window, Lacey could see high clouds scudding across the sky, half-obscuring the sun and casting crazy shadows beneath the two large eucalyptus trees that marked the entrance to a main driveway. Those trees had become familiar to her over the past few hours as she stared out the window, hoping and praying. She was huddled in one corner of a living room, hands and feet bound tightly, while Serge sat beneath the window opposite, his head resting just below the decaying wooden sill. He looked so relaxed he might even be asleep. She stared mutely at him, trying to figure out his next move.

The room contained a few pieces of dusty furniture, left in position as if the person had just got up and stepped outside. A scratched wooden coffee table in front of a filthy couch and an old television set on an equally shabby sideboard. A dent on the left-hand side of the couch marked where the owner of this property might have once sat—in his favorite spot—and the watermarks on the coffee table hinted at many cups of coffee being sat down without a coaster. No one had lived here in quite a while, however, that much was blatantly obvious.

In her imagination, Serge might've taken her many places to *talk*, as he so eloquently put it, but this abandoned farmhouse hadn't been on her list of likely locations. Last night, he'd ordered her to lay her head down on the back seat as he drove and keep out of sight, so she had no idea where they were going until he'd pulled up behind this old place and told her she could sit up. They hadn't driven far, only twenty minutes or so, and that limited the area to somewhere around Burnie. It was dark when they arrived and Lacey could see nothing of their surroundings except that they were in an isolated spot somewhere in the country.

She'd flinched away when Serge had opened the car door and asked her to step out. But then she'd gritted her teeth and followed through with his order; she was the one who'd willingly put herself in this situation. Serge had taken her lightly by the shoulder and guided her up a set of rickety stairs and in through a door that was half hanging off its hinges. It was surprising the way he was so gentle with her, touching her respectfully, not pushing or cursing at her. She wasn't sure if she was reassured by his treatment, or not. And just because he was being nice to her, didn't stop her cataloging every angle, every movement he made, waiting and watching for a chance to escape. His congenial treatment hadn't extended to leaving her feet unbound, however; he was clearly smarter than that. The second she'd sat in the corner, he'd politely but firmly told her to put her legs out, feet together, then he'd used two more cable ties to make sure she wasn't going to walk out of this room anytime soon.

Last night had possibly been the longest night she'd ever endured. She guessed the old place no longer had electricity running to it and Serge didn't bother to provide any other form of light, possibly because he didn't want to attract any attention. So they'd sat in the dark; to what end, Lacey had no clear idea. The silence stretched between them, and Lacey was happy to let it flourish at first; it gave her more time to think. But it didn't seem to make Serge uncomfortable. In fact, it was the exact opposite.

Meanwhile, her mind was whirling like a dervish, until finally, she could stand it no longer. "I thought you wanted to talk to me," she'd challenged after half an hour of maddening quiet. Better to get it over and done with, because this dark solitude was driving her crazy.

"Why don't you try to get some sleep. We can chat in the morning." He sounded almost bored as he spoke.

Lacey gave a most unladylike snort. Sleep wasn't an option. It seemed he was waiting for something. But what? For Nico to come? Was he using her as bait? Had that been his intention all along? She was beginning to think so. That his attempt to contact her, to draw her aside, had in fact been aimed at getting Nico to take notice of him. As if he wasn't already doing that. But now, Serge had taken it to a totally new level.

This had always been a possibility, but Lacey had hoped that by talking to Serge, she might begin to understand what he wanted, perhaps even talk him out of whatever he had planned. But he'd stymied that idea by simply not engaging with her.

When Gabe had abducted her, he'd been very happy to purge himself of all his misdeeds, as well as gleefully revealing his plans for plotting her demise, so at least she'd known what was in store. But with Serge, she was at a complete loss. Were they just going to sit here all night? Waiting? If that was the case, she needed to warn Nico somehow. Because whatever Serge had planned for Nico, it couldn't be good. But Serge had divested her of her phone, as well as the burner she'd brought along just in case. So that option was out. How else could she send him a signal to stay away? Set the house on fire? But that'd bring everyone running toward them, not away.

When Gabe had her tied up and helpless in her Kombi van, she'd done a lot of praying that Nico would find her and rescue her. But now, she needed the opposite to happen and wished him as far away as possible. Hope that he didn't use those incredible smarts of his and figure out where Serge was holding her.

Her mind turned back, almost unbidden to that time when Gabe had taken her. She didn't want to think about it, about how similar her circumstances were this time. Her hands and feet had been bound together, just like now, but Gabe hadn't been as thorough as Serge, and had stupidly left her access to a drawer full of cutlery inside the van so she could cut through her bindings. Back then, she'd had to save herself by jumping out of her Kombi van at the last second as it plunged over a cliff. Nico had come too late to stop Gabe driving it over the edge, but he'd been there to help her out of the tree where she'd landed, broken and bleeding. If she'd been able to extricate herself out of that dire situation then, she could do it again. Save herself, and save Nico in the process.

It'd help if she knew where they were. And why Serge had picked this place to stage his ambush—if that's what this was going to be. It must have some meaning to him, Nico, or both. Otherwise, how was Nico supposed to work it out?

The sun remained stubbornly below the horizon as the night drew on. Lacey must've dozed a few times, because she found herself jerking awake more than once. Propped in the corner, her head resting in the crook of the two walls, she let her body relax and prime itself for when she might need it. At first, she'd searched around her for anything she could use as a weapon, or to help her escape her bonds. But it'd been fruitless, as every time she even moved a muscle, Serge turned his piercing gaze on her.

A few more times over the course of the night, Lacey had

tried to engage the man who sat like a stone carving across from her. But he politely shut her down each time, only answering in monosyllables. All that military training had clearly stood him in good stead, and was still evident in the way he held himself, using an economy of movement, but remaining focussed and ready. It looked to Lacey almost as if Serge might still consider himself a soldier, and this was his latest mission. Like a sniper waiting silently for hour upon hour for his target to appear between the sights. He sat like a curled viper, loose, but ready to strike at a moment's notice, the gun resting easily in one hand cradled in his lap.

The sun was sluggish to rise, but Lacey thought she could finally see the sky outside turning a soft gray, then a pastel lilac. She shifted position to get a better look out the window, trying to stretch cramped muscles within the confines of her bindings. Her left calf muscle threatened to cramp, and she grunted, pushing her foot straight to circumvent the spasm. The heat of the day began to penetrate through the thin wooden plank walls into the dingy room. Surprisingly, her usual nausea did not make an appearance this morning. She decided that her stomach was so empty, and so tied in knots from the night's stress, that it didn't have the capacity to want to empty itself.

Glimpses of her surroundings through the cracked windowpane showed her open paddocks and farmlands stretching away between scattered patches of gum trees. The area looked familiar, but not enough for Lacey to pinpoint exactly where she was. Serge continued to sit there, wearing black from head to toe, and somehow looking cool and stylish, as if this was exactly where he wanted to be and how he wanted things to go.

Lacey licked her lips and wished she had a bottle of water as sweat ran freely between her shoulder blades. But the urge to pee was getting stronger with every minute. Serge hadn't offered her a bathroom break all night, and she wondered if he just expected her to pee in her pants. It probably wasn't good for the baby for her to get dehydrated. With that theory, it was as if she'd allowed a chink in her armor to open, and thoughts of her unborn baby rushed in. Not only was dehydration bad for the baby, this whole damned situation was bad for the baby. What had she been thinking, agreeing to Serge's terms? With hindsight, she could see her judgement might've been skewed. Because it wasn't only her life she'd traded in exchange for Taylor's. If this ended badly, she'd made that selfish decision for her unborn child as well.

If she told him she was pregnant, would he let her go? Would the fact she was carrying his grandchild soften him, break through that impenetrable wall he held around his heart and his mind? Would he want to preserve his heritage? Or would telling him do the opposite and make him want to destroy it?

Either way, she needed a drink and a toilet break, and perhaps asking for those things might break the stalemate that'd formed between them. Up until now, pride had kept her mouth shut, but this wasn't just about her anymore.

Just as she opened her mouth to ask Serge for some water, he preempted her, by saying, "Do you think Nico will work it out? Where we are? I mean, I left him enough clues." Serge's words shocked her, and she snapped her mouth shut. This was the first time he'd spoken to her in hours.

"What?" she croaked, then tried to swallow through her dry mouth.

"I'm just wondering if Nico is indeed as smart as I thought he was. I was hoping he might've been here by now," he continued.

Well, at least that confirmed what Serge had been thinking all along.

"Nico has been taken off the case. It tends to be a conflict of interest when the serial killer you're hunting is your own father," Lacey spat. But she was silently wondering if Nico would indeed work it out. She couldn't see how. But she needed to make Serge think it was definitely not an option. Perhaps she could sway him away from his idea of an ambush. "How the hell do you think he's going to *work it out*?"

"Ah, a little thing like being taken off the case shouldn't worry him." Serge waved a hand as if swatting away a gnat. It was the first time Lacey really noticed his French accent. She'd almost forgotten about Nico's heritage. Nico had lost his accent soon after he moved to Australia as a ten-year-old child. Nico's mother, Catarina, still had her French lilt, however. Lacey loved to listen to her talk over the phone, that flowery, nasal quality that was romanticized in so many movies and novels. But Serge's voice was more guttural and hard-edged.

"So, you lied to me," she accused. "You never really wanted to talk to me at all. You're just using me as bait."

Serge merely shrugged in the face of her growing ire. "You are right, of course. You are the prize that will draw my son in. And I don't need you to talk to me, I already know everything I need to about my son. I've been studying him, watching him, learning about him. He is extraordinary, is he not?"

"What?" Lacey was completely lost. What was this man talking about? "Studying your own son. Why would you do such a thing?" Then she nearly laughed at the stupidity of her question. This man was a serial killer. He'd done a lot of sick things in his life, taking the time to stalk his own son was probably one of his lesser evils.

"So I could learn everything there was to know about him. And you of course too, because you are important to him. And it was worth it. He is my bright light. My shining star.

He's turned out to be everything I hoped for. My other two children, not so much. But Nicolas, he's so determined, so ferocious." Serge smiled, a ghastly smile, all hard edges and hard eyes. There was no humor in it.

Lacey grunted. From all of Nico's accounts, Serge was a terrible father, and he'd certainly never been full of praises such as these. Why had he suddenly decided that Nico was the greatest son who ever walked the earth?

"How long have you been…studying him…us?" Lacey asked, suddenly troubled, wondering exactly what Serge had seen. Had he been peering in windows at them both, while they'd been oblivious to his gaze, carrying on their lives, eating dinner at the kitchen table, sitting out on the front veranda toasting the sunset with a glass of wine, making love in their cozy bedroom? She shuddered at the thought of what this voyeur had seen.

"A while. At least two years."

Oh, shit. That was around the same time Serge had relocated from the mainland to Tasmania. Did that mean he'd come here with that sole purpose in mind? To reconnect with his youngest son? If it was, he had a fucking strange way of doing it.

"We know it was you who broke into our house before Christmas," she accused.

"Yes, I made sure Nico understood it was me," Serge replied loosely. "It was a shame. That night was a missed opportunity. I was hoping you might have been home. Alone," he added with a small smile. "But you and that dog foiled my plans."

"What do you mean?" She lifted her head sharply.

"Maybe if you'd come home earlier that night, then this might all have been over by now." He waved his gun in the air, but Lacey failed to grasp what he meant.

"What would be all over by now?" she asked. Then a

sudden realization struck her. "Were you planning on abducting me? Is that why you were there?" Serge merely nodded, and Lacey's whole body shuddered at the thought of how close she'd come to disaster that night. Hell, she'd been about to chase him into the dark night. What an idiot she'd been.

"But because that plan failed, I had to concoct another strategy to get Nico's attention. And I think this one worked well, don't you? Perhaps even better."

It took her a few seconds to work out the meaning behind his words. "You mean abducting those poor innocent girls, murdering one of them and leaving the other one forever traumatized? That was your new plan?" Then the irony hit her. Instead of having to take her by force, Serge had induced her to hand herself over without a struggle, meek as a lamb. He'd achieved his goal in the end, and those two poor girls had ended up paying dearly for it all.

"Yes. And it was a good one." Serge shifted position slightly, easing out one of his legs, then gave a small grin. "I got to feed the monster one last time, and I made my son work hard to catch me. Such fun, this game we play."

Lacey felt physically sick. Game? This wasn't a game; this man was playing with people's lives. And monster? What did he mean by that?

Before she could ask, however, he went on, "I thought I would add a few unconventional details this time. I don't normally like to inflict harm. Quick and clean is the only way to do it. Give them what they need and then leave."

Again, her stomach heaved as his words hit her; the way he was so casual about carrying out a murder. So blunt. But she was a cop, and she needed to clear her mind of her own roiling emotions and analyze his words like a cop. She assumed he was referring to the way he killed the women he took cleanly, without any other form of interference such as rape or torture. Except where Taylor was concerned. He'd inflicted harm on Taylor. Was that what he meant by unconventional details? The million and one cuts all over Taylor's body.

"But I wanted to make Nico work harder. And to make you feel sorry for her. I knew you wouldn't be able to resist her. Your compassionate side is so strong."

Lacey shrank against the wall. Oh, God. Serge had cut Taylor just to draw her in. To make sure she'd do just about anything to try and protect her. He'd tortured her with some sick notion of attracting Lacey's attention. And it'd worked. But how did Serge know so much about her? Just through studying her and Nico, as he claimed? He must be a master at working out human motivations if that were the case. Nico had warned her that Serge was smart, but this was something else again.

"You're a sick, sick man," she whispered.

"I understand that," he replied simply, surprising her with his candor. "That is why I need Nico."

"Why? What do you want with Nico? Why can't you just leave him alone?" she spat, wanting this conversation to be over. This man *was* a monster, just like he claimed, and she suddenly wished she'd never wanted clarification in the first place. Understanding why he did these things was almost scarier than not knowing.

"Because Nicolas will be my savior."

What the hell did that mean? She stilled as she considered his words. This man was a serial killer. His son was a homicide detective. There wasn't going to be any happy family reunions when they finally met. Nico wasn't going to greet his long-lost father with open arms. But the outcome Serge had in mind still wasn't clear to her. Did he want Nico dead, or not? If she were to help Nico, she needed more information.

"Don't hold your breath." Her voice was full of mockery. "I'm not sure why you think he'll find us so easily. Nico is good, but not even he is that good. And even if he does, he won't fall for your tricks."

"I have laid a trail of breadcrumbs. Only the smartest detective will be able to work it out. But I think Nicolas is that smart," Serge said with the hint of a smile.

"A trail of breadcrumbs?" she repeated. What kind of clues had he left? Because up until now, he'd been exemplary at leaving almost no traces, as if he prided himself at staying ten steps ahead of the police. So, what had changed? Her mind began to churn through the possibilities. What was so significant about this house? Why had Serge chosen this place to forge his final stand?

"What does this cottage have to do with it all?" she asked. "Why did you bring me here?"

"Ah ha, at last you are beginning to think like a detective." He gave that ghastly smile again. "That is the brilliant part. Once Nicolas figures that out, the rest will fall into place."

The man was talking in riddles, and it was pissing Lacey off. "Why don't you just stop all these games and tell me where we are?" she spat. Enough was enough. "I'm not about to go blabbing it to anyone now, am I?" She indicated her bound hands as evidence she was going nowhere.

Serge lifted one eyebrow and considered her for a moment. "This property once belonged to Vincent's son," he replied, surprising her with his direct answer.

Vincent? Who was Vincent? Then it came to her. That was the old farmer; Pacca's given name. But what did he have to do with anything? He'd been the one to report the screams in the night. Then Danika's body had been found on Cutter's Road, the old track traversing his farm, and Taylor had clearly been set free in the same place. Was he complicit in the murders somehow? An accomplice to the crimes? Or merely covering up evidence? But what was his motivation? What was Serge holding over Pacca's head to make him do such a thing? Clearly something to do with his son. But as far as she knew, Pacca had said he hadn't talked to his son in years.

"So, it wasn't a coincidence you dumped the body of that poor girl on his property then?"

"I don't like the word *dumped*." Serge's face crumpled into what could only be called a pout. "It was her place of rest. I treated her with nothing but respect. She is free from the mortal coils of this world now."

Lacey's anger surged hot and intense and she wanted to spit in his face. "Respect! She was a young girl in the prime of her life, with everything left to live for. You didn't treat her with respect. You murdered her." Lacey was shaking with rage. How could this terrible excuse for a human being think he was doing that young girl a favor? She didn't care that his mind was so twisted he probably had no concept of the horror of his crime. She was going to speak her truth.

Serge's face crumpled again, but this time it wasn't pouting, this time he was angry. "Murder is such a crass word." A flush spread up his neck.

Yes, but that's exactly what you did, she wanted to yell at him, but something stopped her, maybe the fact his face was now suffused with red, his eyes going so hard they could be made from obsidian. This guy was clearly messed up, delusional, and unable to separate reality from fantasy. So instead of confronting him, she changed tack again, going back to why he'd chosen this place as his dumping ground.

"Okay." She drew in a deep breath, then another. "So tell me, why is Vincent's son's property so important?" As she spoke, she twisted her wrists, trying to ease the spasm that threatened to shoot up her arm at being held in one position for so long.

"Because I did a favor for Vincent a while ago, and now it's time he paid me back."

Okaaayy. Serge was nothing if not cryptic, but Lacey decided to persevere. Even if this conversation was making her physically ill, she knew any information she could garner might be helpful later on.

"What sort of favor?"

"I put out the trash for him."

Lacey almost rolled her eyes. Why did he have to talk in riddles? But she'd keep playing along. Serge liked games, it seemed. She'd take a leaf out of Nico's detective playbook, and keep it cool and professional.

"What do you mean by *trash*?"

Before Serge answered her, he lifted his eyes above the windowsill to peer outside and she followed suit. Nothing moved, there wasn't even a breath of wind to rattle the gum leaves in the branches. It was becoming stifling in here.

When Serge was satisfied nothing and no one was out there, he said, "Vincent killed his son, Alexander. He asked me to get rid of the body for him."

What the…? This revelation posed so many more questions than it answered. Why had Vincent killed his son? How had he killed him? And how had he known to ask Serge to hide the body for him? Was Serge in the business of cleaning up other people's messes? And what had Serge done with the body? A cold shiver walked over her skin, despite the closed heat of this room.

"It was good timing, actually. I needed a body double to make people think it was me who died in the car that day," Serge continued, oblivious to the range of emotions coursing through Lacey.

Oh, God. Serge had used Vincent's dead son to help him fake his own death.

Serge got a faraway look in his eyes. "I did a good job of ramming the car into that tree, got the angle right and everything, then jumped free right before it hit. But the damn thing wouldn't ignite. There was plenty of gas leaking everywhere, but no spark to set it off. So I gave it a helping hand."

By all accounts, the body in the car had been burnt beyond recognition. And because all the evidence pointed that way, the coroner assumed it was Serge in the vehicle and it was decided no autopsy was needed, and therefore, no DNA evidence was collected. But even if they had run a postmortem, any signs of how Vincent's son had really died would've most likely been wiped from the body.

This sounded like the storyline to some multi-million-dollar thriller movie she might see at the box office. Serge had just admitted not only to faking his own death, but to committing arson to cover up his tracks. And he'd done it with such cool calculation, like it meant nothing to him. Nothing to his family.

Almost as if reading her mind, he added, "They were better off without me, you know. I knew what I was becoming. I needed to get away. It was the best solution all around."

Lacey wasn't sure Nico would agree with that assessment.

"Even though I did Vincent a favor, and he gave me what I needed at the time, I could never forget. Vincent shouldn't be allowed to get away with murder. With killing his own son."

What was Serge gabbling on about now? Wasn't he the embodiment of a hypocrite? He was a serial killer. Had murdered at least four women, possibly more. And didn't he also intend to murder his own child? Wasn't he drawing Nico in with the intent to kill him? But that one statement gave her pause. Gave her hope. If in his sick and twisted mind, it was okay to kill innocent girls, but not okay to kill your own flesh and blood, then maybe Nico had a chance. Serge had also mentioned in his ramblings that he'd set Danika free when he'd murdered her. For some reason, he believed he was doing the women a favor by killing them.

Lacey didn't even pretend to understand what was going on in his mind, but perhaps she could use this newfound information to her advantage.

"You're right," she said slowly. "No one should be allowed to get away with that. Family is sacred." She was picking and choosing her words with care. "So what did you—"

Serge held up his hand, and stupidly, she stopped talking. But then she heard it too. The low drone of a car engine. Someone was coming. Lacey tried to wriggle a little higher up the wall so she could see more out of the window. The engine cut out so suddenly that Lacey wondered if she'd imagined it. Was it Nico? Had he figured out Serge's little game after all?

Before she could properly react, Serge had dashed across the room and slapped a bit of duct tape over her mouth. She hadn't even had time to think about screaming out a warning.

Her eyes pleaded with Serge, but he merely turned away and went back to stand by the window, watching with that hawklike gaze.

CHAPTER TWENTY

Nico sat in the chair opposite the old farmer as he'd poured out his tale of despair. Once Pacca had made up his mind to tell the truth, it was as if a tap had been turned on, and the words just spewed from his mouth. Pacca's story was one of violence and betrayal. And if Nico had had the time, it would've made for an intriguing listen. But as it was, Nico prompted him for the pertinent facts and no more, silently urging him to get on with his story, waiting impatiently as Pacca's flow of words was often punctuated by a hacking, wet cough. The old man didn't sound well.

In the beginning, Pacca and his only son, Alexander, had been close. Alex had left the farm to start his own business as a house painter when he was eighteen, but Pacca knew that trade was slow and his son wasn't doing too well. Alex had never married, and lived a bachelor's life in town, *sowing his wild oats* as Pacca put it, but never settling down. Then, after Pacca's wife died twenty years ago, the old man had struggled to cope with the farm on his own. So when Alex suggested he move back home to help out his dad, Pacca had agreed. The farmer had then consented—stupidly as it turned out—to make Alex a part owner of the farm, so he was assured of an income if anything happened to his old dad.

Pacca had already started dabbling in farming the alpacas, and was beginning to show a profit, but Alex didn't like the new trend and thought he should go back to farming barley and potatoes, as they'd been the staple crops since his grandfather before him and brought in solid money.

They began arguing all the time, usually ending in shouting matches. Pacca wouldn't be swayed, hoping to prove to Alex that he was right about the alpacas being the most profitable way to earn money. They were the livestock of the future. Their fleece is highly valued and worth its weight in gold, they also produced milk and cheese products, and alpaca meat is extremely low in fat and in high demand at some of the ritzy restaurants on the mainland. But Alex went against his father's express wishes and ploughed up one of the prime pastures, planting potatoes without permission. Things deteriorated from there. Pacca tried to throw him out of the house, but Alex wouldn't leave, saying the place was half his now.

Finally, Pacca had taken out a second mortgage on the farm and paid Alex off, just to get rid of him. But Alex hadn't gone far. He bought the property next door, and taunted Pacca from there, while trying to turn the property into a viable farm by growing barley and potatoes, just like he wanted. But it turned out, Alex was a crummy farmer; his land was too small to turn a profit, and he didn't understand agriculture as well as he thought, so he was always hassling Pacca for more money. Which his father gave him, begrudgingly, getting deeper and deeper into debt, while the rift between them deepened.

But Pacca missed his only son, worried that they would both end up lonely old men, staring at each other over the fence that kept them apart. And he always hoped they could reconcile. One night, after a few whiskeys for dutch courage, Pacca had gone over to confront Alex, and try to come to some sort of agreement. "He was my only child. My flesh and blood. I just wanted it all to go back to the way it was. I can't believe he treated me that way," Pacca had complained.

Pacca hadn't even made it past the front door when things had turned nasty. Alex had committed the cardinal sin, and punched his father in the face. This had been seventeen years ago, and Pacca had been younger and stronger then. So, in shock and rage, the farmer had flown at his son, shoving him backward, not realizing he was standing at the very edge of the top of the stairs leading down from the veranda. Alex had hit his head on the way down and never got up. He was already dead by the time Pacca knelt by his side.

Pacca had stared down at his male child, his only heir, the one who was meant to continue in his footsteps, and wept. When he finished weeping, he tried to decide what to do.

In a terrible twist of fate, Pacca understood that he'd just inadvertently solved all of his problems. Without Alex around, he was free to keep farming how he wanted to. He also stood to inherit Alex's land, as he was the only surviving next of kin. Without Alex bleeding him dry, his money troubles would disappear. Or they would disappear, if Pacca could make his son's body disappear. There was no way he was telling the police the truth, they'd put him in jail for the rest of his life for murder.

Nico was going to refute that statement, as it would surely have been looked upon as self-defense, and Pacca may have served only minimal time. But he asked a more direct question instead, because he needed to get to the heart of the matter as he still had no idea how his father and Pacca knew each other.

"How does Serge factor in all of this?"

"I'm a Vietnam vet, didn't you know?" Pacca had looked at him then, a hint of pride on his face. But that soon disappeared when he went on to say, "Me best mate was conscripted, and so I joined up in solidarity. That's what you did in them days. Never let a mate down." Pacca's gaze turned inward as if reliving those days after he'd been shipped off to fight in another man's war. "Nigel died over there in that godforsaken jungle. And I came home wounded, a changed man." He patted his knee as he said this. That explained the old man's limp. Nico wished he'd looked into all this earlier instead of putting that investigation on the back burner. Apart from giving him a deeper insight into Pacca's past pain, his military service may have raised a red flag in Nico's mind as well.

"I was pretty messed up, but for a long time I wouldn't admit it, and I wouldn't tell anyone," Pacca continued. "And it was dreadful the way some of those bastards behaved toward me when I came home from the war. It was like I was a pariah or something. I tried to forget about it and just get on with the farming, but when they finally built that memorial for us vets in Canberra, I went over to see it. It was kind of like an apology by the government, you know?" He stopped as another coughing fit overtook him, and Nico winced as the old man turned and spat into an old tin sitting at his feet.

Yes, Nico knew all that, in theory at least. How badly the Vietnam soldiers had been treated when they returned home, in both America and Australia. And how the government had erected a national memorial on Anzac Parade for the vets. Nico had even visited it on a school outing once. Nico's mind had been computing all the variations in his head, but when Pacca mentioned Canberra, he had a lightbulb moment. He suddenly had an uncanny feeling he knew where this was going.

"I joined a veterans' group over there and made some good mates. We'd meet up at least once or twice a year in Canberra. To support each other and stuff, you know. We weren't picky about who could join either, as long as you'd served in some manner. The group got big toward the end. We had guys in there from the Korean War, and the—"

"The Gulf War," Nico finished for him. Oh. My. God. That was the connection. And Nico had never even known his old man attended these meetings. But of course Serge wouldn't have wanted his family to know. That would've been admitting to a weakness.

"And you met Serge through this group?" he asked, even though he'd already guessed the answer.

"Yeah." Pacca nodded, but there was something unfathomable in his gaze. "A lot of the guys were wary of him when he first joined. I mean some of us—hell, maybe even most of us—suffered from some form of PTSD. And we knew some guys with severe mental problems. But that group was there to help. But with Serge... There was something else. Something really dark inside him." Pacca raised his red-rimmed eyes and stared at Nico. "Something a little scary."

Nico nodded because he knew what Pacca meant. Serge may have kept most of his darker side at bay around his family, and perhaps they only experienced the mere tip of the iceberg. But it must've been there, buried deep, waiting to come out, to kill.

"I was really the only one to befriend him. Even though he was quite a bit younger than me, we clicked, you know? We would talk for hours about death and dismemberment and the way the eyes of a child could stare at you, wide open and still accusing, even after they were dead. It might sound morbid, but for us it was cleansing, like squeezing all the pus out of a pimple." Pacca nodded as he remembered. "He always said he owed me a debt of gratitude. For my compassion. For my understanding. Not that I really understood him. And not that I think I really helped him, that man was seriously mucked up. But he said that if I ever needed a favor, no matter what it was, that he would help out."

"So what did Serge do for you?" Nico asked. "What favor did you ask?"

"I called him and asked him if he could dispose of a body. And he said yes, like I knew he would. That man was capable of anything." Pacca seemed to sink in on himself at his confession, but Nico was trying to put the pieces together. Had Serge already been planning to fake his own death? And perhaps Pacca's call was a sign. Because he now had a spare body to act as a proxy for the car crash. Or maybe he'd come up with the idea on the fly on the drive down here to retrieve Alex's body. Because he would've needed a way to dispose of him.

"Serge agreed to take care of it. Cover any evidence of the death and then just disappear. It was almost too easy," Pacca said in a whisper.

There was more, but Nico was only half listening as the old man went on to tell him that Serge had only one stipulation; he was not to report Alex missing, as this would alert the authorities. And Pacca held up his end of the bargain. If anyone asked, he'd just tell them that Alex had met a woman on the mainland and decided to go and live with her. Then his story changed to include the fact that father and son had become estranged. Alex hadn't had many friends, and so no one really asked about him. But the catch was that for Pacca to be able to claim his inheritance, he had to report Alex missing and then have him declared dead. Which Serge had explicitly forbidden. So the house just stood there and went to rack and ruin. In a strange kind of way, Pacca said he was glad. He was loath to go near that house; it felt dirty and tainted, and Pacca knew he was better off without it. The money he'd gain from selling it would never make up for the death of his son.

Serge had actually imposed two stipulations; the second was that Pacca never breathe a word to anyone about what had happened that night. And up until right this very second, Pacca had kept his mouth shut about the death of his son. Meanwhile, the guilt had been eating him up inside.

The farmer had wanted to keep talking, telling Nico it was as if a huge weight that he'd been carrying around this whole time had been lifted from his shoulders. But Nico had the information he needed, and he was already heading for the door. Because now he knew where he needed to go.

Serge was in Alexander's abandoned house. He was sure of it.

Everything Serge had done with the two girls all led back to this location, as if he'd been pointing a giant finger at the spot all along. And maybe he had. Now he could see clearly, Nico wondered why his father had been so transparent. Had he been baiting Nico? Taunting him because he'd been so close, yet so far? Perhaps this was what Serge wanted all along, for Nico to come to him. Well, he was going to get exactly what he wanted, because Nico *was* coming for him.

"He had a family, this broken man. I never met them, but I always felt terribly sorry for them," Pacca said as Nico reached for the front door.

Nico brushed aside the old man's compassion. He had what he needed. He had the connection now. If Pacca had guessed that Nico was Serge's son, he wasn't going to confirm it. And he certainly wasn't going to take his pity.

While Alex's property was adjacent to Pacca's, it was accessed from the main dirt road at the end of Cutter's Road, where all the rest of the properties had driveways. Nico drove the cruiser along the back road to the turnoff, taking it slow, not wanting to alert Serge that he was coming. The midday sun beat down on the windshield and a paddock of almost ripe barley swayed in the slight breeze as he drove past, looking for all the world like he was just out cruising on the perfect summer's day. But inside his head dark clouds circled, a voice clamoring for him to drive faster. To get there before it was too late. Saving Lacey was all that mattered.

He left the cruiser at the front gate, deciding to walk in, so he had time to get the lay of the land, as well as hopefully arrive unannounced. Because Serge would be waiting for him, of that he had no doubt. On the drive over, he'd conducted a quick internal debate about the pros and cons of calling Shadbolt to let him know what he'd found. Or calling in Linc or Gorman as backup. Both those ideas had been rapidly discarded. He was here now, and he wasn't going to ask permission to go in and rescue Lacey. He also wasn't waiting for backup to arrive.

The police had door knocked this whole area when Danika's body had first been discovered, talking to neighboring property owners and other locals, asking if they'd seen or heard anything, but they'd turned up nothing. An empty house wouldn't have raised any warnings, it would merely have been cursorily checked and then disregarded. Serge may have used Alex's house as his staging center, but in his usual precise manner, made sure all traces of himself and his crimes were erased and left that same night. Possibly gone back to sleep in his other bolt-hole a few streets over from where he and Lacey were completely unaware of him or his crimes, as they also slept in their own beds.

The farm house came into view as he crested a low rise, and wanting not to announce his arrival, he stepped off into a dry paddock that may have once held a crop but had now been overtaken by weeds and small shrubs recolonizing the space. Slipping his service weapon out of his shoulder holster, he hunched over so he remained hidden behind the bushes and stalked forward, one foot at a time.

As he got slowly closer, the house—a cottage really—

became more distinct, and he could see how run-down and unloved it was. Pacca had been right; it certainly looked like no one had been here since the terrible night of Alex's death. Although if his hunch was correct, Serge had been here, he'd just hidden his presence well. The front door was hanging off one hinge, and some of the windows were cracked or broken. A heat haze shimmered off the bare dirt of the driveway, which was marked with two large gum trees on either side of the entrance to what once would've been the front yard.

As stealthily as he could, he snuck toward the building, all the while scanning the area for danger. A couple of small outbuildings peeked out from behind the main structure. One looked to have been a garage, its roof now collapsed inward, and the other some kind of large shed, also looking worse for wear. Serge could be anywhere in the vicinity.

At last, Nico made his way to the shelter of a stand of acacia shrubs running along the fence line of the front yard. He was panting now, the sweat running freely down his back as the hot sun beat down mercilessly out of a never-ending sky. His bullet wound was a throbbing knot of heat and pain, but he ignored it. Centering himself, he hunkered down in the shrubbery to catch his breath and scrutinize the homestead. He stared at the house, hoping for some sign to point him in the right direction. Suddenly, he caught a flash of movement at the side of one of the front windows. It was so quick he might've easily discarded it as nothing at all. But Nico knew better. Serge had slipped up and given away his position. He was hiding in the front room. Was Lacey in there with him? Or did he have her tied up and sequestered somewhere else? Maybe in one of the outbuildings. The other option—the one where Lacey was no longer alive—was too horrible to contemplate, and Nico put it out of his mind.

What was the best way to breach this place? Alone, and with no backup, he needed to be smart about this. Should he enter through the back door and try to take his father by surprise? Sneak through one of the broken windows and suss out the lay of the house first. Or just charge through the front door and hope like hell he didn't get shot before he could take Serge down?

The decision was made for him, when the front door swung all the way open, its rusty hinges squeaking loudly, as if in invitation. He tensed and raised his weapon, waiting for an attack, waiting for Serge to come out guns blazing.

Instead, he heard the deep, clear tone of his father's voice echo over the dusty yard. "Come in, Nicolas. We've been expecting you."

So much for arriving unannounced. Serge had clearly been onto him from the moment he appeared on the property. He straightened and walked cautiously across the open yard, keeping his gun up and gaze trained on the open door. Nothing moved inside.

"Come in, come in," Serge crooned. "I promise I won't shoot you."

Yeah, right. But what other choice did he have? Taking a deep breath, Nico stepped into the room, his eyes taking precious seconds to adjust to the dim interior. What he saw froze his blood. Lacey was tied at wrist and ankle, her mouth bound with tape. Serge stood above her, gun resting against her temple.

"Put the weapon down." Serge tilted his chin in Nico's direction, his gaze brooking no argument.

It was a no-brainer. He couldn't take the risk that Serge would follow through and shoot Lacey in the head if he didn't do as he was told. He slowly leant down and placed his gun on the floor, then stood, hands raised in surrender.

"Good boy," his father murmured appreciatively, and Nico was nearly sick at the condescension in his tone. It was the same tone he'd used on him as a twelve-year-old boy. Almost as if Serge couldn't see—or couldn't accept—Nico was now a man. A man who was prepared to do anything to save his woman and his unborn child. "And your phone too."

Nico gritted his teeth as he put his cell next to his gun on the floor.

"Well done," Serge warbled as if to a well-trained dog. "Now, let's take this outside, like the two civilized men that we are."

Serge raised his gun to point it at Nico and indicated that he precede him out the door. Lacey's gaze tracked them both as he led Serge out the door, her eyes wide with panic as she made grunting noises of objection. There was nothing he could do to help her at the moment, so he sent her a telepathic message, telling her to stay calm and he'd come and get her when this was over. Whatever *this* was.

When Nico was standing in the middle of the dusty yard, he turned to face his father.

"Are you going to tell me what this is all about?" he demanded, using his calm, authoritative voice that sounded nothing like a man who had a gun currently pointed at his chest.

"Yes," Serge replied simply. Then, much to Nico's surprise, he took a few steps backward, emptied all the ammunition out of his gun, and placed it all on the top step of the veranda. "You and I are going to fight to the death."

"What?" This wasn't what Nico had been expecting. He didn't know what exactly he had been expecting, but this wasn't it. A fight to the death?

"Why?" he sputtered. Why would his father put himself at any kind of disadvantage? Up until a few seconds ago, Serge had held all the cards. Why would he give that supremacy away? It was most unlike the man he'd used to know. That man had demanded absolute compliance from his children through the sheer force of his iron will and his cruel conduct.

And reveled in the power it gave him. Nico narrowed his eyes suspiciously at his father.

"Come on, I'll give you first shot." Serge tapped his chin and took up a fighting stance.

He really meant to do this. For some crazy reason he couldn't fathom, Serge wanted to fight Nico. He had no idea what might happen if he refused, and he was going to do everything in his power to keep Serge away from Lacey now that he was out of the house.

So he took a step forward and put up his hands. If Serge was offering first shot, then he was going to take it. If he could hit him hard enough, this whole thing might be over before it began. Nico ignored the nervous flutter in his belly. Ignored the shooting pain in his side. Ignored that slight twinge of guilt. Guilt that was reminding him this was his father. And a son never hit his own father. Shouldn't ever want to wish his father harm. But most sons didn't have a father like Serge, he reminded himself. And most sons also didn't have a father who'd turned out to be a serial killer. Serge had said this was to be a fight to the death, and so Nico couldn't let anything distract him from the seriousness of this situation. Serge meant business, and Nico needed to treat him like the dangerous fanatic that he was. To forget he had once been the man Nico had looked up to, who he'd wanted desperately to please. The man who was supposed to love him unconditionally.

"I assume we are alone? We won't be rudely interrupted by your police mates? So we can finish this thing once and for all?" Serge took Nico's curt nod as agreement. Nico had no idea what his father wanted to finish, but if it kept him occupied and his mind off Lacey and off his gun, Nico was up for anything. Perhaps he should've called for help. But this thing was between him and his father, and Serge was right on one point; it needed to be finished once and for all.

Nico wasn't fooled. Even though Serge was older, he was probably nearly as fit as him. And might even be better at hand-to-hand combat. But Nico was prepared to fight dirty to gain the upper hand. So he stepped in and landed a hard uppercut on Serge's chin. Then quickly tried to land a few good shots to his lower belly, which Serge managed to block.

Even though Serge had called the fight and told Nico to take the first swing, he could see the older man had been taken by surprise; he hadn't really expected Nico to do it. But he'd misjudged Nico's determination. Nico was going to take every advantage he was given.

Serge stumbled back a few steps, a new light of understanding and grudging respect lighting his gaze. "In it to win it, hey, son?" Serge nodded sagely, then narrowed his eyes. "Good."

Nico almost didn't have time to react as Serge lunged forward on the attack, spearing one hand toward his face, aiming for his eyes, while the other went lower, trying to land a liver shot just beneath his right rib cage. Nico blocked both moves, but only just, and stepped away to regroup. Seemed like Nico wasn't the only one who was prepared to fight dirty today. Nico's newly healed wound protested at the sharp movements he was forced to take. Did his father know he'd been injured up in the mountains six weeks ago? And if so, would he use that against him? Nico couldn't show any pain, any weakness.

They circled each other like two caged lions.

"You look good, Nicolas."

Why was his father speaking? Trying to put him off his game? Nico didn't respond. He had nothing to say to this excuse for a father. When Nico refused to answer, Serge shrugged and then, quick as a snake, aimed a kick, again at Nico's liver. Trying to incapacitate him. The blows came thick and fast then, and it was all Nico could do to defend himself, let alone get a few good shots in.

Punches rained down on him and Nico was forced back one step, then another, but then Serge employed his feet as well, kicking out again and again. As Nico turned to avoid a nasty blow aimed at his face, he was caught unawares when Serge got behind him and managed to sweep his legs out from underneath him in a low kick so that he landed heavily on the ground, the wind knocked out of him. Sucking in great gulps of air, Nico rolled just in time to avoid another kick aimed at his kidneys, grabbing Serge's foot instead and knocking him off balance so that Serge was on his knees in the dirt too. Nico took the second or so that Serge was disoriented to sweep a foot toward his head, his wounded side screaming in pain so that he almost screamed out loud himself. Serge ducked beneath the blow, but then Nico was able to grab him by the collar of his shirt and pull him down.

Then they were both rolling on the ground, grappling for a hold, and it became more of a wrestling match than a fistfight. Serge had his knee on one of Nico's arms, stopping him from throwing a punch. His hand scrabbled in the dirt, hoping to find a stone or a stick to use as a weapon. His next punch caught Serge on the temple, and his weight shifted slightly, and Nico could move his arm. He hurled a handful of dust into his father's face.

"Argh," Serge screamed in pain, and partially blinded, he staggered to his feet, trying to get away from his assailant. Perhaps without realizing it, Serge inadvertently turned his back to Nico as he tried to clear his eyes, holding one hand out in front in a futile gesture to stop any attack Nico might deliver.

Nico took his chance and scrambled to his feet, leaping on his father's back, taking him from behind. Kicking Serge's knees out from beneath, he dropped them both to the ground like a sack of potatoes, then wrapped his legs around the front of his father's, taking Serge in a wrestler's hold—the choke hold, some people called it. His old injury was on fire, the angle of his body pulling on all the barely healed muscles and scar tissue until they felt like they would burst open again.

His father fought like a demon to get free, but they were of similar build and height—equally matched. But Nico had the advantage of youth on his side. Now that he had him, Nico wasn't letting go. He locked one arm around his father's throat, using the leverage of his other hand to pull it tight. And waited.

Serge stopped thrashing and suddenly went limp, not fighting anymore. Now he had the upper hand, rage grew inside Nico like boiling lava.

Nico pulled his elbow tighter on his father's neck so that he could barely breathe. "Why did you come here? What do you want from me?"

After a few seconds of silence, where Nico thought he might not get an answer, Serge gasped out, "I want you to stop me. Because no one else will."

"What do you mean? Stop you how?"

"A fight to the death," Serge answered. "It's simple, really."

"It's not simple at all," Nico hissed. "I don't know why you're doing this."

Serge's breath wheezed in and out of his throat for a few breaths. "I realize something inside me is broken," he finally said. "But I can't do anything about it. You're the only person who can stop this. Tame this monster I've become. Please." The last word came out as a grunted plea.

What sort of twisted logic was that? Serge recognized what he'd done was wrong, recognized the monster within, but he couldn't stop himself, was that it? Couldn't stop his own perverted impulses, so he put the burden on his son's shoulders instead? He'd sought out his youngest son, the one who'd become a homicide detective—the absolute converse of Serge—and decided that he was the only one who could stop him from continuing down his dark path. What a horrible thing to do. What an appalling burden to expect his son to bear.

It was in that moment that Nico realized his father had let him win. Had thrown the fight ever so subtly so that Nico would be the victor. Pretended to be blind so Nico could drop him to the ground and bring him down.

"You want me to kill you? Is that it?" Nico couldn't believe he was even saying this. "To put you down like you're no better than some rabid dog?"

"If that's the way you want to look at it, then yes." His father's words were a mere rasp as he tried to speak past the blockage of Nico's arm on his windpipe. "You are my last act of goodness. The last good thing I created before... Before I let go of my humanity."

It was almost pitiful, the way his father was pleading. The way he thought Nico could be his liberation.

But Nico wasn't having a bar of it.

His father was clearly a sick man. But just because he was mentally ill, did not excuse everything he'd done over the past seventeen years.

"Fine, if that's what you want," Nico muttered in his father's ear.

He increased the pressure on his father's windpipe, ignoring the delighted smile that lit Serge's face as he did so. Serge relaxed, almost as if he welcomed Nico's executioner arm across his throat. But soon enough, instinct took over, and Serge began to fight him, fight for breath. Nico merely tensed his arms tighter, clasped his legs more firmly around Serge's torso. And waited. Serge's movements became weaker and more sporadic. Nico held on for dear life.

Until finally, his father stopped moving altogether.

He released a little of the pressure on Serge's neck. When his father didn't budge, he struggled to push the deadweight of his body off him. He only had about ten seconds or so, and he fumbled around in his pant's pocket until he found the cable ties he'd slipped in there before he left the cruiser.

Nico was suddenly glad Lacey was trapped inside and hadn't had to bear witness to this. His father's indignity. Nico's humiliation. Working quickly, he bound Serge's wrists, then went to work on his ankles. Serge groaned and rolled sluggishly onto his side just as Nico tightened the last tie.

"No!" Serge moaned. "No. No, no, no." He rolled to look at Nico, face suffused with red, spittle flying from his lips. "You were supposed to kill me. I wanted you to kill me."

"Oh, believe me, I wanted to kill you too." Nico spat on the dusty ground beside his father. "So much. After what you've done to those poor innocent girls. After what you put Lacey through. And me." Yes, he'd been sorely tempted to go through with it. To keep squeezing until Serge had no more oxygen left, until the blood stopped pumping through his veins. The world would've been a better place without Serge in it. His mother, brother, and sister would be better off if Serge hadn't survived this day.

But that would've given Serge what he wanted.

And it would've turned Nico into something just as evil as his father.

"No!" Serge shouted again. "You're not the man I thought you were."

"No, I'm not," Nico said with a shrug. It was true. He finally understood what honor meant. What it meant to have integrity. And he finally understood who he was as a man. How far he'd go—or wouldn't go—to achieve a goal. Serge had made one fatal mistake. He'd assumed that rage and hatred would rule Nico's heart, just as it had Serge's. Like father, like son. But Nico had Lacey now, and his unborn child. He had something to live for. Something that meant more than vengeance.

"Perhaps, if you'd had the courage to kill yourself that day in the car crash, instead of faking your own death, you could've stopped your own monster. But instead you chose your son to be courageous for you. And I chose justice over freedom. You will pay for your horrific deeds. A life in a cage is all you have to look forward to now."

"Nooooo," Serge howled, and Nico suddenly understood that this might be Serge's biggest fear. To be locked away forever. Was that why he'd decided Nico should kill him? Because he knew that eventually the police would catch up with him, and he couldn't bear to be locked away. And he couldn't, or wouldn't, do the deed himself.

Nico ignored his father's screams of rage as he hunted for something more to contain Serge until backup arrived. He found an old coil of rope underneath the front stairs. It was frayed and gray with age, but it should hold him long enough.

Serge was still writhing on the ground as Nico walked back, raising a cloud of dust which stuck to his sweaty face, making muddy streaks. Without another word, Nico dragged his father through the dirt to the base of one of the large eucalyptus trees at the edge of the drive, and sat him with his back to the tree, wrapping the rope tightly until Serge could barely move.

When he finished, Nico was shaking with the aftereffects of the adrenaline rush. Sweat poured freely off him, and his mouth was as dry as the dust in this front yard. But they were all minor physical ailments that could be healed by one thing.

Lacey.

He jogged back to the house and up the steps. She was still in the corner, her eyes nearly bugging out of her head, tears tracking unnoticed down her cheeks. Picking up his phone and gun from where he'd dropped them on the floor near the door, he strode over to her.

As gently as he could, he removed the tape across her mouth. The ties around her wrists and ankles required a knife or a pair of clippers, neither of which he had on him. So he merely sat down next to Lacey on the dirty floor and pulled her into his lap.

"All I could hear was you fighting, and then your father screaming. I didn't know what was going on," she sobbed into his chest. "I didn't know if you were alive or dead."

"I'm very much alive, baby," he crooned, feeling his own eyes well with tears. But they were tears of joy. Tears of commiseration. Of hope and deliverance.

CHAPTER TWENTY-ONE

Lacey stared at herself in the mirror, not quite convinced she recognized the person looking back. Perhaps she should go and change back into her comfy jean shorts and T-shirt. Because this didn't feel like her at all. A vein started to pound in her temple and a light sweat broke out on her forehead. What was she doing? They were rushing things, this was all happening way too quick. Lacey glanced at the open window, a slight breeze ruffling the curtains on either side. Beyond it was the ocean. And freedom. Lacey took a hesitant step toward the window.

A knock at the door startled her out of her reverie. "Can I come in, my love?" It was Nico's mother.

Oh, God, should she let her in? Catarina would see right through all the makeup and hairspray, down to how rattled Lacey was. Lacey fanned her face and tried to stop her breath coming in short gasps.

"Honey? Are you okay in there?" Catarina's voice held only concern, not condemnation. Perhaps she should let her in. Maybe her motherly air would help bring Lacey down from the precipice she suddenly found herself standing on. Her sudden need for reassurance was so unnerving. Lacey was an officer in the Tasmanian Police Department. How could a little scrap of lace and silk scare her so?

Lacey took a deep breath and steeled herself. "Yes," she replied, taking one more panicked glance in the mirror before swiveling to face the door.

"Oh, my!" Catarina's hands flew to her mouth as she took in Lacey. "You look absolutely stunning, my love."

"Really?" Lacey wasn't sure. She stood and smoothed down the bodice of the dress. When she'd tried it on, Steph at the bridal shop had assured her that there was no better dress for Lacey on the whole of the island of Tasmania, in the whole world even. The cream silk fell like a waterfall over her hips, over her still flat stomach—she still wasn't showing yet, although everyone knew she was pregnant now—and down her legs all the way to her toes, and the lace bodice fit her like a glove, leaving her shoulders bare. But through her overwrought eyes, it looked completely out of place. How could she think she deserved a dress like this?

"Oh, honey. That dress is perfect. Wait till Nico gets a look at you." Catarina came up and ran a soothing hand down Lacey's arm, and Lacey's pounding heart slowed a little.

"Really?" she asked, staring into Catarina's blue eyes to make sure the older woman wasn't just telling her what she wanted to hear.

"Really," Catarina replied, patting Lacey's hand in sympathy. "It's just pre-wedding jitters, my love. Everyone gets them." Just as Lacey predicted, Nico's mum had seen straight through to the heart of Lacey's near hysteria.

"You don't think the flowers are too much?" Lacey reached up to touch the small headband of white native flowers the hairdresser had nestled into her hair. Her long, blonde hair hung down her back in loose waves, and to Lacey's mind, the hairdresser had fussed for way too long over each individual curl.

"No, no," Catarina crooned. "They look simple and

elegant. Pretty, but not overindulgent." Catarina took her hand and led her over to the chair in front of the mirror. "You look amazing," she told her again. "There's not going to be a dry eye in the house when you walk up that aisle. And remember who will be waiting for you at the other end. My handsome son. And he can't wait for you to become his wife."

"Thank you," Lacey finally replied, deciding to believe the older woman. "And I can't wait to become his wife," she added, immediately realizing it was true. Why had she even questioned it? Of course she wanted to marry Nico.

Catarina patted her shoulder and beamed down at her. Naturally, it was Catarina who'd come to find Lacey at the last moment; her own mother would be too busy holding court with the other guests out in the yard. After only meeting Catarina and her partner, Andy, for the first time two days ago, Lacey knew she would get on well with her soon-to-be family-in-law. Catarina had called Lacey *honey* and *my love* right from the start, and Andy had given her a huge bear hug the moment he'd met her. Her own mother would never use any such term of endearment or hug her like that. She tried to stop the disloyal thought, but it came anyway. If only her mother could've been as caring and empathetic as Catarina. But there was no point in wishing for things that were impossible. Elora was who she was, and Lacey would either have to deal with it, or move on.

After much deliberation, she and Nico had decided to invite her mother and father to the ceremony, but under strict conditions. Elora was to keep her thoughts to herself about the choices Nico and Lacey were making, and not to interfere in any of the wedding arrangements, because Elora would try to take over if she was given the slightest chance. Silently, Lacey believed her mother would break the rules before the end of the night—a leopard like Elora never changed her spots—but she couldn't find it in her heart to exclude her mother from such an important occasion, and so was prepared to ignore any fallout. This was her wedding and nothing was going to take away her joy today.

It'd been three weeks since Nico had defeated Serge and finally put him in jail. But a lot had happened in those three weeks.

Those few seconds, when he'd pulled her into his lap after he'd triumphed over his father, were etched into her mind forever. She'd had no words to explain how scared she'd been. How helpless she'd felt. Hearing the two men battling like vikings outside and not being able to see what was going on. Not knowing who was winning. Not knowing if Nico was alive or dead.

The shock at seeing Nico appear at the door while Serge had held a gun to her head had been so great she nearly burst a blood vessel in her brain. But that was nothing compared to the shock when Nico had obeyed Serge's words and obediently turned around and headed out of the door. She could hardly believe it. He was leaving her alone and unprotected? So he could what…? Go and fight it out man-to-man outside? The noises coming from outside were incredible, and she was desperate to see what was going on, so she'd started to shuffle and roll her way toward the open door. But the flea-bitten furniture hindered her movements, and she'd only made it a little way before she'd been blocked because the gap between the couch and the wall had been too small for her to fit through. She kicked and screamed through her duct tape at the couch, but her need to at least overhear what was going on outside had outweighed her frustration at being stuck inside. And so, she'd rolled back to her spot in the corner and lay there, trying to quiet the breath that wheezed in and out of her nostrils as she struggled to breathe so she could decipher the noises coming from the front yard.

No words could explain how her heart had soared when it'd been Nico who walked through that door a few minutes later. She couldn't speak because of the tape over her mouth; all she could do was implore him with her eyes. He'd sat down beside her and lifted her so tenderly into his lap, removing the tape as he did so.

"All I could hear was you fighting, and then your father screaming," she'd sobbed into his chest. "I didn't know what was going on. I didn't know if you were alive or dead."

"I'm very much alive, baby," he'd crooned when she'd burst out crying as he touched her, and then his own eyes had filled with tears.

Nico had cradled her as he called for backup on his cell phone, and she laid her head against his chest, listening to his strong heartbeat and felt nothing but gratitude and love. There was nothing with which to cut through her ties, but she'd been happy just to lean against him and let him run his hand over her hair, soothing her like a lost kitten. Once he'd arranged for a unit to get here ASAP to take Serge into custody—Lacey had no doubt the place would be crawling with just about every cop from Burnie station in the next half hour—they'd sat in the corner and savored each other's company. Lacey drew strength from Nico's quite assurance. He had an aura around him that hadn't been there before. An air of supreme confidence, as if he'd just conquered Mt Everest and made it down alive. And perhaps Serge had been his own Everest.

"You are the best thing that ever happened to me," Nico said suddenly, with such vehemence Lacey was taken aback and looked up into his indigo eyes.

"We're getting married as soon as is humanly possible," Nico had murmured fiercely into her ear. "I'm making you my wife, and we're giving this child a family, a name he can be proud of. I'm going to keep him safe, and I'm going to keep you safe. I'm not going to let my father's legacy be my own."

She'd absorbed his words. "It's a him, is it?" Lacey had challenged tearfully.

"Definitely."

"Then I guess I'll marry you. Even though it might be a girl."

And that was that. Nico hadn't so much asked her to marry him as demanded it. But in that moment, it was okay with her. They'd just walked through fire and come out—not necessarily unscathed—the other side. Emotions were running high, but they were both safe, and that was all that mattered.

They'd chosen this date, because it was the soonest they could find a celebrant to marry them. And Nico was at a loose end for a while, since he'd been suspended pending an internal investigation into his actions on that day at the farm. So they could even have the luxury of taking a few weeks for a honeymoon afterward, despite the circumstances. Nico had known full well what he'd been doing by going against direct orders. Shadbolt had been none too happy when Nico had called in for a police car to attend the farmhouse and take the serial killer into custody. And he'd had plenty to say to Nico afterward. But the fact was they had the murderer in custody and Lacey was safe. The only two things that mattered to Nico.

Lacey was still sore at him for breaking all the rules and putting his job on the line to come and rescue her. But he was still sore at her for putting their baby at risk. So in both those aspects they were pretty much even. But neither of them would stay mad for long, because they had extremely good reasons for doing what they did. And everything had worked out okay in the end.

"I think they're nearly ready for you outside," Catarina

said, breaking Lacey's reverie. "Are you up to it, my darling girl?" Catarina's gaze found hers in the mirror.

"Yes. Thank you for your help." Lacey stood and embraced her soon-to-be mother-in-law. At least Nico's side of the family was easy to deal with, and she was so happy to be welcomed with open arms. She pushed away and straightened her shoulders.

"You'll do good." Catarina touched her face lightly, then turned to open the bedroom door and helped Lacey through the doorway; even with such a short train on her dress, it got tangled in everything. Lacey breathed deeply as she preceded Catarina down the dim hallway, heading toward the noise and bustle coming from the backyard.

"If you're sure you're okay, I'll go back and join Andy," Catarina said. "Your father is waiting for you just down there." She pointed through the screen door to where Lacey could just make out the top of her father's head over the railing of the back porch.

"Thank you again." Lacey leaned in for one more hug as Catarina fussed with her hairpiece. Then she was gone and Lacey stood alone on the threshold.

She stepped out onto the porch and surveyed everything below.

The backyard of Nico's cottage—her cottage too now she had to keep reminding herself—was decked out for the occasion. Lanterns hanging on poles had already been lit and a string of fairy lights glowed cheerfully over the arbor which had been decorated with posies of white flowers. The soft light of late-afternoon shone, lending an orange hue to the trees in the orchard behind the arbor. It was a still and balmy evening, the heat of the summer day just now lifting, leaving a gentle breeze and a lilac sky. Music drifted from hidden speakers, and rows of rustic benches marked a makeshift aisle, as many excited faces turned to stare at her, a hush falling over the crowd as they noticed her. The nerves came back a little then as she saw how many people were here, all looking at her.

Linc sat in the last chair of the back row. He turned and gave her such a beaming, sunny smile, almost as if he was the one getting married. "Looking good, Shorty," he mouthed, and she couldn't help but smile back at him, her anxiety melting away with his white, toothy grin. Her gaze drifted to the rest of the rear row of seats, which were filled with other officers. Shadbolt was there with his wife—Lacey had never considered what Shadbolt's wife would look like, but was surprised to see a petite woman with lots of bouncing, curly hair and a broad smile—Gorman and Hickey sat next to him, looking slightly uncomfortable in their suits, the stitches on Hickey's ensemble straining around his biceps and broad chest almost to breaking point. Constable Dawn Lawson was there, and surprisingly even Detectives Saito and Pederson. She was glad they'd decided to come, although Pederson wouldn't quite meet her eye, which didn't surprise her. If Nico had followed Pederson's lead on the case, rather than using his own intuition, Lacey might well be dead by now.

Margie waved at her energetically from her seat three rows back, looking like a bright butterfly in her orange and pink flowered dress. Herb sat beside her, looking almost as uncomfortable in his suit and tie as Gorman and Hickey. And there were lots of other locals, who she and Nico had got to know over the past few months, familiar faces that made Lacey feel calm. They were the faces of her home now.

Family from both her mother's and father's sides were standing in the front row. Aunts and uncles and cousins she hadn't had a lot to do with over the past few years, but like always, a wedding brought them out of the woodwork.

Taylor waved at her shyly, her mother standing ramrod by her side, watching everyone warily. Her poor mother, she may never be able to trust anyone or any situation ever again. Part of Lacey understood where that fear was coming from. But Taylor seemed to be coping much better. She looked bright-eyed and determined in her summery dress, showing off her coltish legs, her long, auburn hair floating around her shoulders, not caring that her scars were on display. Most of them were healed now, but she'd always bear the marks of her terrible time in Serge's hands. She was so beautiful. And so alive. Lacey didn't want to think about the alternative. Serge had let her go, and now he was in jail, where he could no longer hurt anyone. That was the reality, and she shouldn't dwell on what-ifs. Taylor had agreed to fly over from Brisbane for the wedding, and Lacey was so glad she'd decided to come. It felt like she now had some sort of closure on that whole terrible episode.

Lacey glanced down and saw her father standing at the bottom of the steps, waiting patiently. He was going to give her away. It was only fitting, even though she'd questioned her reasoning many times in the past few weeks. A little voice of sedition had murmured that her father hadn't really done much in the way of being a true father, and that perhaps she didn't want him giving her away. But he was her father, and she'd decided not to take that honor away from him. The way he was smiling at her now, so full of pride and standing so tall in his impeccable dark-gray suit, she was suddenly glad she'd stuck with her decision.

But before she took those steps down to her father, she raised her gaze to see Nico proud and tall waiting for her at the end of the aisle. Her brave, beautiful man. Smudge sitting obediently at his master's feet. Her equally brave and beautiful dog.

She'd heard from a little birdie—her sister Sammy had delightedly nudged her elbow and whispered in her ear earlier—that Nico had looked decidedly ill all morning, like he might be about to puke all down his black tuxedo. Lacey didn't blame him, after her own wedding jitters back in the bedroom. She wasn't sure if he was more worried about getting married, or becoming a father, or both, all had happened in a whirlwind over the past few weeks.

The "Wedding March" began to play, and everyone stood. It was time. She stepped carefully down and took her father's proffered elbow. He smiled at her. "You look lovely," he said, and there was no doubting the pleasure in his voice.

Lacey walked on air all the way down the aisle, her father's firm grip on her arm the only thing from stopping her floating away on a bubble of happiness. Fleetingly, she caught sight of Elora standing beside Aunty Pam and Uncle Donald who'd flown over from America for the wedding. Aunty Pam looked a lot like her older sister, but that was where the similarity stopped, because her eyes twinkled with delight as Lacey walked by. Her mother's face, however, was blank as she merely lifted one eyebrow in an arch when Lacey passed. Who the hell knew what that was supposed to mean. Her mother was a closed book most of the time. But Lacey was too happy to care right now. Her brother, Matty, lifted his chin and gave her a wink of appreciation, making her forget about her mother. It was so nice to have him and her sister here to share in this day. It felt like perhaps her family might be wobbling their way back to some kind of normality.

In the front row on the opposite side of the aisle, Catarina waved a lace handkerchief in front of her face, her eyes already damp and the ceremony had yet to begin, her arm linked tightly through Andy's, seeming to use him to hold her upright. Beside them, Gaëlle was practically jumping on the spot with excitement.

Nico's younger sister had been a godsend. She'd arrived a week ago to lend a hand planning this hasty wedding, and she'd been in her element, helping Lacey choose the flowers, dealing with the furniture hire company, stringing all the fairy lights in the garden and so much more. She was also the spitting image of Nico, except where Nico rocked the tall, dark, and handsome image, she was petite, blonde, and bubbly. Their facial expressions were the same, and she had the same way of piercing you with her stare, lasering all her focus on you while she listened to what you had to say. Her boyfriend, Oscar, had arrived yesterday, escorting Catarina and Andy across to the island on the ferry. They'd been going out for nearly six months now, and Gaëlle had confided in Lacey that her biological clock had started ticking all of a sudden a few months ago, and while she didn't want to scare Oscar, she was hoping this wedding might nudge him in the right direction. All of Nico's family were staying here, in the house with them. Which meant the little cottage was bursting at the seams. But it was a happy house, full of light and laughter, and Lacey didn't begrudge one second spent getting to know Nico's family.

Lacey lifted her head to see Sally-Ann on one side of the altar, along with Lacey's sister, Sammy, both looking pretty in their chosen outfits. Lacey wasn't the sort of bride to demand her bridesmaids wear a certain matching dress. She gave them a color scheme and let them choose whatever suited their bodies best. And they both looked stunning. Sally-Ann twitched at her dress a little nervously, then shot Lacey a warm smile. Sammy looked as glamorous as always, but Lacey could tell even she was a little tense. She hoped some of Sally-Ann's homespun, kind spirit and cheerfulness would rub off on Sammy, who'd been a tad distant all day. But Lacey put that down to Elora's influence. Because her mother wasn't allowed to lecture Lacey, she was taking her spite out on Sammy instead. But as Lacey drew closer, Sammy seemed to draw herself up and beamed at her older sister, a genuine happiness in her smile that lightened Lacey's mood even more.

Tyrell and Brice, Nico's brother, stood next to Nico on the other side. Lacey had been so glad when Nico chose Tyrell to be one of his groomsmen. He was Nico's best ally at work, but more than that, he was also a great friend. Gabriel had been Nico's best friend in Burnie, but after he was incarcerated, Nico hadn't really bothered to find anyone else to replace that bond outside of work yet. It was a shame that Tyrell would be shipping back to America soon.

She barely noticed her father leave her side and walk back to join her mother in the front row. All she wanted to do was stare at the man she was about to marry in front of her.

The celebrant cleared her throat and brought her book up in front, ready to begin the ceremony. A slim woman, wearing a flowing linen dress and lots of bohemian jewelry, the celebrant's voice was soft and calming; exactly what Lacey needed right now.

Out of the corner of her eye, she caught Sally-Ann's appreciative glance in Tyrell's direction. He was certainly a handsome man, but even more so in his black suit and tie, which was a nice foil to his dark skin and white on white teeth. About the same age as Sally-Ann as well. And single. Hmm. She made a mental note to look into that match later. Much later. But maybe she'd just found a reason for Tyrell to stay in Tasmania after all.

"Welcome, family and friends," the celebrant intoned, and Lacey shut everyone else out of her mind. It was just her and Nico, and the words of the celebrant. The woman read the introduction, but Lacey barely heard her, all she could see was the sapphire blue in Nico's eyes.

Then suddenly, she caught the words, "Nicolas Favreau, do you declare before me and before your witnesses here present, that you come here voluntarily and without reservation and that you are free by law to be married to

Lacey Carmichael today?"

"I…" His voice broke, and he had to clear his throat and start again. "I do."

And that's when Lacey's tears threatened to overflow. God, she'd never been a crier. Certainly never cried at weddings before. But then she'd never attended her own wedding before either. Never been about to marry the most perfect man in the world.

Then it was her turn to say "I do" and now her throat was closing up.

Nico had composed himself by the time he had to speak his vows. They'd both written them in secret, and she had no idea what he was about to say.

This time his voice was deep and full of purpose as he spoke. "I promise to stand by your side and respect everything you do. There is danger in our chosen professions, but I promise to love you enough to not interfere or argue with your choices." There were a few quiet chuckles at that one. Everyone knew how overprotective Nico got. But Lacey liked his commitment, even when she knew she might have to remind him of his vows, and probably sooner rather than later. His need to safeguard her was exasperating, but also one of the reasons she loved him so much.

"I also promise to love, guide, and respect our child for as long as we all live," Nico continued, but this time, his words caught her off guard. He'd included their unborn child in the ceremony and it touched a chord deep within her. He finished with, "You bring out the best parts of me. I give you everything I have and everything I am."

And now it was her turn. She could hardly speak to utter her own vows.

She cleared her throat and concentrated on his face. The setting sun caught the scar on his cheek, making it seem more prominent. And making her remember how much she loved him. For all his differences and flaws. His imperfect perfection.

"You are my knight in shining armor, my guardian angel, my north and my south and my salvation. You are my everything." And so much more, but she had to keep this short, otherwise they'd be here all night. And she was impatient to become this man's wife. Then she could whisper all of these things into his ear as they lay cocooned in bed.

"But even though you are all these things, just remember that I can drop you on your ass whenever I feel like it. But I promise not to do it anymore. I don't want our children to get the wrong idea." Matty gave a startled laugh at this from behind her, and more than one person's muffled giggle erupted from the crowd.

"I promise to respect you, and encourage you, walk beside you through whatever life brings, especially when you are in pursuit of justice and what is right. I promise to be grateful for you every single day and to choose you over and over again. Falling for you wasn't a choice, it was an absolute, and I can't wait to start our lives together."

By the time the ring ceremony came around, they were both wiping away tears as Smudge gave a little woof to remind them that he was there, and they laughed through their watery eyes. The dog was the ring bearer, proudly wearing the little black box with the two matching bands nestled within tied around his neck with a ribbon. Nico leaned down and untied the box. Plucking her ring out of the box, he slid it slowly onto her finger. The rose gold band was smooth and unadorned, just the way she wanted it. Nico had promised her an engagement ring, but they were yet to find the time to shop for one.

She plucked his equally plain platinum band from the proffered box and slid it on his ring finger, having to push a little harder to get it over the knuckle. It was the same band she'd planned to propose to him with back on their trip to the Tarkine. Their tastes in simple jewelry was one more thing they had in common.

"You may both now kiss if you wish," the celebrant said.

If she wished? She'd never wished for a kiss so much in her whole life. This kiss was the sealing of a pact, the sealing of a new life together, a new family together, a dream come true.

He lowered his head and took her mouth, his lips warm and soft, placing one hand over her belly at the same time. Telling her without words how much he wanted both of them. Her, and this family they were about to create. Lacey was so glad that Nico hadn't turned out anything like his father. That he'd rejected the urge to kill Serge, even when that was what his father had wanted. Even when perhaps that was what Serge deserved. Proving to himself and to her that he was a good, honorable man. He would make a great father, teach their son, or daughter, how to be honorable too. She couldn't wait to start this new chapter of their lives together.

CHAPTER TWENTY-TWO

Nico stood under the small marquee tucked in by the side of the rear stairs, staring at the wedding cake. He'd needed a few moments alone and found himself in this corner contemplating the three-tiered construction and taking a few deep breaths.

It'd been one hell of a day. A good day. A great day. A euphoric day. But one hell of a day, nonetheless.

The sun had set and the fairy lights had come into their own, lighting the backyard with a soft, warm glow. Now that the ceremony was over, people mingled and chatted with a glass of champagne in their hands while they waited for the caterers to tell them the food was ready. The large shed where he normally parked his Jeep, and where Dotti 2.0 also now resided, had been transformed into a rustic dining hall, with tables spread with white tablecloths, sparkling silver cutlery, table centerpieces made from the green branches from his orchard, and more fairy lights strung across the roof. Nico could see the caterers scurrying to and fro up the driveway, carrying large covered trays, so dinner wouldn't be too far away.

It was the first chance he'd really taken to look closely at the cake and as he leaned forward, he noticed the figurine placed in pride of place on top. Nico had no idea where Lacey had found the cake topper, but it was hilarious. It was a bride and groom, but they were back to back and both holding guns in a ready stance. Amazing. He had a sneaking suspicion that Lacey had help from Gaëlle. His younger sister had dived in headfirst when she'd heard there was going to be a rushed wedding, arriving nearly a week ago to help with all the organization. She was a whiz at these sorts of things and Lacey had mentioned more than once how glad she was to have her help. Gaëlle had retorted that she'd do anything to make sure Nico made her his wife, because then he'd be happy for the rest of his life.

An idiotic smile rose on Nico's face. Lacey was his wife now. They were married. All that soul searching and contemplation about whether he should ask her, and it'd been so much easier than he'd ever imagined. Because he wanted to be with Lacey for the rest of eternity, and everything else was a minor detail.

He knew without even really looking that she was over by the arbor, chatting to Linc and Tyrell, her arms waving animatedly as she conveyed some story or other to them. It was funny how he knew where she was at any given time, almost like she had a gravitational force and he was a satellite forever trapped in her atmosphere.

He'd asked her to marry him while they'd been sitting on the grimy floor of a run-down cottage. Not the romantic setting he'd had in mind at all. And he hadn't really asked, he'd told her in no uncertain terms. But the sentiment had been the same. Stronger perhaps than if they'd been sitting on the beach watching the sunset and sipping champagne. Stronger because there was no more powerful motivation than a near-death experience. He could've so easily lost her that night. And he couldn't let that happen without telling her how he felt. How he wanted to make her his wife, so he would never lose her again.

And now he had the birth of his son to look forward to—there was no doubt in his mind that their first child was going to be a boy. Maybe they could try for a little girl next time. Or the time after that. What was the kid going to look like? Would he take after Lacey, all flowing blonde locks and fiery stubbornness? Or would he be dark haired and a tad moody, like his father? That was half the fun though, wasn't it? The anticipation of seeing their baby for the first time. It was still too early for most people to even notice Lacey was pregnant. But he could see the changes already happening in her body. The lovely ripeness of her breasts, the slight swelling of her belly that she refused to believe was there. Her skin had taken on an extra special luminescence, her eyes a distinctive sparkle. She was still prone to morning sickness—one of the reasons they'd planned an evening wedding—but that didn't dampen her love of the baby growing inside. Lacey was going to make an awesome mum. He needed to remind her of that most days, however, because she was terrified her own mother's narcissistic tendencies would suddenly manifest in her once she had the child. That was never going to happen; Lacey was a completely different person to Elora and had made a concerted effort to be the opposite of selfish and self-centered.

Having Elora as a mother-in-law was going to be a challenge. He raised his eyes and searched her out, finally locating her over by the orchard fence talking to his own mother and Gaëlle. Catarina had a smile on her face that Nico recognized as her fake, get-me-out-of-here smile, and Nico wondered if he should go over and rescue his family. The geese had been locked away in their run in the shade at the side of the orchard for the day—he didn't want them chasing any of the guests or dive-bombing the food, but he could hear them honking their disapproval. Funny, but the geese had taken an instant dislike to Elora from the moment she'd stepped foot on the property. Thank God she and Barry had chosen to stay at the hotel just down the road. Well, more of a luxury resort out on an isolated peninsula, but it was only ever the best for Elora. He wasn't sure how they would've all coped if she'd demanded to stay in the house with the rest of them.

Almost as if she could feel his gaze on her, Elora lifted her cool, blue eyes to his, and then she lowered her finely manicured eyebrows into the hint of a frown. Even from this distance, he could feel her disapproval. In her mind, he was the man to blame for Lacey wanting to stay in Tasmania. She'd already told him Lacey was a different woman now that she was with him. Way too defiant and stubborn. Which made him laugh, because Lacey had always been those things, but Elora had only chosen to see them now because it suited her narrative; Lacey had turned from being the good daughter into someone she no longer recognized. Elora didn't say it in so many words, but he knew she blamed him for Lacey's change of heart last year, when she'd given her mother the ultimatum that'd caused their estrangement over the past six months. Nico wanted to yell at her to take a look in the mirror. That the responsibility lay squarely on her shoulders, but in Elora's world, everyone else was to blame except her. It was going to be a long, uphill battle with that woman, but he and Lacey held the trump card. Elora's first grandchild. And he wasn't prepared to put up with her shit like Lacey had. Elora would always be Lacey's mother, and this baby's grandmother, but that didn't give her a license to control their lives.

Someone cleared their throat behind Nico, and he swiveled on his heel, the smile that was forming on his face falling the second he saw who it was.

Pederson pulled his shoulders back and extended his

hand. "Congratulations on your wedding," he said stiffly.

It'd been Lacey's idea to invite him and Saito to the wedding; she held no lingering grudge against the man. Unlike Nico, who felt a low simmering anger rise in his belly every time he saw him. Pederson had ignored Nico's words of warning and gone off on a tangent, chasing a ghost, while Lacey had been in urgent need of his help. Shadbolt had tried to temper Nico's disgust by saying that Pederson had truly believed the chances of finding Lacey at his hideout in Hobart were high. Nico had merely snorted his contempt.

Pederson had received no formal punishment for his possibly deadly decision. But Nico understood it would be a long while before the indigenous detective would be given the lead on another case. Pederson had an ego the size of Tasmania, but Shadbolt had assured Nico that the younger man was contrite and also determined to learn from his mistakes. It didn't mean Nico had to like him, however.

But he also wasn't a man to leave another man hanging, so he took Pederson's hand and shook it, saying, "Thank you." Then added a formal, "Glad you could make it," when the silence stretched between them. Pederson and Saito would've made the trip out from Launceston to be here for the day, and he had to respect them for making the effort to show up.

Tasman Saito broke the impasse when she appeared from behind Pederson and said, "Congratulations. You two make a great couple." Then she did the most surprising thing of the whole day when she reached up and hugged him. Serious, sober, reserved Tasman actually hugged him. When she stepped back, her face cleared, and she was once again the pragmatic detective he'd come to know. He hoped that she'd be able to step out of Pederson's shadow one day soon and become the exceptional detective he knew was hiding in there somewhere behind all those starched shirts and dark suits.

"I'm glad you think so," Nico said again a little

awkwardly.

After a few more heartbeats, Pederson lifted his chin in acknowledgement and turned on his heel, Saito following his lead. But after a few steps, Pederson looked back over his shoulder and called out, "I hope you get reinstated soon. You're a great detective, with great instincts, and the force can't afford to lose you."

"Thank you," Nico answered, surprised, but the two detectives had already melted back into the crowd. He guessed that was where their main differences lay. Nico was prone to listening to his gut when it came to a case. He'd had enough experience on the job to know when it spoke true. But Pederson was one to go strictly by the book, only going on the concrete facts in front of him. Maybe Pederson just needed more time to learn to trust his intuition. Then he might become a great detective.

But going on his gut and breaking the rules, wasn't always the way to do things. Nico was still dealing with the consequences of his actions from that fateful day. He'd been suspended from duty awaiting the results of an internal investigation regarding his misconduct. That could take up to six months, with no clear idea what the outcome might be at the end. He could lose his badge and be discharged from the force. He'd abused his power as a police officer; his interview with Pacca had been illegal because he'd already been suspended from the case. And his flagrant disregard of the rules when he'd entered Alexander's property without a warrant, or any kind of permission from his superiors, may have put the court case against Serge in jeopardy. The lawyers had already told him that he could never be a witness in the case against his father, as his testimony was tainted. The defense lawyers would surely call his conduct into question and they could even ask for a mistrial on account of his cowboy antics.

But he'd do it all again in the blink of an eye. Because Lacey and his unborn baby were his only priority. And if he lost his job because he had to save her, then he'd just find another career. And he'd made peace with that decision.

Besides, he wasn't worried that Serge would be set free on some technicality; he was a bona fide serial killer, and the mounds of proof against him were growing every day. Taylor's testimony would be key. Even though her memories still hadn't fully returned, there was enough evidence to prove beyond a doubt that Serge had murdered Danika and abducted Taylor—not once, but twice. She was such a strong girl; he was so proud of how determined she was to take the stand at Serge's trial and look him in the eye and tell him that he was indeed the monster he purported himself to be.

Serge was refusing to cooperate, not even entering a plea. He said that the truth would remain between him and his son and that no one else mattered. A forensics team had raked over the old farmhouse with a fine-toothed comb. Serge had done a good job of trying to erase every trace of evidence, but there were some things he couldn't expunge completely, and the team found a few interesting clues as to Serge's movements over the past week. After they found tire tracks going cross-country, they surmised that he had driven to the site behind Pacca's house in his car directly through the paddocks rather than using the road, cutting through fences on the way there, and then painstakingly repairing the damage on the way back. This was why they could find no tire tracks on Cutter's Road. Following the trail, they then deduced he'd parked the car a way back from the road and carried the girls one by one to the crime scene. He'd woken Taylor with a drug that reversed the effects of the ketamine, taped her eyes open, forced her to watch as he strangled her best friend, then drugged her again while he completed his other tasks of cleaning up the scene and arranging the girl in the right position, then carrying a comatose Taylor back to the car. It was Taylor's screams as she watched her friend dying that had woken Pacca, just as Serge had hoped. He would've known of Pacca's nightly ritual of drinking himself senseless and knew he wouldn't come to investigate that night.

Pacca too, might well be a witness who'd help to put Serge away. Now that Pacca had confessed to killing his own son, the old man was determined to try to make amends for all his wrongdoings. And if putting Serge away could help Pacca ease his own mind, then Nico was all for it. Pacca would stand trial for the manslaughter of Alexander, but with the time passed since the murder, the extenuating circumstances of the way Alex had lied and tried to cheat his own father out of his farm, and the fact that Pacca was dying from lung cancer—something he'd revealed in a post incident interview—Nico was confident Pacca would be given a non-custodial sentence. Living with that much guilt for the past seventeen years had probably been punishment enough. Pacca was a broken, lonely man, with no family left and nothing in his old age to look forward to except to die from a terrible disease. Lacey felt sorry for the old bugger, but Nico was still finding it hard to conjure up any true compassion. Pacca had withheld vital evidence and for that, Nico would never forgive him.

The other two cold cases that'd been uncovered on the mainland would take a lot of unraveling, but Nico was sure they'd pin them on Serge eventually. This court trial could drag on for years, but in the end, justice would be served.

In jail, Serge would hopefully get the help he needed—not that Nico was sure he deserved it after all the atrocities he'd committed—but it might help him reconcile exactly how damaged he'd been by everything he'd seen and experienced in the Gulf.

PTSD was an insidious disease, manifesting in many ways,

and Nico had to accept that Serge couldn't take the full blame for his murderous spree. He was a sick man. But in Nico's mind, that'd never fully excuse his father for his actions. Serge had enough awareness to understand he was becoming a monster. But not enough balls to stop himself from following through on his urges. He blamed the monster in his head for driving him to kill those women, but they still had no clear idea why he'd chosen the women he had, and why he'd moved on to sex workers because Serge refused to say anything and wouldn't even speak to a court-appointed psych. Hopefully in time, the whole truth would come out about Serge's macabre choices, but for now, they were left merely to guess at his motives. If only Pacca had been of more help to Serge when he'd joined the veteran's group. Perhaps he could've made a difference if he'd urged him to get help, maybe even stopped him before he started killing. But then he couldn't put any blame on Pacca. No one had any real idea of the demon that lurked in Serge's subconscious.

"Hey, dude, got your speech ready yet?" Brice thumped him on the back scaring the shit out of him; he'd been so absorbed in his own thoughts he hadn't heard his brother approach. When Nico turned to glare at him, Brice handed Nico a glass of champagne and took a large gulp from his own glass. "Nice bubbles, by the way. The proper French stuff." Brice held his glass up and clinked it against his brother's.

"I know," Nico said, taking a gulp of champagne. "And to answer your other question, sort of," Nico hedged. The honest answer was not really. But he didn't need to write it down; he knew that when it came to talking about his new bride, his words would flow straight from the heart. "What about you? Have you got your best man speech ready?" Nico challenged.

"Of course," Brice scoffed, and patted his pocket. Nico had

no doubt that Brice had been working on that speech since the day he'd found out his younger brother was getting married.

"Can I ask what's in it?"

"Nope." Brice smirked. "All you need to know is that there's some good stuff. All your dirty laundry is going to get aired tonight, don't you worry about that."

Nico rolled his eyes and grimaced at his big brother. "Is that really necessary?" Brice had been his best man at his marriage to Marietta as well, but he didn't remember him being this ebullient, or this mischievous. Actually, now he thought about it, Brice had been decidedly sour-faced throughout the whole ceremony. No one in his family had really liked Marietta. That should've been the biggest red flag for him, but he'd been so blinded by lust and too young and full of his own self-importance to take their warnings seriously

"Of course it is, bro." Brice pounded him on the back again. "And by the way, just so you know, you lucked out. I don't know how you managed it, but you got an excellent woman there."

"I agree." It was Nico's turn to smirk, but he knew what Brice was trying to say in his roundabout way. He liked Lacey. He approved of her. And that meant the world to Nico.

Before he could put his sentiments into words, however, Brice said, "Hey, be a good brother and introduce me to your lady friend over there." His gaze was focussed over Nico's left shoulder.

"What?" Nico swung his head, confused.

"Over there." Brice pointed to a group of his workmates standing near the entrance to the shed, watching the covered trays of food arrive with hungry gazes.

The group contained Sally-Ann, Tyrell, Gorman, Hickey, and… "Oh, you mean Dawn?" Nico turned to stare at Brice.

"I thought you said you'd *never* get involved with a police officer. That we're too career oriented and self-righteous."

"Yeah, I know what I said. But you didn't tell me how downright gorgeous some of your colleagues are." Brice's gaze hadn't shifted from Dawn's face. Now that Nico took the time to notice, Dawn was looking rather fine in her knee-length, dark-blue dress, hair left to flow long and smooth over bare shoulders, and smoky, kohl-lined eyes. Nico was so used to seeing her in her uniform, hair pulled back, and no makeup that he barely paid any attention to her physical looks; it was her sharp mind and great police skills that interested him.

But now he reassessed her in this new light. Perhaps if Brice was distracted by Dawn, he might forget to make jokes at Nico's expense during the speeches. And if Brice fell in love with a Tasmanian cop, he could do worse than move to Burnie. Nico would love to have his big brother close by.

"I can do better than that," Nico said, elbowing Brice in the ribs. "My wife is in charge of seating arrangements. How would you like to sit at her table?"

"Yep, that'd be great." Brice's face had gone a little flushed and Nico had to hold back the urge to laugh. His brother was a bit of a Casanova, he'd never settled down, and all his relationships were short-lived. Perhaps Dawn might be the answer to taming his brother's wild ways.

Nico, Brice, and Gaëlle had had a long talk over a group video call the day after Serge was arrested. They'd brought their mother in later, but first they wanted to sort out a little of how they felt about their father being a serial killer. And about Nico being the one to capture him. None of them blamed him one bit for being the one to bring their father down. They congratulated him.

Brice was pragmatic about the whole thing, saying he was just glad the bastard was behind bars now. Gaëlle, being the youngest had a misplaced belief that Serge had good reasons for faking his own death, and had held out hope that he wasn't the serial killer after all. She wanted to believe in the fantasy of a father who could do no wrong. But they'd been shattered when Nico had rung and confirmed her worst fears. She was bouncing back quickly though, at least on the outside. And his mother… She'd taken the news hard, as he expected her to. Nico was eternally grateful to Andy, who'd been Catarina's rock while she grieved for her husband and his heinous deeds all over again. They all promised to keep reminding each other that it was not their fault that Serge had turned out like he had. Nico hoped that one day he'd start to believe it.

A small hand slid around his waist and settled in the small of his back. "Hey, husband," Lacey whispered in his ear.

"Hey, wife," he whispered back, realizing it was the first time they'd had two minutes alone since last night, and she leaned into him, pressing her palm against his cheek and looking deep into his eyes. The surrounding noise subsided until he could almost imagine they were alone here, standing beside a gorgeous cake beneath a canopy of emerging stars.

"Whatcha doing?" she asked.

"Just taking a moment to breathe," he replied.

"I know what you mean, it's been a whirlwind. But in a good way," she amended, blowing a long tendril of hair away from her eyes. The flowers in her hair were so cute; they made her look younger, carefree, like a beautiful garden nymph. He'd already told her how ravishing she looked ten times over, but he could still barely believe that she was his.

"Today has been very special," he agreed. "But… And don't take this the wrong way… I can't wait until it's over. Because I have a secret. I have this urgent need to go inside, undress you, and hold your naked body next to mine all night long." He didn't even need to make love to her. It was enough to know she was there with him. He could sleep soundly in the knowledge they were both safe and heading for a bright future together, with his arms wrapped tightly around his soulmate.

Her jade-green eyes lit up, reflecting the glow of the fairy lights. Then a look of contemplation turned to one of mischief as her lips turned up on an impish smile.

"Well, I have a little secret of my own. I'm not wearing any underwear," she whispered in his ear.

"You're wh…?" He could hardly believe his ears. But his cock heard her all right. It was already standing to attention, and he had to turn around, so his back was to the rest of the guests. This pregnancy thing certainly had its advantages, one of the major ones being that all those extra hormones turned Lacey into a horny little minx. This new, lascivious Lacey was a buffet of fresh and exciting menus to be sampled nightly. God, she smelled divine, like roses and apples and vanilla all combined, and he wanted to taste her so bad.

"You can't do this to me," he moaned.

"I'm sure no one will miss us if we just nip inside for five minutes." She bit her bottom lip and stared up at him from beneath lowered eyelashes.

Was she serious? The look on her face said she was. He was paralyzed by indecision. Surely they couldn't. Could they?

"Ever since I put this dress on, I've been wondering what it'd be like to have sex with my new husband in my new dress."

"You're killing me," he moaned again.

"I know." She gave a slow, wicked smile.

"Lacey, we can't." He couldn't believe he was saying this. Couldn't believe he was the one showing restraint, because if the way she was kissing his neck was anything to go by, she meant what she said. Even though he wanted to. Oh, so much.

"Spoilsport," she said with a small pout, but then her eyes cleared and she seemed to regain some sensibility once more, and he knew he was right to stop this.

"You have to distract me. I can't turn around." He looked pointedly at his groin, and she followed his gaze down to where a large bulge strained at the zipper of his pants.

She giggled, and raised an eyebrow, but when he cast her an anguished glance, she relented. "Okay. I've been dreaming up a little plan, but I need your help," she said, pulling back a few inches from him. "So get your thinking cap on."

"Right." He tried to redirect his thoughts away from what Lacey might look like astride him, wedding dress hiked up to her breasts, while he lay on the bed wearing nothing but his white shirt. "What am I thinking about?" he asked almost in desperation.

"Sally-Ann and Tyrell," she replied triumphantly. Her smile told him he should know what she was talking about, but he was completely lost.

"What?"

"I think Sally-Ann would be great for Tyrell. We need to get them together. I noticed the way she was looking at him earlier."

"Oh." He nodded. Sally-Ann had been so intent on setting Tyrell up with one of her friends, but he had rejected every one. Maybe Lacey was right. Maybe the woman for him had been right under his nose all along. "Right."

"I think I'm going to go into the shed and make a few changes to the seating arrangements," she said, her lips curving up at the idea of her secret conspiracy. "And I need you to start dropping subtle hints to Tyrell. Like, how lovely Sally-Ann looks out of uniform, that sort of thing."

Nico nodded sagely. He could do that. "Sure. But while you're changing the seating arrangements, I promised Brice a little favor as well." He went into detail about how Brice had an immediate, almost visceral, reaction to seeing Dawn. Lacey absolutely loved the idea, as he knew she would. By the time they'd come up with their little plan of action, he was pleased to discover his erection had almost disappeared.

Almost, but not quite.

"We should get back to our guests," Lacey said, not without regret. "Some of them are starting to stare." She tipped her chin and Nico saw a gaggle of the older ladies from around the neighborhood with their heads together all looking in their direction.

"Yes, I guess we shouldn't scandalize the guests. Especially when we have to see them every day," he replied, taking a step back and pulling on the hem of his suit jacket to get it straight again. "But just know this," he said, leaning in to kiss Lacey lightly on the cheek. "I'm making you a promise. Two more hours. Three tops. Then you're mine. And I'm a man who keeps his promises," he growled. The cottage would be full to the brim with his family tonight. Hell his mother and Andy were sleeping in the spare bedroom down the hall. But he didn't care a whit if anybody heard what they were up to. It was their wedding night. And Nico meant to make sure to be grateful for every single second of it.

They were driving down to the Tarkine tomorrow morning to spend three glorious nights under the stars in their special place. Then they were moving on to spend another week in the Saffire luxury resort in Freycinet National Park. He couldn't wait to start their honeymoon. But he wasn't going to wish tonight away either. Surrounded by their family and good friends, tonight was a time to celebrate. With the woman he loved more than anything else in the world by his side, he was invincible. This was the start of something new, intense, and deep and significant. The next chapter in his life. And he was more than ready to step up to the plate and be the husband and father he wanted to be.

"I'm holding you to that promise," Lacey said as she took his hand in hers and led him away from the cake tent toward the group of guests all gathering at the garage door. The crowd parted to let them through, a few of them raising their glasses in their direction and shouting, "To Lacey and Nico," until there was a chant ringing around the garden. "Lacey and Nico, Lacey and Nico." The sound hit him straight in the chest. He drew his wife into his arms and they beamed at the people all around who wished them the best of life to come. And in that moment, Nico knew it would always be them, him and Lacey, together forever. Along with whatever family was gifted to them.

EPILOGUE

SEVEN MONTHS LATER

It's a boy.

A happy, healthy, bouncing baby boy.

Nico tells Lacey he knew it all along.

Lacey tells Nico that she loves him and Samuel to the moon and back.

When Samuel comes home, Smudge will not leave his new baby brother's side, appointing himself protector and soulmate for the rest of eternity.

Also by Suzanne Cass
NEW
Dark Tides Series
Mystery and Romance collide.
Into the Rain
Rain Washed
The Clearing Rain

Stormcloud Station Series
(A Stargazer Spinoff Series)
Small Town Romantic Suspense
Clear Skies
Starlit Skies
Crystal Skies
Dawn Skies
Tangled Skies
Outback Skies

Stargazer Ranch Romance Series
Small Town Romantic Suspense
Combustion: Prequel Novella
Wildfire
Firelight
Snowbound: Christmas Novella
Snowfall
Cloudburst
Silverstorm

Island Bound Series
Mystery Romance (on an Island)
Books can be read as stand-alone
Bound by Truth
Bound by Silence
Bound by the Stars

Colors of the Earth Series

Small Town Romantic Suspense
Books can be read as stand-alone
Shadows in the Dust
Shadows in Deep Blue
Shadows of Red Earth

Romantic Suspense
Single Title
Island Redemption
Glass Clouds
Chasing Bullets

Love in the Mountains Novella Series
Small Town Short Romance
Novellas can be read as stand-alone
Rain on a Tin Roof
Lost and Found
Rescue his Heart

Please Leave a Review
The greatest gift you could ever give an author is to leave a review. You will be helping other people to discover this book and making a difference to me as an Independently Published Author. If you liked this book and want other people to read it too, please leave a review.

About the Author

Suzanne Cass is an Australian author who writes rural romance and romantic suspense abounding with passion and danger.

Her debut novel, Island Redemption, won the Romance Writers of Australia Emerald Award in 2016. Suzanne was also a finalist in the 2019 Romance Writers of Australia RUBY award.

She had always had a fascination with the tough resilience of people who live in our amazing red-dirt outback country. When not writing about the characters that inhabit her head, Suzanne can be found roaming the Perth beaches with her border collie, or encouraging from the sidelines as her two sons play sport.

Visit her website www.suzannecass.com or subscribe to her newsletter via: www.suzannecass.com/contact

Or you can stay in touch via my website
www.suzannecass.com

Facebook: www.facebook.com/suzannecassauthor/
Instagram: www.instagram.com/suzanne.cass/
Pintrest: www.pinterest.com.au/suzanne_cass/

Acknowledgements

This book is as much about the trials and tribulations we all encounter within our families as it is about finding love. No family is perfect. All families are complicated and just because we are blood related to someone doesn't mean we get on with them; in certain cases we may even learn to hate and fear them, as happens to Nico with this father. Lacey, too, has a troublesome relationship with her toxic mother and she has to learn to put firm boundaries around her life and her heart to keep from being dragged under by her mother's controlling habits. I'm sure every reader has at least one family member that causes them pain or heartache, and can perhaps relate to the characters in this book. But in the end, Nico and Lacey come to terms with their noxious parents and they hope to build a future family that is better, happier, and more healthy of their own.

There is a team of people who I couldn't do this without, beta readers (big thanks to Rebecca, my best typo hunter ever) and my ARC team, who are essential to an Indie Author like me, for their wonderful reviews.

Big thanks to my editor, Nicole at Evermore Editing for keeping my commas in check and my sentence structure so well structured!!!!!

To Gary who is my greatest cheerleader, and my two sons who are such amazing young men.

And to you, the readers, it sounds so trite, but thank you for reading my books. I wish I could reach out and hug you all personally. You are the reason I keep writing.